A FENCE AWAY FROM

FREEDOM

A FENCE AWAY FROM

FREEDOM

Japanese Americans and World War II

ELLEN LEVINE

G. P. PUTNAM'S SONS ★ **NEW YORK**

*In memory of Fusa Shibayama Sumimoto,
and for Michi and Walter Weglyn.*

Photograph credits:

Frontispiece, courtesy Library of Congress
Chapter 1, page 1   courtesy Dollie Nagai Fukawa (upper and lower)
Chapter 2, page 11   courtesy National Archives
Chapter 3, page 29   upper: courtesy Clem Albers: National Archives
                        lower: courtesy National Archives
Chapter 4, page 45   courtesy Clem Albers: National Archives
Chapter 5, page 84   upper: courtesy Lillian Matsumoto: National Japanese American
                        Historical Society (San Francisco) Archives
                        lower: courtesy Manzanar Committee
Chapter 6, page 92   courtesy Fusa Shibayama Sumimoto and Art Shibayama
Chapter 7, page 114   upper: courtesy U.S. Army: National Archives
                        lower: courtesy Dollie Nagai Fukawa
Chapter 8, page 130   upper: courtesy Hopwood Photo of Cheyenne in the
                        Wyoming Eagle of Cheyenne, June 1944
                        lower: courtesy Harry Ueno
Chapter 9, page 164   upper: courtesy Library of Congress
                        middle: courtesy National Archives
                        lower left: courtesy Dollie Nagai Fukawa
Chapter 10, page 184   upper: courtesy Chris Huie

Photographs in the insert are used by courtesy of the subjects,
unless otherwise noted.

G. P. Putnam's Sons, Reg. U.S. Pat. & Tm. Off. Published simultaneously in Canada.
Printed in the United States of America. Book designed by Donna Mark.
Map on pages 242 and 243 by Andrew Mudryk. Text set in Bembo.

Library of Congress Cataloging-in-Publication Data
Levine, Ellen. A fence away from freedom : Japanese-Americans and World War II /
Ellen Levine. p   cm. Includes bibliographical references (p.) and index.
        1. Japanese Americans—Evacuation and relocation, 1942–1945—Juvenile literature.
2. World War, 1939–1945—Personal narratives, American—Juvenile literature.
3. World War, 1939–1945—Japanese Americans—Juvenile literature. [1. Japanese
Americans Evacuation and relocation, 1942–1945.   2. World War, 1939–1945—
Personal narratives, American.   3. World War, 1939–1945—United States.]   I. Title.
D769.8.A6L45 1995   940.53′1503956073—dc20   95-13357   CIP   AC
ISBN 0-399-22638-9   10   9   8   7   6   5   4   3   2   1   First Impression

CONTENTS

Photograph Section between pages 113 and 114.

In 1991 Karen and Jeff Campbell, friends living outside Cody, Wyoming, urged me to write about Heart Mountain, the former prison camp for Japanese Americans near their home. They were appalled that their young sons had learned little in school about the camps in general, or Heart Mountain in particular. In the fall of 1992, I visited the camp site with the Campbells. All that remained were the shells of two barracks and the chimney of a former building. Shreds of tar paper flapped on the outside boards, and dust swirled inside the barracks, blown by steady gusts of wind. Heart Mountain itself rose up in the distance.

There have been several moving books written about the internment—histories, novels, picture books, accounts of the experiences of a few families. But after my visit to the former camp, I began to get a real sense of the scope of the event. Not just one face haunts Heart Mountain and the other camp sites, but tens of thousands.

To convey this scope, I needed the small details of the event multiplied many times. And so I interviewed dozens of people who had been interned. Almost all were between the ages of six and twenty-five at the time of their forced evacuation from Hawaii and the West Coast. For some, I was one of the few people they had talked to about their experiences. All were extraordinarily generous in sharing their memories. Sometimes they laughed in telling certain stories of past difficulties; more than a few cried when speaking of their parents. I am most beholden to them all.

Some gave me additional help, providing me with many documents and suggesting other people I should speak with: Sue Kunitomi Embrey, Frank Emi, Sohei Hohri, Kay Uno Kaneko, Mits Koshiyama, Kenji Taguma, and Dr. Clifford Uyeda. I am particularly

indebted to Sumi Seo Seki, who was tireless in her efforts to supply
me with written materials and contacts. And I am most grateful to
Ernest Uno for speaking the words that became the title of this book.

In a friend's phrase, this has been for me a venture of the heart. I
thank the Campbells for starting me on this journey, and my editor,
Refna Wilkin, for seeing it through to the end. I'm grateful to design-
ers Donna Mark and Cecilia Yung; and to Anne and Inger Koedt
who visited Heart Mountain with me and, as my first readers, offered
many insights. Many others have helped along the way, putting me up
on my travels; copying law cases for me; providing contacts, clippings,
tapes, books, food, friendship, advice, and other succor: Ter DePuy;
Ann Diamond; Grace and Olive Goodman; Myrna Guy; William
Hohri; Esther Kartiganer; Lise Kreps; Susan and Bailey Kuklin; Sara
Liebman; Trish McCall; Alison Pease; Elizabeth Schreiber; Grace
Shimizu; Jeff, Jake, and Emma Staniels; and Carol Williams. Very spe-
cial thanks to my writers' group: Marvin Terban, Barbara Seuling,
Fran Manushkin, Peter Lerangis, Sandra Jordan, Miriam Cohen, and
Bonnie Bryant. And thanks to my sisters, Mada Liebman and Dori
Brenner.

Catherine Crank, at the Battenkill Peacemakers' Lanterns of
Remembrance event; and Frank Hodge, Joan Duval, Sara Idleman,
and Tom Havens, at the Hodge Podge Conference, "The Effects of
War on Children," provided me with my first public forums for
speaking about this subject. I am also most grateful to Irving Neuge-
boren. Even more important than his insights, of which there were
many, Irving cheered me during difficult periods in the research and
writing. It is a great sadness for me that he died before the manuscript
was completed.

Finally, it is hard to imagine writing this book without the endur-
ing support of Michi Nishiura Weglyn. Her book, *Years of Infamy:
The Untold Story of America's Concentration Camps* was the first to
broaden my knowledge about the magnitude of this event. There
aren't words sufficient to acknowledge her personal generosity.

INTRODUCTION

In 1942, just months after war was declared, more than 110,000 Japanese Americans on the West Coast were removed from their homes under orders of the United States government. U.S. soldiers herded them onto buses and trains. They were driven to racetracks, stockades, and fairgrounds, where they were temporarily quartered, and then moved to prison camps, hastily constructed in desolate areas of the United States. On February 19, 1942, President Franklin Roosevelt had signed Executive Order 9066, which authorized the removal. On that date, the president committed this nation to a journey of shame that it has taken nearly fifty years to correct.

Two months earlier, on December 7, 1941, Japan had severely damaged the United States Pacific fleet at Pearl Harbor, Hawaii. That act of aggression triggered America's formal declaration of war against Japan, on December 8, 1941. At the time, there were approximately 127,000 people of Japanese ancestry in the continental United States. Nearly 90 percent lived on the West Coast, 80 percent in California. About 150,000 people of Japanese ancestry lived in Hawaii.

In the months after Pearl Harbor, the government issued a series of orders restricting the rights of Japanese Americans, ostensibly to protect national security. Government intelligence agencies, however, had reported and continued to report to the president and his aides that the Japanese community in America posed no threat to security. Nonetheless, political leaders on both the national and state levels indulged their personal biases and pandered to those of others. Along with newspaper and radio commentators, they incited and encouraged the rising tide of anti-Japanese rhetoric by repeating stories of subversion by American Japanese that were absolutely false.

Government officials lied not only to the American people about the dangers to be expected from the Japanese community living in its midst, but also to the courts of the nation. The United States Supreme Court, for example, relied on misleading government reports when, in 1944, it upheld the conviction of Fred Korematsu for failing to report for evacuation.

Supreme Court Justices Roberts, Jackson, and Murphy wrote vigorous dissents in the *Korematsu* case. Justice Murphy argued that the reasons given for the forced evacuation "appear . . . to be largely an accumulation of much of the misinformation, half-truths and insinuations that for years have been directed against Japanese Americans by people with racial and economic prejudices." He concluded,

> I dissent, therefore, from this legalization of racism. Racial discrimination in any form and in any degree has no justifiable part whatever in our democratic way of life. It is unattractive in any setting but it is utterly revolting among a free people who have embraced the principles set forth in the Constitution of the United States. All residents of this nation are kin in some way by blood or culture to a foreign land. Yet they are primarily and necessarily a part of the new and distinct civilization of the United States. They must accordingly be treated at all times as the heirs of the American experiment and as entitled to all the rights and freedoms guaranteed by the Constitution.

Forty-four years later, with the passage of the Civil Rights Act of 1988, the government officially apologized to Japanese Americans for their evacuation and imprisonment. Congress backed that apology with monetary redress to surviving camp prisoners. In 1990, nearly fifty years after Executive Order 9066, the first redress checks and letters of apology were sent out.

This is a book of remembrance. It is not meant to be an exhaustive or academic history of the wartime experiences of Japanese Americans. Rather, through the voices of those who were young at the time, it tries to paint a broad canvas to convey the magnitude of an event in which thousands of people, convicted of no crime, were locked up in prison camps in a country proud of its democratic traditions. It is remarkable that so many of the voices are not just those of victims but also of people able to keep a sense of personal dignity and find some pleasures even in a life behind barbed wire.

There is no assurance that such an event will never happen again. Without the knowledge of what happened to Japanese Americans, why it happened, and what could have prevented it, the same thing may well occur again. The question is only against whom. The answer is a group that is powerless, that has no strong political voice, that we perceive as different from ourselves.

The voices of the young people in this book are typical of those who suffered the indignity of being labeled "disloyal," not because they *were* disloyal but solely because they were of Japanese ancestry. To prevent another such explosion of hatred in our midst, we must listen to them.

NOTE TO THE READER

We speak to one another often without thinking about the words we use. But words, of course, are what convey our meaning. The words used by governments are chosen to convey particular political meaning. The U.S. government called the expulsion from the West Coast an "evacuation," as if the removal had resulted from a flood or an earthquake and not from a political decision. Chief Judge Denman of the U.S. Court of Appeals, Ninth Circuit, wrote in 1949, in the case *Acheson v. Murakami,* that "the beguiling words 'evacuation' meant deportation, 'evacuees' meant prisoners, 'relocation center' meant prison and their single rooms, some crowding in six persons, meant cells, as they in fact were." In the novel *Obason,* about the experiences of Japanese Canadians during World War II, author Joy Koyama speaks of language used to "disguise any crime."

About the use of words in this book:

  • The term "Japanese American" is generally used to include both U.S. citizens and resident aliens living in America. When the term refers only to citizens, it is so defined in the text. As with Italians, Scandinavians, and other ethnic groups in America, the phrase "Japanese community" is used to mean both citizens and resident aliens of Japanese ancestry.
  • The words "prisoners" and "internees" are used interchangeably, as are "prison camp" and "internment camp."
  • The government called the prison camps "relocation centers." Some officials, however, including President Roosevelt on at least one occasion, referred to them as "concentration camps." In this text, they are most often called prison camps.

Facing page: *California elementary school class
before Pearl Harbor;*

Dollie Nagai.

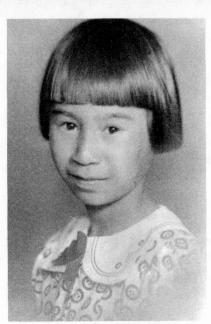

1

THE YEARS BEFORE
PEARL HARBOR

California was given by God to a white people, and with God's strength we want to keep it as He gave it to us," said the president of the Native Sons of the Golden West, a white nativist California group, in the years between World War I and World War II.

Most Japanese Americans lived on the West Coast, the vast majority in California. Many cities on the Coast passed their own laws discriminating against the Japanese. Like African Americans, in some parts of California Japanese-American children lived in segregated neighborhoods, attended segregated schools, and were prohibited from using certain public facilities.

Almost all trade unions prohibited the Japanese from joining, thus preventing them from working in many different types of jobs. V. S. McClatchy, a newspaper publisher and head of an anti-Japanese organization, claimed that because the Japanese were superior workers, they were an economic threat to Americans and therefore should be excluded from the United States.

Newspapers and magazines across California promoted vicious hate campaigns that contributed to an atmosphere in which physical violence was not uncommon and murder not unknown. Statewide, there were restrictions on the purchase of land by Japanese immigrants, and California law prohibited Asians from marrying Caucasians. Federal law prohibited Asian immigrants from becoming American citizens. (A person born in the United States is automatically a citizen, regardless of ancestry.) In 1924, Asians were excluded entirely from emigrating to the United States.

Although there was a long history of discrimination on the West Coast, in some communities before the war Japanese-American children and children of other races and nationalities lived as neighbors, attending school together and playing with one another. The young people whose stories are told in this chapter grew up on the West Coast or in Hawaii. They were elementary and high school students or recent high school graduates at the time of America's entry into World War II. They are *Nisei*, meaning "second generation" in Japanese, born in the United States and therefore U.S. citizens;

and *Sansei*, meaning "third generation," children of the Nisei.★

Some were too young to experience directly the discrimination of the prewar period. Their innocence was shattered after Pearl Harbor. Others had learned from personal encounters and from their parents that some caution was prudent in their dealings with the white world. Some were defiant in the face of petty racism, others frightened or humiliated. Many turned at least part of their anger into a temporary but corroding self-hate. For others, their anger turned into a belief in the superiority of traditional Japanese culture. These prewar stories provide the setting for the eruption of bigotry during the war years.

★   ★   ★   ★   ★

Mits Koshiyama

Mits grew up in the Santa Clara Valley in California, the third of seven children. His parents were farmers.

My parents came to America in the early 1900s. I think they would have become citizens if they were accepted. They had no plans to go back to Japan. Why would they come to a strange country like this against all odds if they weren't coming here to better themselves and their children? But all the laws were made to keep them aliens in this society. They couldn't buy land. Intermarriage was forbidden. They couldn't vote. The government made these laws so our parents would stay aliens, and then they charge that because they wouldn't assimilate, we are dangerous.

Before the war, since Japan was the aggressor in Asia, people in California hated the Japanese. I don't care if you were a citizen or not. We had a pickup truck, and most of us had to ride in the back. When we drove to town, people on the sidewalks would holler, "Go back home, you Japs!"

★Japanese born in Japan are the *Issei*, which means "first generation" in Japanese, the first generation to live in America. *Yonsei* is the Japanese word for the fourth generation. *Kibei* is the word used for Nisei who, although born in America, lived in Japan and went to school there for at least five years.

My father and mother were brought up to accept it. *Shikataganai,* it can't be helped. But for us, the citizens, it hurt you inside. We wanted to be accepted as Americans. We had no ties with Japan. It's hard for a Caucasian to believe, but we had no connection.

Because of discrimination, we hated everything Japanese, even rice and stuff like that. I used to tell my mother, "Why can't we have bread like everybody else? Bacon, eggs in the morning. Why do we have to eat rice? Why do you have to read the Japanese paper? Why do I have to be foreign?"

Ernest Uno

Ernie grew up in Los Angeles in a largely white community. He was a young teenager in the years before the war.

At home we spoke English. I knew very little Japanese. What I learned was conversational, just with my mother. She was more conversant in Japanese than she was in English. My dad had a real skill in learning languages. He wrote beautiful English. He never insisted that we learn Japanese, and that's why I never went to Japanese school. His rationale was that he came to the United States to raise us as Americans. This is the country of our nationality.

I had heard the word "Japs" before Pearl Harbor. Quite a bit. We needed a large house because of the number of kids in the family. As we were moving into this neighborhood—it was strictly a white community—a woman came from across the street and very indignantly shouted at my mother's face, "I don't want to have nothing to do with you Japs. Don't you ever come across the street to here!"

Joe Norikane

Joe grew up in a small town about thirty miles south of Sacramento, California.

We were all Oriental in school. There were three schools segregated by law. We were segregated until the war. One day in the fifth or

THE YEARS BEFORE PEARL HARBOR

sixth grade, some Chinese boys ganged up on one Japanese boy. The teacher lined up everyone in the room and went up and down staring at each of them. She said, "Why did you fight?"

One said, "The Japanese boy called me a Chink."

She looked at us and said, "You're no Chink and you're no Jap. You're 100 percent Americans. Understand? I don't want name calling." She was a Caucasian. Then she said, "Any questions?"

This Japanese guy Charles was standing next to me. He said, "If I'm 100 percent American, why aren't we with the white schools?"

She stared at us. Then she said, "That's none of your business. That's how it is." That's how I know about being 100 percent American.

Frank Emi

Frank was born in Los Angeles. His family moved out of the city when his father began farming.

I grew up in San Fernando. There was the grammar school and O'Malveny School. All the white people went to O'Malveny and all the nonwhites went to the grammar school. San Fernando was a pretty racist town. We'd go to the theater, and all the nonwhites would have to sit upstairs in the balcony and all the whites would sit downstairs.

When I was in the Scouts, about twelve years old, I was the only nonwhite in the troop. One time the whole troop went swimming. I wasn't allowed in because I wasn't white. I still remember sitting in the balcony, watching them. Not even the troop leader did anything. I guess in those days they didn't think too much about civil rights.

In high school there was no feeling of racism. Around that time we were able to sit wherever we wanted in the theater. My best friend at the time of high school was a Jewish kid named Sam. We used to pull a lot of pranks and do things together. We were sort of rascals.

Then we moved from San Fernando to Long Beach about the time

I was starting eleventh grade. I was on the football team. One instance sticks in my memory like fire. We were out for football practice, and there was another Japanese kid on the team. They were scrimmaging, and he had his helmet knocked off. The assistant coach turned to the head coach and said, "Hey, coach, Joe's helmet's knocked off. Maybe we better stop the scrimmage and have him put it back on. He could get hurt."

The head coach says, "Aw, it's all right. If he gets killed, it'll just be another dead Jap."

Yosh Kuromiya

Yosh attended elementary school in the 1930s in Monrovia, California.

School was predominantly Caucasian. Very few Mexicans. At the high school level, blacks were able to join with the rest of the community, although in the grammar school, they had a segregated school. The city swimming pool was segregated. Mondays were set aside for the blacks, because they cleaned out the pool on Tuesday. A friend of mine who's Japanese went to the pool regularly on the white days. I didn't want to risk the humiliation of being turned down, so I avoided going. I wouldn't go to a barbershop. I had heard of Japanese being turned out. I was even afraid to go to a restaurant.

I graduated from high school the same year as Pearl Harbor. I was very much aware of the hysteria beginning to build up—headlines in newspapers, hate signs that would crop up every once in a while, the classic "Jap" caricature, the "Yellow Peril." All that hatred and venom was directed on us just because of our appearance.

This was actually going on long before the threat of war. In those days you didn't think to raise the issue. As a child, you assume that's the way it is. As you grew up, you began to realize you're never going to live up to the image of Anglo-Saxon facial features and everything else. That was never going to happen. You try to salvage something of your own unique culture. I've always had a very strong sense of appreciation for the Japanese culture. I admired a lot of the characteristics, the integrity, of the Japanese culture. And I denied a lot of the negative aspects of it because I wanted something to base my own validity on.

Nami Nakashima

Nami was born in Long Beach, California, and went to school there. Her father was an Issei and her mother, Mexican American. At that time the Cable Act, passed by Congress in 1922, provided that any American-born woman married to a person ineligible for citizenship (for example, Asians) automatically lost her U.S. citizenship. The act was repealed in 1936.

Nami also married a Mexican-American man. Miscegenation laws in many states prohibited interracial marriages. These laws were enforced until 1967, when the Supreme Court ruled in the case Loving v. Virginia *that such laws were unconstitutional.*

My mother was Mexican-American, born in California, and my father was Japanese from Japan. They met in Los Angeles. At that time it was a "no-no" to marry out of the race, but they fell in love. It was very hard to get married. You had to go three miles out to the high seas and the captain would marry you, or else go out of the country. In 1939, my husband and I couldn't marry here. He's American-born Mexican, and I'm half Japanese-American. We had to go across the border, down into Tijuana, Mexico.

When I was growing up, my parents saved a little money and thought they'd better farm. Lo and behold, the oil gushers came, and my parents happened to have a lot with oil on it. Immediately, my father purchased some other land in my sister's and my name because they couldn't own anything. Everything was bought in the children's name. It couldn't be in my mother's name because when an American citizen married someone of the Asian race, you lost your citizenship.

At that time, Long Beach was known as "Iowa" because there were a lot of retired farmers here. They were prejudiced, yes, but there were some very nice ones too. I can't say they were all discriminating against us. But an Oriental couldn't get a job in Long Beach. I couldn't get a job in Kress's. Japanese who were university-educated were still working in farm stalls, selling at the market downtown. My mother always said, "You're not going to sell vegetables." I guess you'd call it proud. She'd see all these kids who had gone to the University of California at Berkeley, and there was nothing here for them. They sold vegetables.

Noboru Taguma

Noboru was born in 1923 and grew up near Sacramento. His parents were truck farmers.

There were seven kids in the family. I was the eldest son. We spoke Japanese at home. My parents probably knew "hello." They had no time to learn English.

We lived near Russian people, and they seemed to hate the Japanese. Maybe they hated us 'cause they were defeated by the Japanese [in the Russo-Japanese war of 1904–5]. I don't know. We tried to avoid them, but they came after you.

In school you sat in alphabetical order. I was by the big Caucasian football players. I used to help them out on the tests, so they protected me. Whoever tried to hit me gotta face those two big ones. Two hundred fifty or three hundred pounds!

Mary Sakaguchi

Mary was born in Fresno, California, number five in a family of seven children. She was a teenager before the war.

My father was quite well educated, but he was the fourth son, so he didn't inherit anything. There's primogeniture in Japan—the oldest gets everything. When I asked him, "Why did you come to America?" he said, "When I was in school, my teacher used to say 'Go to America. It's a land of opportunity.'"

When I was in the sixth grade, I had a classmate, Hiromi, who had a farm not far from ours. He was the only other Oriental. One day my class was taken on a trip to the swimming pool. I didn't have a bathing suit, so I couldn't go, but my friend did. At the pool, they said he couldn't swim with the rest of the kids. One of the teachers took Hiromi to a movie for three hours.

Hiromi's family made enough money to go back to Japan and buy land. This was their dream because they couldn't buy land in America. I went to see them off. I never saw my classmate again. About fifteen years after the war was over, his older brother and sister came back. I asked them what happened to Hiromi. They said he joined the kamikaze pilots and died during the war. I often thought that humiliating experience where he couldn't swim with the other kids made him do what he did later.

In school they always teased you and called you "Jap." I got so I could do judo. If anybody said that to me, I would knock them down. One day I was sitting in the bus that would pick us up after grammar school and take us to Japanese school. All of our parents got together and set up these schools. We were waiting to pick up a boy who lived in a white neighborhood. This white, blue-eyed, blond little kid who couldn't have been more than seven or eight years old saw us in the bus and starts to yell, "You Japs!" and all kinds of things. As he's saying this, he's backing up. Right behind him was a garbage can, and he fell right into it. We all laughed and laughed.

Mary began medical school shortly before the war started.

It was unusual in my day for a woman to get into medical school or even to have the ambition to be a doctor. I never really wanted to be a doctor. I wanted to be a bacteriologist, to do research, like Arrowsmith [in the novel of the same name].

My second year in UCLA I went to my adviser. He was the kind of man who bragged that his wife was DAR [Daughters of the American Revolution]. People heard him walking through the halls saying, "Goddam foreigners." He looked at my grades, which were very good. "What do you want to do?"

"I want to be a lab technician."

He said, "If I were you, I'd quit. Because of what those damn Japanese are doing in Manchuria, you'll never get a job."

Then I went to Dr. Green. I said, "Is it true if I'm Japanese I'll never get a job?"

She said, "Why don't you be a nurse?"

My mother said, "Oh, no, don't become a nurse and don't be a teacher. It's too hard."

I said, "Mama, can I be a doctor?"

She said, "Yes," and I got into University of California at Berkeley in 1941. The war started, and in March of '42, I had to leave school and go to [prison] camp.

Lillian Sugita

Lillian was born in 1928 in Honolulu. The experiences of the Hawaiian-Japanese community were very different from those of Japanese Americans on the mainland.

There were five kids in my family—my brother and four of us girls. My father and mother were Niseis. I'm a Sansei.

We came from a very sheltered family, although we were very rambunctious, very uninhibited—like typical kids, but still innocent. The boys grew up very different from the boys on the mainland. In Hawaii, they didn't have to face all the discrimination as they do here.

The Japanese community in Hawaii was very big until the war. And there were Chinese, Filipinos, Koreans—a lot of Asians. I think it was almost 50 percent Asian. In Hawaii we thought we were the majority, the others were the outsiders.

Facing page: *FBI agent searching home of Japanese-American family, December 1941.*

2

PEARL HARBOR

On December 7, 1941, in a surprise early-morning raid, planes of the Imperial Japanese Navy bombed the United States Pacific fleet at Pearl Harbor, Hawaii. Despite Japan's earlier and ongoing military aggression in the Pacific area, the American forces were completely unprepared and suffered devastating losses.

Responding to this outrage, President Franklin Roosevelt declared war on Japan. Within hours and days of the attack, FBI agents in Hawaii and in the West Coast states of California, Washington, and Oregon had rounded up hundreds of Issei elders, ministers, school-teachers, businessmen—anyone in a position of leadership in the community. The stated reason was national security. Many of those arrested remained in special high-security camps for the duration of the war; others were released after shorter periods of detention.

The Japanese-American community had been under watch for years by the FBI and various military intelligence units, which had conducted extensive studies both in Hawaii and on the West Coast, assessing loyalty and looking for spying activities or other sabotage. Nothing had been found. In October 1941, President Roosevelt ordered yet another study. The investigator, Curtis B. Munson, noted, "For the most part the local Japanese are loyal to the United States. . . . We do not believe that they would be at least any more disloyal than any other racial group in the United States with whom we went to war." Indeed, he said, "There is no Japanese problem."

But the American war fleet at Pearl Harbor lay in ruins. How was the government to explain to the American public the total lack of preparedness? Incompetence was the true answer, but one that Navy Secretary Frank Knox was unwilling to acknowledge. He knew there was no evidence, not a single instance, of sabotage by any resident Japanese alien or Japanese American in Hawaii or on the mainland. Nonetheless, returning from a review of the Pearl Harbor disaster, he announced to the press on December 15, 1941, "I think the most effective Fifth Column work of the entire war was done in Hawaii, with the possible exception of Norway." Thus began the federal government cover-up of the real information on the Japanese, that they were a loyal, hardworking, overwhelmingly apolitical community.

Those early-morning bombs shattering the peace in Pearl Harbor fractured the lives of the tens of thousands of Japanese living in America. Families lost their fathers and husbands, who were arrested and imprisoned, and the community lost its leaders in the early roundups. These first FBI raids were swift and unannounced.

The Japanese were subjected to curfews and travel restrictions, unannounced searches of their homes, and escalating hostility from many of their Caucasian neighbors. The Chief of Police in Hood River, Oregon, posted the following notice. The ignorance and bigotry it reflects are startling:

> As you are well aware the sentiment of the American people at the present time is not as friendly as it was some time ago. This feeling has not been brought about entirely by the American public alone, but by the careless and needless action on the part of the Japanese nationals and those citizens of Japanese descent. Therefore at this time I wish to take this means to give you a few suggestions. . . . Stay at home, travel only in the day time, when using the telephone do not converse in Japanese. If you feel you cannot speak English good enough have your son or daughter talk, do not drive about for leisure, when in town you meet another Japanese do not greet him in the Japanese custom by bowing. You're in America. Greet him in the American way by shaking hands. . . . Do not congregate in one place. Meetings should not be held. Even church should now be limited. You should not be considered a sinner if you limit your church activities to a minimum. Stay at home and work, a busy body has no time for idle gossip. Early to bed early to rise makes a man healthy, wealthy and wise. We are at war with your homeland. Hysteria is created to a large extent by the actions of you people. Limit your actions and hysteria will die a natural death.

The press, particularly the Hearst papers, contributed to the hate-filled atmosphere, printing stories of farmers growing tomato plants to point to military installations, and brush fires set in the shape of arrows, also allegedly to direct Japan's air force to America's strategic areas. Editors, reporters, and columnists refused to draw the obvious distinctions between the Japanese who bombed Pearl Harbor and those who lived in America, two-thirds of whom were American citizens because they were born in the United States and the majority of whom were eighteen years of age and under.

Nami Nakashima, then twenty-five, remembers the newspapers. "They were very slanted. They'd have these cartoons of awful Japanese with big glasses and four rows of teeth. Sharklike. It was terrible."

Seventeen-year-old Sumi Seo remembers the hate:

The movies were showing these Tojo caricatures. It made everybody hate anything Japanese. The Sons and Daughters of the Golden West wanted to get rid of us. Insurance companies canceled all the insurance on the Japanese. Earl Warren was running for governor, and running against us. Everybody turned, just like that, regardless of how friendly they were before the war.

And six-year-old Jim Matsuoka remembers the fear. "We couldn't open the doors of our houses because we were simply afraid. There were a lot of rumors going around that people were being beaten."

★   ★   ★   ★   ★

Kay Uno

Kay and her brother Ernest grew up in Los Angeles. Kay was the youngest of ten children.

I was nine at the time of Pearl Harbor, and I was in third grade. That Sunday we were on our way home from church and we had the radio on in the car. Everybody was excited. We said, "Oh, those Japs, what are they doing that for?" We didn't think of ourselves as Japs.

When the war happened, my parents were really torn. Japan was their country. They were Japanese, and they couldn't have citizenship here. Buddy, my oldest brother, was in Japan, and my relatives were all there. But all of us kids were Americans. In a lot of ways, my parents were very American. They flew the flag for every national holiday. My father was born on the Fourth of July, and he celebrated the Fourth in a big way.

We lived six blocks from where I went to school, and I always walked. All the merchants and everybody knew me. "Hi. How are you?" Monday, they turned their backs on me. "There goes that little Jap!"

I'm looking around. Who's a Jap? Who's a Jap? Then it dawned on me, I'm the Jap.

After Pearl Harbor, the kids began to shun me. My friends. One person started it, and then pretty soon it went throughout the school. My classmates were the last ones to leave me. My teacher and the music teacher were both very supportive all through the time. When I had to leave, one of them gave me a gift, a gold leaf pin. It was the first real piece of jewelry I ever had. I still have it.

There was the curfew at eight. You had to be off the streets and in the house. It didn't bother me, but it was hard for my sisters and brothers. People couldn't travel more than a certain number of miles. We had a friend, Chris. Going to work was outside his range, so he moved in with us. When the evacuation came, he evacuated as part of our household.

There was a lot of tension in the house with the FBI coming. My family would shoo me off upstairs or into the kitchen or the back yard. But I knew something serious was happening. Big ears, I listened.

The boys all made model planes bought in Woolworth's. My father had sent a model to my oldest brother, Buddy, who was in Japan. The boys had them hanging in the bedroom window and on the table where they were working. They had the model plans tacked on the wall. The FBI took all of that away. They said my father was a spy, sending airplane plans to Japan.

When Father was taken, we knew it was because of Buddy. A few years later my dad told me they were accusing him of poisoning the American food chain because he was working for an insecticide company. They also said he was directing farmers how to plant signals, and he was spying on crop-duster airports that were strategic airfields. Some of the airports became training fields, but not until after he was gone!

One of these days somebody's got to write a comedy about these FBI men making up all these stories and trying to find out who this man, my father, is. A friend said it's too serious and too sad. I said, "I know, but at a certain point you have to laugh."

Frank Emi

Frank was twenty-five at the time of Pearl Harbor.

It was morning, and we had just opened up our grocery store. I had turned the radio on and I heard this news flash that Pearl Harbor has been attacked. We didn't know where Pearl Harbor was. It didn't mean much.

I remembered the Orson Welles show, the radio drama of the War of the Worlds, where everybody went panic-stricken. They thought we were being invaded by Martians. I thought it was another drama like that, a dramatization of a war with Japan, especially in the climate the newspapers had been painting. I listened and thought, They sure make it sound real. They'd have music going, and then all of a sudden "Bulletin—Flash!" Just the way I heard it on the Orson Welles show.

Then, as the day wore on, I turned to different stations, and they were all saying the same thing. It dawned on me that we *were* at war. The climate had been getting more ominous by the week. Right away we wondered, What's going to happen to our parents? They weren't allowed to become naturalized citizens. Now they were enemy aliens. I wasn't concerned about us. We were Americans. We never thought anything would happen to us.

When my parents were farming, we had a good friend and neighbor. She was a very religious, Christian person. She used to send us kids a book every year at Christmastime until Pearl Harbor. After that, she wrote a very nasty letter saying, "You Japs started this war!" We never heard from her again.

Our store was in an area that was practically all white. Business went on as usual. We had steady customers, all Caucasians. They told us, "Don't worry. You're not the enemy." If we didn't have the evacuation, I don't think we would have been bothered too much, at least in our little area. Some other place, maybe out in the farms, people might have been shot.

Sumi Seo

Sumi had just turned seventeen when the war broke out.

We were in San Pedro [California], right on the coast. My father was a farmer. On December 7, my mother, myself, and my dad were out working in the celery fields. We learned about Pearl Harbor in the afternoon when our Caucasian neighbor came by. He had a gun and he started shooting at my dad. He was yelling, "You Japs started the war. You bombed Pearl Harbor!" Who knew where Pearl Harbor was? I didn't.

I was in the eleventh grade. Monday I went back to school. I saw the kids in the hallways and started talking to them. They turned their heads and looked the other way. The white kids didn't want to have anything to do with us because of all these rumors. They said enemy airplanes were flying here. They said Japanese submarines shut the refinery over in Santa Barbara. They said the Japanese army was getting ready to invade.

These were people who were friends. They gave me the silent treatment. You never forget those silent treatments. A lot of people say, "Why don't you forget and forgive?" But when somebody gives you the silent treatment, you cannot. It's in you for life.

Ernest Uno

Ernie was sixteen and a junior in high school.

The next day I went to school. There was myself and one Korean boy in the class. An English teacher immediately started to tell horror stories of how she heard from a friend of a friend who said the Japanese living in Hawaii had signal flares for the Japanese bombers. Her friend's friend came up with these stories almost daily.

A couple of weeks after Pearl Harbor was the Christmas break. I went back to school in January. Although there weren't a large number of Japanese students, we were pretty much told it was best not to come back. Life would be made uncomfortable for us. The school administration, the vice principal, and all the students let us know. The vice principal was up front in telling us he didn't like the Japanese.

Amy Hiratzka

Amy was eighteen at the time of Pearl Harbor and lived on the Coast, halfway between San Francisco and Los Angeles.

After church was over, my brother and I saw our mother and father off. They were going to Los Angeles. It was about four hours away. Later our mom told us she heard about Pearl Harbor on the car radio. My father pooh-poohed it all the way down. They saw placards: "Pearl Harbor Bombed!" They hadn't reached Los Angeles yet, but on the streets there were newspaper extras—"War with Japan!" My father said, "Never. Never!"

At 10:00 P.M., three FBI men came to our house through the back and cut the telephone wires. In those days we didn't lock our doors, so they were able to come in. My younger brother and myself were alone in the house.

They said they wanted Paul Masuo Hiratzka. "Why do you want him? Who are you?" They opened up their coats to show us the badge. I told them he went to a meeting in Los Angeles, and our mother had gone with him to do her Christmas shopping, and that they were at the Olympic Hotel. I was crying by then.

They searched the house. The only thing they took was a picture of my uncle, who was an admiral in the Japanese navy. They said they would have to take us down to the police station. In the years that have passed, my brother and I say we were taken hostage.

We were at the police station until four-thirty in the morning. No one talked to us. We didn't know what was happening to my parents. Then they heard on the police radio that Paul Masuo Hiratzka was taken in.

The night of December 7, my parents had gone to a banquet in Los Angeles. The next morning, the police broke down the hotel door. My father said he would go in style, and he wore his tuxedo to the jail. Then they released my mother, so she was able to come home.

For three months we had no idea where my father was. Finally we heard from him. We got a censored letter. They cut out words. He was detained in the "dangerous alien enemy" camp in Missoula, Montana.

Ben Tagami

Ben was a freshman in high school.

I went to school on Monday. We used to eat lunch with other kids, but all of a sudden it just slammed down on us. None of the kids would associate with us. Before Pearl Harbor, I had good friends who were Caucasians—an Italian kid, a Jewish kid, an Okie, and a couple of Mexican kids. We all used to hang around together. I was the one Japanese. The day after Pearl Harbor, they were civil with me, you know, but they weren't that friendly. The son of the junior high school principal and I used to run around together. I had had dinner over at their house. Not after Pearl Harbor.

I still played basketball. The teammates were not friendly anymore. During Christmas vacation we went to a basketball tournament. The coach and one of the players on the other team said they wouldn't play us. "You got a Jap on the team. We won't play with this Jap." Glen Davis was a student at the other school. He stood up for me. He said, "This guy is not a Jap." He had never met me and he stood up for me. He was a star athlete there. In fact he was the star athlete in the country, an all-American. The coaches finally consented and allowed me to play.

We had an anti-aircraft battery right near the house. These army guys would come over, and we'd feed them. One night about two months after Pearl Harbor, they saw a car come out from the orange orchard. The people in the car started shooting at the house. The army guys got us out of the house and stuck us into a pipe in an irrigation ditch. We were in there maybe three or four hours. When we went back into the house, there were holes in the walls.

Yosh Kuromiya

Yosh was eighteen and a high school graduate.

I was studying art at Pasadena Junior College. Monday I was back in school. We heard that in the Imperial Valley area, a man came to the door of a house. When the parents opened the door, he blasted them with a shotgun. Immediately after that a girl in one of my classes left school and never returned. I think it was her parents or relatives of hers who were shot.

Then they started picking up some of the older generation. Most of my friends' fathers were picked up. It's a wonder my dad wasn't. He took his turn in being part of the committee running the Japanese language school. We packed a little bag for him and set it by the front door, and said, "Well, I guess you're next." It was all a joke to us. We really didn't take it seriously.

I didn't think it had that much to do with me. I said, "What's the big fuss about my being of Japanese heritage? We didn't bomb Pearl Harbor. We're Americans." I was surprised when they insisted on associating us with the enemy. Even when they posted restrictions that you can't travel more than five miles from home, and the curfew, I really couldn't believe it. I said, "Gee, what's going on here? They can't mean me. I haven't done anything." I thought, This will all blow over. It's just a temporary hysterical overreaction. I never took any of it seriously, not even the evacuation itself. I thought we'll be back as soon as this thing blows over. I was so naive.

Betty Morita

Betty grew up in Hood River, Oregon. She was eight years old.

My dad must have heard from other families that the FBI would be coming. We had apple orchards, and the farmers use dynamite to take out stumps of trees. My father knew he must have a stick or half a stick of dynamite somewhere. A day or two before the FBI came, he and my older brother were turning the house upside down trying to find it, but they couldn't. He was so afraid the FBI was going to find something. But when they came, they didn't find anything.

Our nearest Japanese neighbor, about a mile away, didn't realize that he *did* have some dynamite. They found half a stick in his barn that he had forgotten about. He was arrested right away, taken to the jail, and sent to a camp. I don't know how long he was separated from his family.

Sue Kunitomi

Sue graduated from high school in February 1941. She lived with her mother and seven brothers and sisters in Los Angeles. Her father had died years before the war.

We were at the store that morning, and I was listening to the radio. They broke into the music station and said Japanese planes were bombing Pearl Harbor.

By afternoon my brothers started to come home. This was a Sunday, and they had gone with their friends to play ball. They said, "Little Tokyo is all barricaded. The police are there. Everybody is driving by to see what's happening."

I said, "So it's really true."

It was scary, although everybody in the neighborhood—the Caucasians, the Mexican Americans, the teachers—all came in and said, "Don't worry, you're our friends, and we'll be here for you." We didn't have anybody making threats, maybe because we were in the residential part of Little Tokyo. The business part was bad. By nightfall the FBI had rounded up everybody.

It was a bad time. Fear, mostly. What's going to happen to us? The Issei were now considered to be enemy aliens, even though they had lived here most of their adult life. My mother came before World War I. We kids were Japanese, but we're Americans. Everybody said, "Don't worry, we're American citizens. We're going to be protected." But we didn't know that.

The average person who knew us was opposed to the government's action, but they didn't feel they should say anything. If you did, you were going to be unpatriotic. You were going to be a "Jap lover."

A young man I know told me his grandparents were shot in their bed after Pearl Harbor. They lived up north in a small farming community. Probably none of this ever got in the papers.

There was a large Italian population, but nothing happened to them, and nothing happened to the Germans. When the notice came out it said: "To all persons of *Japanese* ancestry." That's all. You feel like you're a prisoner. You're inside your house and you can't go out after eight o'clock. You don't know whether you even dare to step out on the front porch. Then General DeWitt [Commanding General of the Western Defense Command] issued a public proclamation exempting other aliens of enemy nationalities [Germans and Italians] from curfew restrictions and travel restrictions. Only the Japanese [were still affected].

In the beginning, some of the newspapers and radio commentators were sympathetic. But as the months went by and the United States and Britain were losing [in the Pacific theater of war], it was "they" may come and invade the United States. People really felt that, although the military had enough information to know that Japan didn't have any plans to do it.

The newspapers began talking about sabotage at Pearl Harbor, and that the Hawaiian cane fields had arrows dug in the ground. Ridiculous kinds of things. People talked about flashlights signaling enemy planes. Some of this stuff is unbelievable. DeWitt was going crazy. Even as we were reading the stuff, it seemed incredible people would believe this, but they did.

We wondered, What's going to happen to us? Probably everybody will turn their guns on us. There was a lot of talk like that especially among the Isseis, particularly after the whole community leadership was gone. By Monday morning after Pearl Harbor, there was nobody left. People could not get money out of their bank accounts. They couldn't open their stores. They couldn't do business because the family head was gone, and in most cases the father was the only one who knew what was going on. My mother was giving credit to everybody because nobody had money to buy anything. Overnight they were completely impoverished, not just in terms of money, but in their whole life.

Clifford Uyeda

Clifford grew up in Tacoma, Washington, and went to college in Wisconsin in the late 1930s.

My major was English. I finished all my requirements for the degree, but with the war in Europe starting, you wish you had something concrete to do, rather than just being able to appreciate literature. I thought medicine might be interesting.

I had applied to medical schools in various places. Two weeks after Pearl Harbor, I got an acceptance letter from Boston University. I sent letters to the other medical schools saying, I've already accepted one, so you can cross me off.

Then I get a letter from Boston University, saying, "The Admission Committee has reversed their decision. Here's your deposit back." I

wrote back and said they should give me the reason. They said, "Circumstances beyond our control." I knew it had to be because I'm
Japanese-American.

Dollie Nagai

*Dollie was the youngest of five daughters. She was fourteen at the time of
Pearl Harbor.*

My father was in the wholesale produce business. The banks were
freezing accounts. My father lost the business because people didn't
pay their bills, and then he couldn't pay his bills.

After Pearl Harbor, my mother told us to bring all the books out
that were Japanese. She had a big bonfire. I saw all my children's
books and records go up in flames. I was crying. She said, "We can't
keep them here. The FBI may come, and we don't know what's
going to happen."

It wasn't a Japanese neighborhood we lived in. It was German, Italian, and others. I went to the Christian church. In school we had a
mixture. It was a real integrated school, and you made friends with
everybody. My best friends were a girl who was half Mexican, half
German, a Chinese girl, and two Japanese-American girls.

[After Pearl Harbor] kids I had known all my life asked me, "What
nationality are you?" That really shook me up. I had known them
from grammar school. They knew what I was.

I lived on the west side of town, and I had a Caucasian friend on
the other side. One day I rode my bicycle to the other side to see her.
A young boy went past me and called me "Jap." It was the first time
I ever heard it, and it stunned me. I didn't challenge him. I just went
my own way, brooding about it.

Mits Koshiyama

Mits was a senior in high school.

Before Pearl Harbor, in school my teachers really drilled the Constitution into my head. I wasn't a very good student. About the only

thing that really got drilled into me was no matter what race you are or what you look like, you have certain inalienable rights protected under the Constitution. You have this right to appear in court to prove your innocence. I thought, Gee, what a great government.

After Pearl Harbor, the teachers would never say we were American citizens. Not one of them. None of them spoke up in our behalf. Their use of the word "Japs"—mind you, this is teachers—was terrible. They talked about the principles of the Constitution in social studies, but they didn't understand.

I wish the teachers stood up for us. "Hey, these are just ordinary American students. They haven't done anything wrong. It's wrong to lump them together with the enemy in Japan, which these people have nothing to do with. People are not critical of Italian and German citizens, so why pick on the Japanese Americans?" I wish the teachers would have said that. But they didn't.

In the next months in school, a couple of kids kept on insisting we were "Japs" and we were the enemy. They picked on me every day. "Hey, you Japs have committed a terrible crime and you're going to pay for it!" Finally, I said, "I can't take this anymore. I'm either going to kill somebody or somebody's going to kill me." I told my mother I have to quit high school. She understood. Not one of my Caucasian friends came to see me.

★   ★   ★

The Hawaiian islands were more racially mixed and tolerant than the West Coast of the mainland. Although Hawaii was not free of anti-Asian bigotry, the viciousness and virulence of the hate campaigns on the West Coast were largely absent.

At the time of the bombing of Pearl Harbor, more than a third of the Hawaiian population, some 150,000 people, were ethnic Japanese. Immediately after Pearl Harbor, Hawaii was placed under martial law, with military commanders in charge of virtually all aspects of life on the islands. As on the mainland, in response to the bombing, leaders of the Japanese community in Hawaii were quickly rounded up.

Bert Nakano

My dad had us get up early in the morning. He wanted us to fix a roof. We were on top of the roof when we saw these things starting to pop up in the skies. Black smoke all over. The neighborhood kids said, "Hey, the Japanese bombed Pearl Harbor!"

I came running down to the corner. In our area, there were a lot of Japanese pig farmers. They used to pick up garbage at the military installations and bring it back. They were coming back with stories of bombing. Some of them were injured from shrapnel. They had bandages over them.

The government didn't waste any time. They picked up all the ministers, educators, community leaders, and fishermen. I went back home, and the FBI was already there. They put my dad in a car, and he was gone. It scared the hell out of you. I don't know what they said to him. My mother was crying.

I was fourteen. My older brother was sixteen, and now he became the head of the family because my mother couldn't speak English. When they took my father away, she said, "What am I going to do about money? What am I going to do?"

My dad was taken to the concentration camp at Sand Island. He was jailed almost a year. Nobody got to see him. I was in eighth grade. After he got picked up, everything is a blank. I don't remember going to school, I don't remember anything after that.

Lillian Sugita

One or two weeks after Pearl Harbor, they picked up my father. It was after dinner. There was a knock, and the FBI came in. They said they had a warrant to search the place. My father's business was in another neighborhood, but we had a little office at the house. They ransacked it. It was a shambles. We were upstairs, so scared. They said to my father, "Take your toothbrush." That's all, and he never came back.

He was sent to a little island just off the harbor that was used as a prisoner-of-war camp. They put some Japanese Americans as well as Japanese aliens in a certain portion of that island. That became the detention center until the family was reunited and moved to the concentration camps on the mainland. It was almost a year he was locked up on that island. And for a year we had no idea what was going to happen.

In my parents' situation, because they were [American] citizens, they were given a little bit more, if you can call that anything. We could see my father for about ten or fifteen minutes between the bars. The Niseis had a "privilege" like that. Isseis didn't even get to see their husbands.

After Pearl Harbor, school was out for a few days. The entire island was in a state of emergency. Martial law. Immediately they implemented a blackout. People had to put black shades in their windows. We took it literally. If so much as one little bit of light passed through the crevice, the police are going to come and catch us.

We lived in a mixed community, Japanese and Hawaiians. The kids were fine, but the Hawaiian parents became a little bit paranoid about talking to us. It's sad that people react that way immediately.

You'd see MPs and servicemen everywhere. No matter where you went, they'd be there in full gear. We were told not to go very far, being kids. Before the war, we had gone to Japanese language school after English school, two hours every day, plus all day on Saturday. That promptly closed. The churches closed. Everything was different. Other nationalities went on with their lives, but for us, everything changed.

I was in eighth grade. When we went back to school, it was very tense. There was a certain amount of stigma for us. It wasn't like the masses of Japanese Americans on the mainland. In my school, I was the only one [affected by the roundup]. I was embarrassed. People would say, "Oh, you're going to be sent to these prisoner camps."

After my father was taken, from that day on life changed completely. One of my sisters says that ever since the war started, she's been messed over. We kids were totally in the dark. Back then Japanese parents didn't tell you anything except, "Don't worry about it. Let us do the worrying."

Facing page: *Detainees arrive at Santa Anita assembly center, April 1942;*

Waiting to be evacuated, San Francisco.

3

ON ORDERS FROM THE
PRESIDENT: PREPARATION
FOR EVACUATION

In the months immediately following the bombing of Pearl Harbor, Japan's military forces seemed to be unstoppable as they swept through the Pacific. With each of Japan's successes, anti-Japanese sentiment in America increased. Pressure began to build for the evacuation of all the Japanese, both aliens and citizens, from the West Coast. The Congressional delegation from the Coast states sent President Roosevelt a letter urging the evacuation of "all persons of Japanese lineage." A California state legislature committee added its voice to the calls for removal, along with private groups like the Native Sons of the Golden West. Many newspaper columnists advocated forced evacuation. In a particularly hate-filled column in the *San Francisco Examiner*, Henry McLemore wrote:

> Herd 'em up, pack 'em off and give 'em the inside room in the badlands. Let 'em be pinched, hurt, hungry, and dead up against it. . . . Let us have no patience with the enemy or with anyone whose veins carry his blood. . . . Personally, I hate the Japanese.

In a surprising abandonment of civil liberties principles, Walter Lippmann, one of the most respected columnists of the time, supported the idea of evacuation in a February 12 article entitled "The Fifth Column on the Coast." The article was circulated in the White House. Seven days later on February 19, 1942, President Roosevelt signed Executive Order [E.O.] 9066, authorizing the Secretary of War to establish military areas from which any persons so designated may be excluded.

Within days of the issuance of E.O. 9066, the machinery for evacuation was established. Assistant Secretary of War John J. McCloy and Colonel Karl R. Bendetsen were the chief architects of the exclusion plan. Secretary of War Henry Stimson appointed Lieutenant General John L. DeWitt to carry out the removal. The Tolan Committee (the House Committee on National Defense Migration) began hearings in four West Coast cities to investigate the situation of enemy aliens. The chair of the committee, John Tolan, from California, supported the evacuation of Japanese aliens, but not Italians or Germans. The committee discussed the example of the parents of Joe DiMaggio, the major-league baseball hero. It was noted they were honest, law-abiding aliens who shouldn't be forced from their home. No one discussed the fact that Italian aliens like the DiMaggios could have become citizens and had apparently chosen not to, whereas Japanese aliens were prohibited by law from doing so.

Throughout March, General DeWitt issued a series of proclamations designating the Coast and western states as military areas. At first the government encouraged a "voluntary evacuation" from the Coast, assuring the Japanese if they moved inland to eastern California or interior states they would be safe. But those who moved to eastern California were evacuated in the spring along with everyone else. And when they traveled across state lines, they were often greeted by "No Japs Wanted!" signs. At the Nevada border, armed bands turned them back. Some migrants were jailed by local police officers, others were threatened with mob violence. Most returned to their homes. By the end of March, the voluntary relocation program was officially stopped, and Japanese Americans were forbidden to leave their homes unless and until so ordered by the army.

Fear and confusion were rampant. The community itself was split. In the vacuum of leadership created by the arrest of so many elders, the Japanese American Citizens League (JACL), a Nisei organization, stepped in and became the self-appointed spokespersons for the community. The JACL leadership believed Japanese Americans had to demonstrate their total loyalty to America in every possible way. Officers of the group testified before the Tolan Committee in support of an evacuation should the government deem it necessary. JACL members had, in fact, been providing the FBI and military intelligence units with names of Issei and Kibei whose loyalty JACL took it upon itself to question.

Many Japanese Americans rejected the JACL approach, resenting the group's attack on fellow Japanese, but most were too politically inexperienced to challenge the JACL. James and Caryl Omura, brother and sister, were the only Japanese Americans to testify before

the Tolan Committee against a mass evacuation, arguing it was a violation of Japanese Americans' rights as citizens. Sue Kunitomi remembers some of the internal strife:

> People were accusing others of being informers, selling out the
> community. Some were saying, "What are the JACL doing?
> They're not talking for us." That's why all this antagonism
> against the JACL still exists. If we're in a bad situation, we
> should stick together. We shouldn't be dividing and fighting
> among ourselves. Maybe the leadership had no other alterna-
> tive, but if they had stuck by their guns a little more, maybe it
> would have been all right.

This was a community without a recognized political voice. Most
Nisei were too young to vote, and the Issei, as aliens, couldn't partic-
ipate in politics. Trapped between escalating bigotry on the one hand,
and a small Japanese-American group claiming to be the voice of the
community on the other, Japanese Americans for the most part went
along with the JACL for want of any other leadership.

There was no "good" way to handle the stress of the times. Some
refused to believe the government would strip them of their rights.
Others tried to prepare as best they could for the anticipated evacuation. When the removal orders were posted, it was largely confusion
and sadness that reigned.

As a prelude to the mass evacuations of the spring and summer of
1942, the navy issued the first exclusion orders in late February to the
Japanese living on Terminal Island. Terminal Island, across from San
Pedro, in Los Angeles Harbor, was home to about 3,000 Japanese, at
least half of whom were American citizens. Island residents worked
as fishermen and in the canning factories. Children went to elementary school on the island but traveled by ferry to San Pedro to attend
high school.

By February all the Issei men with fishing licenses had been arrested
and sent to an internment camp in Bismarck, North Dakota. Sumi
Seo lived in San Pedro, across the bay from Terminal Island. Her

friend Charlie, a Terminal Islander, was taken in one of the early FBI raids:

> After Pearl Harbor they came in the middle of the night to Charlie's house. The FBI man shook his leg and woke him up. "Come on, come on, you're coming with us."
>   Charlie said, "What for? Where am I going?"
>   They just repeated, "You're coming with us."
>   Charlie said, "Wait a minute, I'll get my shoes." They wouldn't let him. He went all the way to Bismarck, North Dakota, in slippers.

On February 25, the remaining Terminal Islanders, primarily women and children, were told they had forty-eight hours to dispose of their life's belongings and leave the island. Yukio Tatsumi tells of those frantic days.

★ ★ ★ ★ ★

Yukio Tatsumi

The next day [after Pearl Harbor] they stormed into Terminal Island. In those days we never had our doors locked. The FBI showed up and checked everything. The Terminal Island people were taken right away because they were fishermen. When the war started, the government accused them of spying. When they'd go out fishing for sardines, they had to go through the battleships. The Pacific fleet was right up all along here. That was the same Pacific fleet that went to Pearl Harbor and was bombed. We knew all the names. We used to sit on the wharfs and watch the battleships.

After the war started, we were still going to school on the ferry boat [to San Pedro]. The MPs checked you on the Terminal Island side before you got on the boat. But we couldn't go to a movie because the movies were in San Pedro. I read in the paper that Chinese Americans were walking around with buttons saying "I'm an American Chinese" because they were mistaken for Japanese. There were all kinds of rumors, like if you go to a Japanese restaurant, they'll put poison in your food. They refused to give Japanese people haircuts.

In February, the Navy Department put a sign up that we had to leave in forty-eight hours. Hell, we had to leave everything! There were looters. People came by, and they were like vultures. We went wherever we had friends. That's where we stayed until we were evacuated to camp.

★   ★   ★

In the rest of this chapter, young people from the mainland and Hawaii tell of the days leading up to the evacuation.

Dollie Nagai   (AGE 14)

Word was passed around that they were going to move us. My parents started buying sleeping bags for each of us in preparation for the evacuation. I thought we were going to be traveling around in our trucks and sleeping in the bags. We had to get shots, typhoid and others. The signs were out on the telephone posts. Executive Order 9066. We didn't understand it. We were going someplace, but we didn't know where.

Two things that were important to me were the piano and my bicycle. A Caucasian friend took the piano with the understanding that we were to get it back when we came home. I had to fight for it when I returned. I was an adult then, so I was able to stand up for my rights, and I did get it back. Other Caucasian friends took the bicycle. They were *real* friends. They [helped us and] drove our family to the camp in their own car.

Amy Akiyama   (AGE 8)

Everyone was so busy, and I guess they were distraught. My father was very quiet. Thinking back on it, I think he was very depressed. He said very little.

He was very organized. He packed everything in boxes. He had a pad and he numbered all the boxes and said what was in them. We were leaving our things with two nursery school teachers [Caucasians] who became very good friends of ours. They kept our refrigerator, our phonograph and radio, and a car we had. We were very fortunate. They sent us letters and packages at Christmas.

My father was sent somewhere else because he was not a citizen. I don't know why they took him. There's nothing I can think of that was subversive about him. He was a gardener. He didn't read books in Japanese. He wasn't interested in the community. He was a loner. My mother was left with the three of us. She assured us we would see him later. "He just has to go and talk to some people."

We had very few belongings we could take. My mother said take what you like the most. We took books, and I remember taking a doll. My mother was questioning the whole thing. She would argue every inch of the way. We were in a church in Berkeley. That was the embarkation point. We had tags so that we wouldn't lose each other. We were number 13661. My mother had my brother on her hip and my sister and me. She argued with the soldier who was standing there. She said, "My children were born here, I was born here. I don't understand this. Why are you doing this? How would you feel?" The people in back would say, "Come on, come on, he can't help it," in Japanese.

Ernest Uno   (AGE 16)

Mom said, "Start getting rid of all your junk." I had a Schwinn balloon-tired bike. In those days we worked hard to earn money to buy our own bicycle. I had to get rid of it. I sold it for $5. It broke my heart that that was all it was worth to whoever bought it. It was red and white. It was a beautiful bike.

People were like scavengers. Wherever they knew Japanese families were, they'd come right up. "Hey, you got anything to sell? What do you want to get rid of?"

Sue Kunitomi   (AGE 18)

After the president signed Executive Order 9066, we had all these meetings in Little Tokyo [Los Angeles]. I went to one of them. There were some people who wanted to protest and others who wanted to wait and see what the government was going to do. There was a big debate over whether we should go quietly and cooperate with the government, or whether everybody should go on their own wherever they could. There was a lot of opposition to that because of all the discrimination out there.

I heard some people were going to chain themselves to a telephone pole. They were dissuaded. We kept wondering whether anybody was going to protest. We sat around saying, They can't do this to us. We're American citizens. But we didn't have much power. We had nobody in Congress, we had nobody in the city or state legislature who would say one word for us.

I had a friend whose mother had died a year before. They had to sell her sewing machine. Some woman offered him $5. "I was so mad," he said, "I told her, 'Get the hell out of here!' I took a crowbar and I broke it into little bits and I buried it. I was not going to let anybody buy my mother's sewing machine for $5."

My mother stored her Christmas ornaments with a friend and never got them back. Same thing happened to my brother. They left their furniture with a neighbor, supposedly locked up in a garage. When they came back, the neighbor said, "We sold it," and didn't even offer to give them the money.

We registered at the old Union Church. My mother sent my oldest brother. She said, "I don't know where we're going, but we cannot be separated." He signed all of us up, including his in-laws, nieces and nephews, everybody. All together he must have registered about twenty-five of us. Our family number was 2614.

People who went to Santa Anita left on a Friday in the first week of May. We went down there to say goodbye to all our friends. That was really heartbreaking for the older people. Everybody was saying, "We'll see each other again. The war's not going to last forever." Oh, it was a bad time.

Saturday morning we left. At the train station, there were many soldiers with guns. It was scary. All our friends helped us to take our luggage, so we took more than our two bags apiece. Just before we boarded, a man came up and said he had been asked to buy me a box of candy by one of the young men in the neighborhood. "But," he said, "there are no stores open this morning." He said he was really sorry. I burst into tears. I looked up and there was a soldier staring at me. He turned away.

We had a Caucasian friend who had always lived in Little Tokyo. He was a veteran of the Spanish-American War and he was living on a veteran's pension. Around nine-thirty or ten in the morning, he'd come down and say hello to my mother. He knew everybody in the neighborhood.

He hated FDR because of the evacuation. He said he was so lonely when we left. "I can hear my footsteps behind me," he said. "Everybody is gone. All my friends are gone."

For farmers, the evacuation caused a special distress. Fields were planted, and some crops were near harvest.

Noboru Taguma   (AGE 19)

We were farming ten to fifteen acres. Mr. Todd Hunter was the owner. He was a nice man, really good to Japanese. One year there was a bad frost, and my father couldn't pay the rent. Mr. Hunter knew we had seven children. "Mr. Taguma, you don't have to pay this year, but when you make it next year, you'll pay." A decent man.

We'd grow the vegetables and sell them to a wholesaler. We'd also go to the market, and people would buy directly. We had everything planted. It was all growing. My father looked at the field and said, "Oh, my God, we have to leave everything."

Mits Koshiyama   (AGE 17)

The farm was just beginning to get pretty good when the war started. It was March or April and all the crops were planted. We weren't allowed to crop it. We lost everything. Strawberries were a month away. We had a lot of green berries and a lot of flowers at the time, and my mother said, "We're going to lose all this. All this hard work for nothing." Till the last moment, she thought something might happen. She kept working the berry farm and hoping for the best.

When you lose things like that, which your whole family worked so hard for, it's normal to be resentful. Nobody's going to say, I'm happy we lost it, and I want to cooperate with the government. No way.

Mary Sakaguchi   (AGE 21)

I grew up with my father and mother not able to vote or own land. When the evacuation was announced, we sort of accepted that we were being treated as second-class citizens.

My father had two weeks to try to sell the farm equipment. We were lucky to even get $1,100 for it. We had thirty acres of crops all ready to be picked. We would have made a fortune.

We had a big truck that was only about a year or two old, and a four-door passenger Plymouth. We took the car to a Korean dentist friend and the truck to a Caucasian friend. When we were allowed to come back to California after the war, the dentist said, "I'm sorry, but I sold your car." He wouldn't give my sister any money. I was surprised an Oriental would treat another Oriental that way. The Caucasian fellow gave us back the truck.

We owned our house, and everything was all paid for. My father rented it during the evacuation, but no one ever paid a cent. They knew we couldn't collect.

Amy Hiratzka   (AGE 18)

With Germans and Italians, it was individual cases. We were aware of that. What an injustice! We were the three "enemies," and they just took us. Of course, we were obvious.

There were people who were silent. Then there were people who came forth to help us. Rachel Miller. She was a member of the Episcopal church, and really the only one who stood out from the onset and said, "This is wrong." She told us, "Whatever you have that you want me to take care of, I'll be glad to." We stored all our stuff with Mrs. Miller, and everything was there when we came back.

All the years we had been in the church. They'd give lip service, but they were afraid. It wasn't that they thought we had done wrong, or that they hated us. It wasn't that at all. It was through fear they reacted.

They said we were being removed for safekeeping, for our protection. Ha! On the other hand, they also said sabotage and all that. They were torn. They didn't know exactly where they stood. I see people like that today.

Betty Morita   (AGE 8)

Late at night my father and mother were talking to my older brothers and sisters. They were saying they may be sent back to Japan. My father said, "You have to take care of your younger brothers and sisters." That's the first time I thought, Gee, what's happening? What's really going on? My parents are going to be gone? It was frightening.

I was in the third grade. I remember the last day of school. We were going to have to leave early. My teacher had all the kids in my class go out and pick wildflowers and give me a bouquet. I'll never forget that.

Sumi Seo   (AGE 17)

First they told us we were going to go to Manzanar. They said it was way out in the desert, and there were lots of snakes. Be sure to wear boots. That was my first pair of boots. Then they said it's going to be cold. That was my first coat. We never had to have a coat, only a sweater. We stuffed a lot of sheets and things in an army duffel bag. Each one of us had a suitcase, and that was it. My mother had a small little Buddhist shrine. She put that in her pocket. I had to leave my German Shepherd dog home. His name was Poochie. He was about two years old.

It was over twenty-five years we lived on the farm. We had to get rid of the horses and the farm equipment. The day we evacuated, I saw my father talking to his horses. He was saying, "I hope the next person will take care of you real good." The tears came.

The day we left, there were hundreds of us. All of San Pedro. Then Long Beach. The whites lined the sidewalk and watched us as we moved by—like "Good riddance, I'm glad you're leaving." Nobody waved.

Clifford Uyeda (AGE 24)

My mother was running a store. She said, "We have to keep the store open until the very last moment so we can clear the debts to these wholesalers." You could say, "They're going to put me into camp, so why should I have to pay my debt?" But she felt that's an obligation we should pay.

My wife's father was a tailor. They were evacuated and didn't have a chance to pay taxes that particular year. After the war, the first thing he did was see how much he still owed the government. He wanted to be sure his taxes were up-to-date.

Kay Uno (AGE 9)

I loved to play dolls. When we were preparing to go, the government said we could bring just what we could carry. I thought, I'll take my doll named Hana. We had some neighbors who weren't real close to us. The little girl was about my age, and we used to play together. When I said I was going to take this doll, she said, "No, you don't need it. I want it."

I said, "I'm going to keep this doll with me." I had given her another doll, but it didn't have all the clothes. She stepped on my doll and broke it.

We left in March or April [1942]. I remember having the family number put on me. It was like a dog tag or a luggage tag on a piece of string.

Frank Emi   (AGE 25)

We put our business out for sale, and we had a hard time. People who were interested had us over a barrel. We got some ridiculous offers that really made me very angry. I almost threw somebody out of the store.

We had about $25,000 invested in it, which at that time was a lot of money for us. It was about two years' work that we had put back into the business without taking wages. All we could get out of it was $1,500. It was almost given away.

The postscript was after we came back from camp. I went to the store to see how it was doing. Somebody else was there. I asked the guy, "How much did you pay for this?" At first he wouldn't tell me. But I told him, "We opened up this store and sold it for $1,500 bucks." His eyes were bulging. "Yeah?" he says. "I paid $100,000." During the war, everybody made a lot of money.

Issei, as aliens, were not permitted to own property. If their Nisei chil-dren were not of legal age, some Issei registered property in others' names. This happened in Frank's family.

Luckily my father and mother had their own house, so we were able to store stuff in one bedroom. When my parents bought the prop-erty, it was in a good friend's daughter's name. When I became of age, they transferred it over. During the war, we rented it out, and we locked one bedroom with all our valuable stuff in there. The people who rented it promised to take good care of our things. When we got back, they had broken into the room, and anything of any value was stolen.

Tetsuko Morita   (AGE 13)

Tetsuko grew up on a farm in Sacramento, California, in a family of twelve children.

We didn't have much money, but my father managed to buy a card-board suitcase and get a duffel bag. It was only one week's notice. My mother was worried they'd separate us kids. She cooked lots of rice and sun-dried it. Then she put it in bags for each of us, so we'd have something to eat.

People stood around waiting for you to leave. I was mad all the time. I can still see those vultures. We had a horse, tractors, truck, car, and like everybody else, we didn't have time to sell anything. When we left, they went right in to find something they wanted.

Avey Diaz   (AGE 30)

Avey Diaz, a Mexican American, was married to Nami Nakashima, whose father was Japanese and mother was Mexican-American.

We were married and had bought a new house. We didn't have too much. I came home from work, and here were these three FBI guys. One of them said, "We're going to take your wife to camp."

I said, "You take her, you take me."

He said, "Be my guest."

I didn't feel sorry for my wife. I just loved her. I'm a Latin. That's the way we live. They said, "All right." And I left my house with just the clothes on my back.

Nami Nakashima Diaz   (AGE 25)

We had no idea what was happening. They'd tell us, "No, you don't have to go because you're only part Japanese." Then they'd say, "We have no idea." One Friday night we came home and there was a poster on the front door, "Report at 7 a.m. on Sunday at the Electric Cars Depot." That was Easter morning. They classified my family as Japanese because our name was Nakashima, my father's name. Later we found out anybody who was one-eighth Japanese had to go into camp. We boxed up everything as quickly as we could and took it over to my husband's folks and left it there. We didn't sell anything.

My father lost his whole business. Overnight it was gone. Towards the last part of his life, he had cancer. He sat in front of his fireplace and had all his papers. People still owed him. Some tried to pay him, but when they came back, there was nothing.

Yosh Kuromiya   (AGE 18)

I had a little Model A roadster. I was one of the early hot-rodders that put a V-8 engine in this little four-cylinder car. In shop in high school, I dropped the chassis and jazzed it up. Smoothed out the radiator shell and dropped the headlights, put the loud mufflers on it. That was my pride and joy. It was black. I put my graduation money and a lot of work into it. It was a dumb thing, but that was my whole identity in those days. I was really proud of it. It would have been easily worth $400, $450, but I had to get rid of it. I sold it to the first person who came along. I was in no position to bargain.

Fortunately, the owners of the house we were renting were very considerate and generous. They allowed us to store most of our furnishings and our pickup truck on the premises. When we came back, there were no wheels on the truck, and the place had been broken into and a lot of the things were missing. But their generosity really impressed us. They had nothing to gain by it. Just a matter of simple human decency. It's things like that, people like that, that kept us afloat.

Lillian Sugita   (AGE 13)

Lillian grew up in Honolulu. In Hawaii, out of a population of some 150,000 Japanese, only about 1,100 were evacuated.

We had to take the evacuation notice to school. My teacher said, "Are you being sent to those camps?" He was so moved and angry about it. He said be sure to write to him when I reach there. Later I read in the newspaper that during the McCarthy hearings he was red-baited from school. He was the only person who knew anything about the evacuation. The other teachers had no idea. He was very knowledgeable. Very decent. I admire him so much.

Just to pack to get out of our home was something. We didn't have very long. My mother was working day and night, getting all the things sorted. She was packing for the family of five only what we were allowed. We were all kids. She had no help. Somehow we packed everything. We had to get to the immigration center early in the morning. That's where we saw all the other families. It was kind of nice to think that you're not alone, that there were others going through the same thing.

They rounded you up like cattle. We were in an enclosed fence area, and they gave you a number. "Gather your things. This is your spot. You stay put until we tell you where to go." We're all sitting there and everybody is looking lost, not daring to talk to anybody, just watching each other. We don't know what's going on, and we don't ask questions. My mother is a real strong woman but quiet. She just says, "Behave. We're going to know soon enough."

We spent pretty much the whole day waiting around. When we found out we're going to get on a ship, they brought all the men out. It was chaotic. Everybody's looking for their families. That was the first time I saw my father in a year.

On the boat, I was the only one from my school. We felt lost, but kids being kids, we made friends with the family in the next room. I think we were on the boat about seven days. This was December 1942. We didn't know where we were going. My mother was saying, "We're going somewhere far." That's all she knew.

After we landed in San Francisco, we were put on a train. MPs are going back and forth down the aisle. In some ways, children are funny. You don't want to face up to what it is. We started giggling. We'd laugh about everything. I think we spent all our camp years doing that. Especially when it really hits you. It's impossible to survive, to live with pain day in, day out. You go to the other extreme—everything's a joke. It's a way of hiding.

Facing page: *Food line at Santa Anita assembly center.*

4

LIFE IN THE CAMPS

Beginning in late March 1942 and continuing through the summer, thousands of Japanese families crowded together at bus and train stations up and down the West Coast. Guarded by armed soldiers, they stood by their life possessions, two bags per person. They didn't know where they were going or what awaited them.

Mary Sakaguchi remembers, "We left for camp . . . on a gray, cloudy day, and just before we got on the bus, it began to rain. A mother of two standing next to me said, 'See, even God in heaven is crying for us.' "

For most of the Japanese Americans, the official evacuation took place in two stages. The first move was to an "assembly center" under the control of the army. The second was to a more permanent "relocation center," a prison camp administered by a civilian agency, the War Relocation Authority (WRA).

In order to evacuate the Coast as quickly as possible, the army had to find preexisting structures for the assembly centers. Racetracks, livestock exhibition arenas, and fairgrounds were hastily converted into living quarters. Thirteen of the sixteen assembly centers were in California, the others in Washington, Oregon, and Arizona. The largest center was the racetrack at Santa Anita, near Los Angeles, which at one time housed nearly 19,000. Most people stayed in these centers for three to four months. Some remained for as long as seven months, while the more permanent prison camps were being built.

From the assembly centers, the detainees were then transported to one of ten prison camps built in desolate places with harsh climatic conditions. Eight of the ten camps were in arid areas, stifling hot in summer, bitter cold in winter. Two of the camps were in the remote swamplands of Arkansas. As Sumi Seo says, "How the devil did they ever find places like that to put us in?"

The Japanese in America had been a remarkably law-abiding people. Suddenly, and solely because of their race, they were imprisoned. "The feeling of being prisoners," remembers Frank Emi, "was the worst thing. There was a barbed-wire fence all around, and they had watch towers with armed guards" and guns that pointed inward at the camp population.

The traditional pattern of Japanese life, centered on the family, was disrupted. Barracks at the camps had multiple rooms with walls going only partway up to the roof. Noise could be heard from one end of the barrack to the other. Privacy all but vanished. Bath facilities were communal, with toilets back to back or side by side with no partitions or doors. Everyone washed laundry in communal rooms and ate in large mess halls. As Sohei Hohri said, "Sitting down at the table is a certain kind of celebration. In camp it was a down experience. You finish something because you're hungry, but there's no pleasure in it."

In every camp there were protests, most often strikes against working or living conditions. The riot at Manzanar in December 1942 resulted in many injuries and two deaths. Any inmate thought by other prisoners to be providing information to the WRA camp administrators was considered an *inu,* meaning "dog" in Japanese and used to designate an informer.

With remarkable perseverance in the face of a bitter reality, parents struggled mightily to make life as normal as possible for their children. On the surface at least, they succeeded. Young people attended schools and competed in sports activities. Classes and workshops were organized on subjects as varied as the interests and skills of the prisoner-teachers. Inmates shopped for seeds from Montgomery Ward and Sears catalogues, and planted gardens to cut the erosion and bring some beauty to their desolate quarters.

Still, the fight against boredom and loneliness was constant. Some children and teenagers say they had "fun" in camp, free from the accustomed family discipline. But for most it was a paper-thin veneer of fun covering the pain and stress. One teenage boy talked of having a "great time," but when the government organized a unit for Japanese-American soldiers, he rushed to enlist to "get out of camp as fast as possible."

Although scarred by the experience, these young people for the most part shed tears not for themselves, but for their parents and older siblings. Most were incarcerated in at least two places, an assembly center and a prison camp. The particular center or camp they describe is noted parenthetically.

★   ★   ★   ★   ★

Sumi Seo   (SANTA ANITA, CALIFORNIA)

When we got to Santa Anita, we were in the racetrack. I wonder if you can picture it. It was hot, and you see all these strange faces and soldiers lined up. You go down the line to register with one person, then another. They search your bag. After that they tell you your barracks number and give you a white sack. They had hay in bales at the end of the barracks. You put your hay in the sack. That's your mattress. Then you try to find your barracks, carrying your suitcases and stuff. Finally, when you find the place, you don't know a soul. The rich and the poor. You don't know what to do, what to think. You have to stay in a horse stable, and you get depressed.

Amy Akiyama   (TANFORAN, CALIFORNIA)

When we got to Tanforan, my grandmother and grandfather were already there. They were in the stables with the Dutch door where the horses look out the top. My mother said, "At least they could give you Man o' War's stable!" You could see where they whitewashed over the hay, and where it was coming through the cracks. You had to laugh at it. I think the room was big enough for a horse, and it had two cots. That was it.

Ernest Uno   (SANTA ANITA, CALIFORNIA)

By the time we moved to Santa Anita, they had already built barracks in the parking lot area. We visited in the stables, and thank God we didn't have to live in those things. Those stables just reeked. There was nothing you could do. The amount of lye they threw on it to clear the odor and stuff, it didn't help. It still reeked of urine and horse manure.

It was so degrading for people to live in those conditions. It's almost as if you're not talking about the way Americans treated Americans.

As the buses and trains carrying the evacuees passed through populated areas, the army guards insisted that window shades be pulled down, reinforcing everyone's sense of isolation.

Kay Uno (EN ROUTE)

On the train going to Amache it was hot. When they pulled the shades down, you know kids, we'd peek. We finally got by a window and we all stuck our heads out saying, "Oh, this is cool!" We were getting water in our faces. Turns out it was water from the toilet hitting the tracks and splashing up.

Tetsuko Morita (EN ROUTE)

We went to an assembly center and stayed there one month. Then they packed us off and shipped us to Tule with all the shades down. Even when those MPs were around, I'd peek anyways. I said, "Who cares!" I was in the eighth grade, and we were studying civics. I had just started to learn about the Constitution, and I knew they were doing a wrong thing.

Lillian Sugita (EN ROUTE)

I hadn't heard of Arkansas, and I had no idea where it was. During the day, they would let us pull the shades up, but the minute you got near a town, they made you pull the shades down. We were happy to anyway, because people were gawking at us like we were some kind of monsters.

Babies were always crying. It was very difficult for the adults, I think. But even for us kids something was wrong. Most of the time, we'd sit there depressed. The Hawaiians would get out the ukelele and start to sing. I used to think, "Oh, man, how could they be in such a mood?" My sisters didn't say one word. Two of them just sat there, totally out of it.

We arrived around midnight. It was so dark. Suddenly a bunch of Japanese people came to the train and said, "Welcome! Join the gang!" It was so wonderful to see them. We got on army trucks and rode for at least an hour until we got to the camp.

PHYSICAL ENVIRONMENT

The areas chosen by the government for the prison camps were desolate and marked by stark physical conditions. The barracks were hastily constructed, offering minimal protection against the elements.

Amy Akiyama   (TOPAZ, UTAH)

My mother wept when we got to Topaz. I said, "What's the matter? Why are you crying?"

She said, "All those people meeting us, their hair is all white from the dust." Their eyelashes were filled with this fine dust. Tumbleweed would come loose during a storm and roll for miles and miles through the camp and get caught on the fences. The dust storms were the worst. Everyone would become white. You'd have to cover yourself with something because it was going horizontally at you, like rain, only it was dust.

Mits Koshiyama   (HEART MOUNTAIN, WYOMING)

This was the first time in my life I saw snow. I could imagine, but I had never experienced it. When we got there, it was the coldest in Wyoming's history. People from Los Angeles really suffered because all they went with was a light jacket.

Lillian Sugita   (JEROME, ARKANSAS, AND HEART MOUNTAIN, WYOMING)

It was December, and Arkansas gets very cold. Hawaiians were not used to this weather. Sometimes there was a little bit of snow. Mostly it's a lot of rain. The people already in camp said to us, "We know you guys are cold. We're going to teach you how to warm yourselves up with this potbelly stove." They taught every family how to start a fire with wood and a little bit of coal. This was the support network.

The rooms were so bad. Wind coming in through the cracks, nothing except the army cots and rolled-up army blankets. But we were so happy to see others. Being so alone all this time was more of a trauma. I'd rather be in camp, away from all the stares and the hostile world.

The camp was right in the thick of the swampland. In the wintertime, it's cold, wet, soggy, and mud everywhere. When it rained, it didn't stop. There were huge runoff ditches between the buildings for flood control, but you didn't have pathways over the ditches. They would be flooded in the summer and iced in the winter. We put down planks so we could walk across. I heard of some drownings.

Later, when we went to Heart Mountain, the weather was different. We could see dust storms coming. We'd all dash in the houses, slam all the windows, close up everything. My mother had bronchitis all the time. She was very weak after camp. Asthmatic. When we went back to Hawaii, she was always sick. Towards the end, she had emphysema, and I think that was all from the dust in the camp. We survived. Children are survivors.

Sohei Hohri (MANZANAR, CALIFORNIA)

The most unpleasant thing about camp was the dust. We had a tin cup and a bowl with milk. A dust storm would blow sometimes for hours, and dust would seep into everything. I would see the dust forming on the milk and I'd try to scoop it away. It got to the point where I said, "Aah, just close your mind to it and say, 'Dust is good for you,' and drink it."

Morgan Yamanaka (TOPAZ, UTAH)

I was a voracious reader in school, and I remembered Zane Grey's *Riders of the Purple Sage*. It's in the Sevier desert, and Topaz is in the

Sevier Desert. So I am thinking of Zane Grey's beautiful painted desert. I think the desert is not as bad when left alone, but they built the relocation center. With bulldozers and construction, the desert sand became fine, ground-up dust. Comes rain, you walk on it, and your shoes get higher and higher. It was like mud cement.

Betty Morita   (PINEDALE, CALIFORNIA, AND MINIDOKA, IDAHO)

Pinedale is close to Fresno, and it was hot. They fed us in shifts. We had to stand out in line and wait I don't know how long. I'd see older women passing out. We weren't used to that kind of a heat. We slept on cots on a concrete floor, and they'd hose it down because it would get so hot.

In Minidoka it would rain and be so muddy. Our dad made these special shoes so we could walk through the mud. On top, it was the regular shoe. Then he'd make platform soles out of wood.

Yosh Kuromiya   (HEART MOUNTAIN, WYOMING)

It was very desolate. We felt we had been completely abandoned by civilization. But after being there awhile, I began to appreciate the beauty of the place. The mountain ranges in the distance, the bluffs. As dry as it was, it had its own unique beauty.

I used to do watercolor paintings. I don't think I ever finished one of them. I don't know whether it was unconsciously deliberate or not. There was always this big question mark. Who are we? What are we doing here? I shouldn't be out here painting pretty pictures. There's more to be said than that.

Dollie Nagai   (JEROME, ARKANSAS)

When we arrived at Jerome, they put as many people as possible on a truck to take us to our barracks in Block 45. They shoved us, pushed us, rammed us all in like cattle. I felt like an animal.

We were near bayous. It was all forest, and they said, "Don't go out there because it's dangerous." One time my childhood friend and

I were walking outside and one of those great big huge buzzards came swooping down. We ran back to "civilization."

CAMP FACILITIES

Much of camp life centered on the basics: eating, sleeping, cleaning. Communal mess halls offered simple and sometimes unpalatable meals; and bathroom facilities, while remembered years later with jokes, at the time were uniformly deemed miserable in every camp.

Amy Akiyama   (TOPAZ, UTAH)

My mother said, "We don't have a kitchen now. We're going to eat in one big room. It'll be fun." It was awful. Breakfast was always the same. Oatmeal mush and something like grits. I remember my brother saying, "What is this?" He had never had oatmeal where the spoon stood up. And lines. Lines to go to the bathroom, lines for this, lines for that. Lines for everything you did.

At first the toilets had no partitions. Eventually, the women were so vocal about it, they did put some in, but not doors. A lot of people brought something they'd hang.

Mary Sakaguchi   (MANZANAR, CALIFORNIA)

I used to long for an egg. Every morning my mother had fixed us eggs for breakfast, and we always had a lot of milk and fresh fruit and vegetables. That's what I missed. The food was so bad, we called it "SOS" food—Same Old Slop. Everybody would get diarrhea. We called that the "Manzanar Twins"—Diar and Rhea. Everybody had the twins.

Joe Norikane   (MERCED, CALIFORNIA)

The rest rooms at Merced were bad. It was one long place with holes, no divisions. You all sit, and then the water automatically fills up in this tank. The tank tilts, and the water goes all the way down this trough behind you. If you're sitting on the last hole, the water comes up and splashes right on you. You never sit in the last one. But if everything's filled up and you have to go there, you better finish before the water starts coming down. That's the thing everybody always talked about. They said, "I'm going to remember this."

Lillian Sugita   (JEROME, ARKANSAS)

By the time we got to camp, there were doors on the bathroom. I mean, can you imagine! People must have had problems.

In the mess hall, it was a buffet line. You pick up your plate, and the guys plunk the food down. "Next!" When you sat down, the lady would come with milk or coffee. For the kids it was always that powdered milk. We didn't drink it.

About a week after we got there, we said, We're not going to eat with our parents. All the kids would meet and we would sit at our own table. That's where this terrible breakdown of the family happened. You're not with your family at mealtime or the rest of the time.

CAMP SCHOOL

Schools were set up in some of the assembly centers and later in the camps. Eight-year-old Amy Akiyama said, "We looked forward to school because that would kind of suck up the day. It was something to do." In many states, working in a camp school was a desirable job for Caucasian teachers. The federal pay scale was higher than the states'. For Nisei volunteer teachers, regardless of how many advanced degrees they might have, the pay was $16 a month.

Dollie Nagai   (JEROME, ARKANSAS)

The school was in a barracks divided into classrooms. Study hall was in the mess hall. I was taking Latin, biology, civics, algebra, and geometry. We didn't feel the Caucasian teachers were qualified, although some probably were. The biology teacher would use "ain't," but the Latin teacher was very, very good, and the homeroom teacher was a real warm person.

Kay Uno (AMACHE, COLORADO)

The school was in English. Pledge of allegiance and everything. We were Americans. We participated, and we were proud to sing, especially patriotic songs. We were very patriotic in camp. I was too young to see the irony of it.

There was a compound for the civilians who worked for the camp, and the teachers lived over there. But for a while our camp was so new, they didn't have any fence between us and them. The teachers would shortcut by our barracks, and we'd all go together to the school. There were rumors they were going to put up a barbed-wire fence. The teachers were so much fun. They pantomimed going through barbed wire in the morning because they didn't want it there, and we would all laugh. They were Caucasian, and they were really nice people.

Jim Matsuoka (MANZANAR, CALIFORNIA)

Our grade school teacher called us out for an assembly. She started to speak about Pearl Harbor and she broke into tears, sobbing as she described the bombs raining down. I have no problems with that. But even as kids we knew there was an association, that somehow *we* were a part of that bombing. We didn't need to hear that. She was laying buckets of guilt on us. There we were, kids, and we were absorbing that stuff.

Sohei Hohri (MANZANAR, CALIFORNIA)

On the whole, the high school at Manzanar was not a very good school, mainly because of the very uneven quality of the teachers. At the beginning, they were all Caucasian. Some of the best were young kids out of teachers' training. Some I thought really couldn't hack it at regular school. They were about ready to be retired, and this was their last gasp.

Before the questionnaire [see Chapter 8], I was a very studious, quiet student in class. After, I used to ask what I thought were awfully disruptive questions. In English class, I'd say, "This is just garbage. Why do we have to study this? This doesn't pertain to us at all. Literature is being foisted on us." Then I'd start swearing. I don't remember the teacher's name, but she's kind of a special angel to me.

She said, "You've got a point, but if you only say swear words, you're not going to get anything across. There's a legitimate point about literature. Make your point clear." I had to think about that and the fact that I did enjoy reading.

The idea of attacking the school system actually was a healthy thing. Questioning the very assumptions—maybe there shouldn't be schools, maybe there shouldn't be education, maybe the whole educational system has to be restructured. There's nothing inflammatory about thinking things.

CAMP ACTIVITIES

Despite the devastating blow of the expulsion from their homes, a large number of people in camp were remarkably creative in their attempts to bring some pleasure and beauty to their barren world. Many attended classes, participated in group games, and created individual activities to "suck up" the time.

Amy Akiyama   (TOPAZ, UTAH)

Topaz was a lake bed, so there were seashells. People collected the shells and made pins and things. They'd have craft shows and display them. Some people would carve things out of local wood or whatever they could get their hands on. At the base of the mountain, there were hundreds and hundreds of arrowheads. They were beautiful. Of course the more perfect ones were the most desirable. And they were in all colors.

My mother took us to movies in camp. We all took our own cushions and sat on the floor. The film would flicker, like home movies, and break down. Everybody would wait. I don't remember any movie going smoothly. And she took us to plays. They were in Japanese and highly melodramatic. We would die, we thought they were so boring.

Sue Kunitomi (MANZANAR, CALIFORNIA)

They had bulldozed everything in order to build the barracks. Nothing was growing, not even sagebrush. In between every two blocks, they had what they called a firebreak. It was flat land, and when the wind blew, it created tornado dust storms. Later the government gave everybody grass seeds. People planted lawns and flowers in between the barracks. They ordered through catalogues, or friends would send seeds.

People wanted to beautify. They put in little gardens in front of their doors. They dug ponds and put in goldfish. The director arranged that we could go outside the camp and have picnics. As long as people are not on the highway, nobody's going to know we're out there. Where would you go anyway? You'd get lost if you went up to the mountains.

Kay Uno (AMACHE, COLORADO)

You had to watch your toothbrush. Some people in camp would steal them, especially if you had a black, red, or white handle. If you left it in the bathroom and went to use the toilet, when you came back, your toothbrush was gone. Sometimes when they sawed off the handle, they left you the brush part. They used the handle to carve rings, crosses, birds, and other things.

Harry Ueno (MANZANAR, CALIFORNIA)

I worked in the mess hall from five o'clock in the morning to one or one-thirty. Then I had a lot of spare time. When the dinner bell rang, everybody came and lined up. People were standing around in the dust with the sun baking them, waiting for quite a while. So I said to a friend, "Hey, let's dig a pond over here. Maybe there's water there or we can pipe it in, and I'll bring a lot of rocks." With a pond where there's beautiful water coming down and a rock to sit on, maybe the people will have a comfortable feeling.

So my friend and I started digging a pond. One man said, "What are you doing?"

I said, "We try to build a pond."

"Let me draw it," he said. "I got experience making a pond." We dug pretty deep, probably five or six feet down, and almost 75 to 80 feet around. We needed chicken wire with cement on it to hold the bottom. There used to be an old chicken coop around. We had a bunch of old people working the camp farms. We asked them to bring it.

I asked one of the construction workers, "You handle a lot of cement. How about bringing some?"

"No, no," he said. "A lot of people went to jail for taking cement."

So I went to see the camp director and I asked him for cement. I tell him honestly it's for the people, not for me. "O.K.," he says. He gives me a pass for three sacks. I didn't know how many I'd need, but I know three won't do nothing. The truck driver told me, "Don't give the slip to the watchman. Just show him you got permission for three sacks." Then he went back and forth eight times, three sacks each trip.

The whole block pitched in. They went for the big boulders for people to sit on. The administration let us use the army truck. It took about a month and a half or two months. We made a wishing well with a little bucket on the top. Water was dripping in like a waterfall.

There were small, natural ponds with a lot of carp where the people dump the garbage at the other side of the hill. So the garbagemen brought the carp and we put fish in the pond. We made it pretty good. We planted some trees in the background for the green.

People sat out on the rocks, and they enjoyed it.

Morgan Yamanaka (TOPAZ, UTAH)

My father made a Japanese house in the barracks. He made armchairs out of tree limbs. In the window he put a circle in a plaster board, so the light could come through. Every Japanese home in Japan has a *tokonoma,* a place where you display an art object, one scroll at a time, one flower arrangement at a time. In the camp, he made a beautiful *tokonoma.*

My father's hobby was Japanese swords. The heating system in camp was all coal. Somebody had to feed the coal into the burners so that every block had hot water. He took that job with a purpose of making swords. He got the springs of an old truck and started forging them. He made three swords.

Mary Sakaguchi (MANZANAR, CALIFORNIA)

We kept ourselves busy. They had knitting, sewing, and carving schools. They even had a beauty school, where you could learn to become a beautician. I was so depressed, I couldn't do anything except go to work every day [in the camp hospital] and then go home. Many years later I thought I could have learned to be a beautician. Then at least I could have done my own hair.

Sumi Seo (JEROME, ARKANSAS)

I missed my friends. Before the war, we'd had a platform in front of our house where we'd load our vegetables. Shug, Pat, Charlotte, Kay, Peachy, and I would sit there. Kay, Peachy, and I were Japanese. The others were Caucasians. When I got to camp, I wrote to everybody I could think of. We were so hungry for people to write to us, for some kind of news from outside.

There was only one girl who wasn't scared to write. Charlotte Owens. She wasn't afraid of what other people thought. I don't know why she was different. Maybe because her parents were never really prejudiced about us. She's the only one who wrote to me.

When I saw that first letter, I was so happy! A letter from the outside is like gold. A lot of people didn't get letters, especially from whites. She told me they were real busy with the war effort, and they had blackouts. A lot of the letter was censored. Anything they write about the war effort, they don't let us hear about it.

After the war, when I came back, everybody said, "The mailman said if we write you, we were helping the enemy." A friend just returned the postcard I wrote to his sister. That's fifty years ago. "Hope to hear from you." That's what I wrote. She never answered.

Young children and teenagers sometimes describe the camp years as "fun," and indeed some of it was, as family discipline broke down.

Amy Akiyama   (TOPAZ, UTAH)

In the laundry room we used to play jacks because there was a cement floor. I never met so many friends. We used to play baseball. I remember breaking a window and running away. I also remember staying up later than I was ever allowed. After dinner was the time to play. You gobbled down your food and went off and played until you got called. All this freedom just to run around. There was nothing to do but run around wild. You couldn't get lost. I remember the older kids, teenagers, hanging out together. They weren't bad or naughty, but they did things in groups.

Ernest Uno   (SANTA ANITA, CALIFORNIA, AND AMACHE, COLORADO)

Older kids thought about the more serious part of it, but we were a bunch of kids. I was a teenager having a helluva good time horsing around. I never saw so many cute Japanese girls in one place at one time. We were running around, looking for girls to whistle at.

We kids thought maybe the war would be over and we'd go back home after a couple of months. Because I figured things were so tentative and I didn't give a damn, I didn't try even to go back to school. Although they set up the school in camp, I was a dropout. I just bummed around.

Lillian Sugita   (HEART MOUNTAIN, WYOMING)

I was sixteen, and we were going to high school dances and having all that fun. Forgetting. Just forget and have fun. I was taking a lot of art classes. Other people were doing Japanese dances, but I couldn't do it. Ever since I was eight, I had studied Japanese dances and an instrument. I was very serious about *shamisen*. It's a three-string instrument, kind of like a lute. You play it on your lap. It's part of a Kabuki orchestra.

In camp I refused to play. I didn't want to associate it with camp.

Kay Uno (AMACHE, COLORADO, AND CRYSTAL CITY, TEXAS)

Amache was my first snow. I had my first snowsuit. Oh, it was wonderful! Christmas in Amache. That was really something. This is one of the good times. There was Santa Claus, and a Christmas program. I made a crepe paper sailor uniform. A bunch of us did a little baton routine to "Anchors Aweigh," and we got candy and presents from the outside. The Christian churches were wonderful. They sent things in so everybody got a little something.

Some reporter from either *Life* or the *Saturday Evening Post* came and saw this big cesspool, which was for sewer treatment. They went back and wrote we had a fabulous swimming pool and the government was treating us so well.

We had to make camp fun. You'd die if you didn't. When you write letters in camp, you're not supposed to mention any names and places. My father was terrible. When he was in the other camps, his letters would come with holes in them. When I got to Crystal City, they did the same thing to our letters. When we wrote to my sisters and brothers, we'd put in names and descriptions of places we'd know they'd cut out. We would put in patterns just for the fun of it. I remember doing a Christmas tree once.

But you can't help thinking of yourself as prisoners with the guard towers and everything. We had some fun in camp, but we wouldn't wish this on anybody. It was making the best of a bad situation. I think that was my mother's legacy to us. She always tried to make the best of things.

Even for the kids "having a ball," there was the always present under-current of tension. They might deny their own pain, but whether seven years old or seventeen, they recognized their family's grief.

Amy Akiyama   (TOPAZ, UTAH)

I think it was devastating for my father. He became more and more withdrawn. He used to be more talkative to the children. He used to draw for us. In camp, he'd do a lot of sleeping. My mother would try to get him to go to sumo wrestling, just do something, get out. He'd say, "No, that's O.K. You people go." He never said, "Don't go," just "No, that's O.K. You go."

I don't have any unpleasant memories except I know that my father suffered. And my grandfather died in the camp. My mother said she thinks he died of a broken heart. The old people were too old to play baseball or any of those active sports. We all went to the funeral. It was a Buddhist funeral, and they burned a lot of incense. I can still smell it. My son used to burn incense, and it brought back this awful memory of hearing the Buddhist priest chanting and seeing the profile of my grandfather in the casket.

I keep saying for me at the time it was fun. But I also keep hearing my mother's voice and seeing my father in bed, and I think of my grandfather. I have these mental images of old people sitting outside of their barracks on the benches, not doing anything. Passing the day, every day, like that. They go to the mess hall, they eat and come back. They had this routine till they passed away. I think a lot of older people died earlier than they might have if they weren't in those camps.

Kay Uno   (CRYSTAL CITY, TEXAS)

My brother Bob graduated from Federal High School in Crystal City [Department of Justice–administered camp]. He wanted to pursue his education, but here he was in camp. He got very depressed. My brother Edison found him sitting near the fence with suicidal thoughts. If he went over to the fence, maybe they'd shoot him. He didn't want to go back to Japan. He couldn't go to school. What future did he have?

Ben Tagami (MERCED, CALIFORNIA, AND JEROME, ARKANSAS)

In the camp, I felt like I was a "Jap," the ones they used to have signs for that said, "No Blacks, No Mexicans, No Japs, No Jews, No dogs allowed here." Those were common signs in those days. They had them all over the South. They always put in the dogs.

Camp was demeaning. I felt like I was a piece of shit, actually. As kids we made the best of what was available, but still deep down it felt like I was filthy. I was never cleansed of that feeling.

When we went to camp, we took the neighbors with us. Their sons had sold everything, but they didn't give their mother or father any of that money. At the assembly center, the woman started accusing my mother of stealing their money. To be accused of stealing is a shameful thing. My mother couldn't take it, and my dad wouldn't protect her. He knew she hadn't stolen, but he kept saying, "If you're dumb enough to think that way, then suffer for it." If he had stood up for her, it would have helped. He told me, "Your mom's crazy," and he would have nothing to do with her.

Mom went through hell. She finally cracked and had a nervous breakdown. Among the Japanese, mental illness is a shameful thing. It got so unbearable, we had to move to another portion of the camp to get away from my dad and these people.

My mom cried all day, all night. Kids my own age would hide from me or point fingers. In October they put us on a train, and we went to Jerome, Arkansas. In Jerome everybody in the barracks could hear my mother crying. They were hollering. I'd keep telling her, "Hey, don't cry no more."

We were the family with the "crazy woman." Everybody in the block knew it. They wouldn't say it in front of me, but they'd talk behind my back. You'd better believe it was tough. My brothers and sister didn't know what was going on. All they knew was that Mom and Dad was always fighting. I was ashamed.

All this wouldn't have happened without the evacuation. I know for sure it was the stress that did it. If we could have stayed even one month to harvest our strawberries, we would have got back around five, six, or seven thousand dollars. Before we left for camp, my mother had paid off all the debts. We were broke.

In camp I got a job cooking. I asked the man who was running the kitchen to teach me how to play poker. One day I went to the fire station, where they had a big poker game. I got in the game and won a couple of hundred dollars.

I came home about one o'clock in the morning and woke up my brothers and sister. I got the Sears catalogue out and I told them, "Pick what you want." My mother woke up. She couldn't believe where I got the money. She got a dress, and I got a shirt and a pair of pants. I think we spent $80 or $90, and I gave the rest of the money to her. We never told my dad.

Jim Matsuoka   (MANZANAR, CALIFORNIA)

I was six or seven. You couldn't help but know that something was wrong when you were stuck into a place like that. One day my mother was chasing me around because I did something wrong. She was a warm person, and I never saw her cry a lot. All of a sudden she burst into tears. That really stunned me. I couldn't figure out what was wrong. Little bits of things becoming frayed. The tension and stress poking through.

Angie Nakashima   (JEROME, ARKANSAS)

People who were older and a little more mature suffered more. You know how young people are. They can take anything and bounce back. Kids are very resilient. You don't worry about tomorrow. You have your friends. You don't have the sense or wisdom to know any different. So it was no big hardship for us.

It was a hardship on my dad and mother. My dad lost everything. He turned gray almost overnight.

Betty Morita   (TULE LAKE, CALIFORNIA)

My teacher from Hood River said she happened to be close to Tule
Lake, and so she came to visit me and the other Japanese boy who
was in my [third-grade] class. I felt so ashamed that I couldn't really
greet her. I felt ashamed that I'm put in a place like this. I really don't
remember what she said to me. It was nice to see her, and yet I felt
uncomfortable.

Bert Nakano   (JEROME, ARKANSAS, AND TULE LAKE, CALIFORNIA)

Because he was number-one son, my older brother had to look after
my mother and take care of two younger brothers. He had a helluva
lot of responsibility. He grew up real fast. In camp, when we kids had
breakfast or dinner, we always ate with friends. My mother was very
lonesome. Most of the time she took the food home to the barracks.
After a while my brother said, "O.K., you guys are going to bring
the food home to the apartment. We're going to eat as a family."

My mother had nothing to do. She felt like a failure. A mother is
supposed to bathe the kids, take care of them, clothe them, feed them.
She's not doing that. Of course she's going to think she's a failure.
Especially if she's traditional, born and raised in Japan.

She suffered so much. That's the kind of thing that really hurts.
Every time I talk about her I get shook up. I think we understood
deep down inside how much she was suffering, and we couldn't cope
with it. We didn't want to cope with it. That made it that much more
deep within yourself.

Nami Nakashima Diaz   (SANTA ANITA, CALIFORNIA)

My husband [who was Mexican-American] and I mainly stayed
together. We were amongst a sea of Japanese faces when we went
into camp. I was very uncomfortable. We felt we stuck out like a sore
thumb. The Japanese are basically very polite. They're not going to
do anything real outwardly rude. But of course there was always talk

behind your back. You knew, especially in my day, you were looked down on. Intermarriage was still a "no-no" for the Japanese [as well as the Caucasians].

I really didn't do much of anything. I was probably in a state of shock and depression. Why didn't I take my violin and practice? I could have put that time to use, but I didn't want to do anything. I was just unhappy.

I wouldn't work because I didn't ask to be sent there. I felt resentful. My husband was angry. He was there, and he wondered, What for? What did his wife do? Nothing, but happen to be born Japanese, and for that she was in camp.

I could never figure out what they thought we were going to do. Born and raised here in a typical American home. Middle-income people. Then to have this happen, you wonder why. What'd I do? It was really hard to understand. I was seething inside. I know there's a lot of hate in the country, but my father's been here since 1906. I was born here. Yet you're surrounded by this fence with barbed wire on top and an armed guard. And they didn't like you hanging on the fence, looking out, wishing you could go.

Dollie Nagai   (JEROME, ARKANSAS)

I was angry in Jerome. Why did it happen to us? Why are we here? I'd go for walks in the camp in the evening and I'd talk to myself. I wasn't angry at the government. I was a strong Christian at that time. I couldn't understand why God would let this happen to us. "Why did you let this happen? Why do we have to be like prisoners?" I used to quote Psalm 23. I'd keep telling myself there's nothing to be afraid of.

I never shared any of that. Isn't it funny that none of us really talked about our feelings in the camp?

Mary Sakaguchi   (MANZANAR, CALIFORNIA)

When I got into camp, I used to have palpitations. I said to my mother, "My pulse is so fast, it's 100 to 120 a minute."

My sister, big brother, and father all died within seven months. My sister developed terrible asthma in camp. She was twenty-six years old.

My father in the meantime had developed stuffiness in his nose. The Manzanar doctors told him he must have a cancer there.

My brother was a thoroughly Americanized boy, Eagle Scout, scoutmaster, black belt in judo. He got room and board teaching judo at dental school. He graduated in 1941 and went into practice in Gardena. The day after Pearl Harbor he tried to enlist. They told him, "We don't need any Jap dentists in the United States Army." It was probably a terrible emotional blow, because he felt very American. I think that must have eaten away at him. He had an intestinal obstruction and was sent by car to Los Angeles County Hospital from Manzanar. He died four hours after surgery. He was thirty-one years old.

When all of this happened, I couldn't cry, I couldn't feel any emotion at all. You couldn't afford to cry. You had to hold everything together or you'd fall apart.

Sumi Seo   (JEROME, ARKANSAS)

The worst thing about the camp was we felt we didn't have a country. We didn't know what we were, American citizens or Japanese. We could have been very helpful in the defense work. Sitting in the camps like that didn't do us any good.

In the camps some internees were aware of the politics of bigotry raging outside. Because they were often cut off from detailed news from the outside, the fragmentary bits of information they learned stirred deep anxieties.

Nami Nakashima Diaz   (SANTA ANITA, CALIFORNIA)

Things were getting a little bit scary in camp. Everybody was beginning to wonder what they're going to do with us. When they first took us, my father believed they were going to get rid of us somewhere. There was a rumor they're going to move us. A lot of people figured they might put us on the high seas and shoot us.

Yosh Kuromiya   (HEART MOUNTAIN, WYOMING)

When we first got to camp, I had faith that it's going to all be resolved. It can't possibly continue like this. In the meantime, there were some unsettling reports. Statements or suggestions made by different political figures, such as separating the camps into male and female so that there wouldn't be any new generation, and the Japanese problem would be solved. Also we heard there was consideration of using us as potential hostages for a prisoner exchange. I thought that was just so far out, more evidence of the war hysteria.

> *There was some truth to these rumors. Oklahoma Representative Jed Johnson talked of proposing legislation to sterilize all the Japanese in the camps. And some writers* argue that an explanation for the evacuation and imprisonment of Japanese Americans in camps was indeed to create a pool of hostages for possible exchange with Japan, and as a form of reprisal to counter Japan's treatment of captured Americans and Europeans.*

WORK

For many in the assembly centers and camps, employment provided some relief from boredom and stress. Workers were paid on a scale determined by the degree of skill necessary for the job. Salaries were raised when the inmates were moved from the assembly centers to the camps. In camp, a mess hall worker, a teacher, and a doctor, for example, were paid $12, $16, and $19 a month, respectively. Most jobs were related to the operation of the camps, but there was other work as well. Despite the fact that they were America's "unwanted," many prisoners worked on projects for U.S. military forces.

------

*Weglyn and Hohri, *see* Bibliography.

Ernest Uno (SANTA ANITA, CALIFORNIA, AND AMACHE, COLORADO)

In Santa Anita we made these camouflage nets [for the military]. The grandstands were a perfect place to hang them up. They put these pulleys up, and we were assigned to crews. I guess that's where a lot of us first got hay fever. That burlap was horrendous, the stuff that came out of it. We'd weave burlap strips into these big nets. We had races between the crews. It was a diversion. It sure took the drudgery out of day-to-day doing nothing. And it was drudgery. Some people suffered real psychoses.

You could see life going on as usual right outside the fence. People in their cars, driving back and forth. I definitely thought of myself as a prisoner. We were just a fence away from freedom.

I got a job in camp [Amache] in a silk-screen print shop, making posters for the navy: "Loose Lips Sink Ships," all these kinds of things. That was an interesting experience. There was a young [Caucasian] gal that came. She knew the art of silk screening, and she was assigned to set up this silk-screen shop and hire as many people as possible to grind out these posters. I really felt I learned a trade doing that, and it was fun. Something to look forward to. I got paid $16 a month.

Avey Diaz (SANTA ANITA, CALIFORNIA)

They wanted to make me work making camouflage nets. I told them I was getting paid good money outside, $12 an hour. I said, "Look, you pay me $12 an hour and I'll work. Otherwise I'm not going to do anything."

"This is your country," they said.

I said, "Look where you got me." I didn't work.

Morgan Yamanaka (TOPAZ, UTAH, AND TULE LAKE, CALIFORNIA)

You look for work, but what can you do? [Before the war] I had helped my father clean house. Not a marketable skill. So they asked me other questions. "What did you do?" I read four English newspapers every day I was going to high school.

They asked, "Where did you read them?"

"At the local firehouse." We lived across from it, and they took the four papers. I went there to read every day.

"Good, you're a fireman." At least I knew what a two-inch hose was. Nobody else knew. At Topaz I was a fireman. When I got to Tule, I became a fire captain. Recognition of talent—knowing what a hose was. I never went to a fire, thank God.

Because of military-service and war-industry needs, there was a shortage of hands on the sugar beet and potato farms. The WRA was asked to permit recruiting of workers from the camps. Thousands of young Nisei prisoners left the camps for temporary farmwork, bringing in the crops in Oregon, Idaho, Utah, Montana, and Wyoming. Without them, the crop yield during the war years would have been disastrous.

Mits Koshiyama   (HEART MOUNTAIN, WYOMING)

In Powell and Cody they had a lot of farmers. Most were German Americans. Nothing [like the evacuation] happened to them. These people didn't want Japanese in any area around there. But when it came to harvesttime, they needed help. Suddenly we were Japanese *Americans.* "Please have the Japanese *Americans* come out and help us harvest." When the government asked us to go out and top the sugar beets and pick the potatoes, I said, "Yeah, I'll go." When the farm harvest was over, we were "Japs" again. "Send them back to camp. We don't want them around." But the year passes quick. Again they had this harvest problem. They said, "Can we have those Japanese *Americans* again?" Politics are laid aside when it comes to making money. The only time I can safely say we were accepted in Powell and Cody was during harvesttime.

In some camps, the administrators on occasion issued passes for brief trips to nearby towns. A trip to town from camp could be an experience of

kindness, a precious moment of freedom, or a painful reminder of the
bigotry raging against Japanese Americans.

Dollie Nagai   (FRESNO, CALIFORNIA)

When I was in the assembly center, I had braces on my teeth. Because
there was no orthodontist in camp, the doctor made arrangements to
come in. He was curious about the camp, I think, but after a few
times, he arranged for me to go out to his office. The Fresno Assembly Center was maybe three miles from where I lived. This is my
town!

I would be taken by an MP or a woman guard. The woman was a
stickler for rules, but the MP was so nice. He would say, "What
would you like to take back to camp?"

I said, "I want a milkshake."

"We'll get you that."

I told him, "But we can't take food in."

He said, "You leave it to me," and he hid it under the car seat. I'll
never forget that.

He said, "I'll meet you back here," and he told me what time.
"You go shopping and do whatever you want. I'll pick you up."

Once I said, "What if I run away?"

He said, "You're not going to run away." Really, a human being.

Sumi Seo   (JEROME, ARKANSAS)

I worked at the hospital in Jerome. My first job was as a messenger.
We'd deliver letters or notes to different departments. Then you'd
come back to this one area and sit there until the next message. One
day I got brave and I said to the doctor, "I've never been out. I'd sure
like to go to Little Rock and do some shopping." He and a white
nurse used to go to Little Rock to a conference. Before I knew it, he
had my pass all ready for me.

In Little Rock we were in a hotel, and the maids kept looking at
me. One of them asked me where I was from. I thought, This is a

day I could really tell a big lie, and they'll believe me. So I told them I was from Hollywood. They asked me if I was a movie star, and I said, "Yes, I am." They didn't know I was Japanese, and I never told them. They saw me with the doctor and nurse, and they thought I was a big shot. I played along with them, and I felt good. I *felt* like I was a movie star. I was so relieved to be out in the world.

That was the first time I had ever seen a magnolia tree. I was raving about that tree. Then they took me to lunch. I did a little shopping downtown and went back to the hotel. I was real friendly with the maids, and they were so excited. I felt like a queen.

Lillian Sugita   (HEART MOUNTAIN, WYOMING)

Five of us girls from the block took passes to go to this little town, Cody. We were around fifteen years old. We thought, Oh, this is great. We're going to go out there and have a soda. We got on the bus, and everybody is staring at us, I mean like something from Mars. We started giggling and laughing throughout the whole thing. We went into a drugstore and sat down, ready to order. Nobody would come. Finally they brought this sign that says, "We don't serve Japs." We looked at that and we didn't know what to do. One of the girls said, "Oh, shit," and we all started laughing. We said we didn't want anything anyway.

We were devastated. All we did the rest of the day was wait for the bus so we could get back to camp. Even after we got back, we laughed. We made a big joke about it. We didn't know how to deal with it. After that we became so acutely conscious. Even after the war, it was just as bad. When I went to Chicago, the minute someone is looking at you, you think, I know what he's going to tell me, "Get out of here!" It's a terrible feeling.

PROTESTS

There were disturbances at every camp—strikes, riots, shootings resulting in injuries and deaths, and acts of individual protest. Some hostility was directed by the prisoners against other Japanese Americans thought to be FBI or WRA informants.

The protests started in the assembly centers and continued in the camps. The first big riot took place in Santa Anita assembly center. There are many different versions of what happened, and there is probably some truth in each story.

Mits Koshiyama

Everybody says Japanese Americans accepted it and were very docile and didn't fight for their rights. But I remember at Santa Anita there were riots over the food, and working conditions, and sanitary conditions. Japanese Americans weren't as quiet as our leaders portrayed us to be.

There was a strike because people said they got tired of eating cabbage and weenies. They wanted other food. I remember one incident where they claimed there was a Korean American planted as a spy for the government. I don't know the true story because nobody really tells you the truth at the time. Big crowds beat him up and were surging all over. The army brought in half-tracks. That's a truck with tank wheels and machine guns. They patrolled all the streets.

Sumi Seo

Not too long after we were in Santa Anita, they started searching us for contraband. They hired white guys from the outside. They were searching for scissors, knives, cameras. I heard one of the fellows found some money. Instead of putting it in his pocket, he put it in his hat to hide it. A little boy saw that and ran to his mother, saying they're stealing money. People started beating up that guy. There was a riot. They had two or three big tanks with guns on them driving around. After it quieted down, they had a jeep with a gun going around.

The JACL became the spokesmen for us. They knew English. They knew the law. Isseis didn't know English. And we were not like today's kids. God, they are smart. They know the laws. We didn't know anything.

JACL before the war was a social club, and it was the uppity-ups. When we got into Santa Anita, the uppity-ups all had to come down. They were one of us. But in camp there were some Niseis that had high positions. They were mostly JACL people. Who wants to dig ditches? Who wants to work in the mess hall cleaning silverware? "We want a good job in the administration building and show our importance." Some worked for the government, telling on others. They were called *inus,* dogs. When you have any contact with the administration, people think you're telling on them. They beat up a few of the JACL *inus.*

Morgan Yamanaka

The riot at Santa Anita was a nonincident that became an incident. You go to the mess halls to eat, but what about the young mothers with babies? They need to heat their milk. So they got extensions and got hot plates and plugged into the one bulb hanging down. Once that starts, other people start doing other things with that one bulb, and the fuse went out constantly.

So the order went out from the top administration to pick up all these hot plates. Well, the Nisei internal security became overzealous in picking up all these hot plates. That in itself was a nonincident. The real incident was the frustration of being there. That to me was the issue—letting off steam.

Camp guards on several occasions shot at prisoners who were near the camp perimeters. At Manzanar, a guard claimed he ordered a man to halt. As the prisoner started to run away, the guard said he was forced to shoot. The Japanese man, who was seriously injured, told a WRA investigator he was collecting scrap lumber and hadn't heard the guard's order. The investigator concluded, "The guard's story does not appear to be accurate, inasmuch as the Japanese was wounded in the front and not in the back." Other shootings occurred at Tule Lake and Topaz camps.

Amy Akiyama   (TOPAZ, UTAH)

There was one old man who was very sweet with the kids and played with them. A puppy wandered into the camp, and he adopted this little baby thing. The puppy, knowing no boundaries, ran out through the gate. The man thought he was going to lose it and ran after the puppy. The soldier shot him. He killed him.

There were also individual, nonpolitical acts of protest.

Sumi Seo   (SANTA ANITA, CALIFORNIA)

One month after we got into Santa Anita, my brother Masa, who was seventeen, and three others ran away. They went over the barbed wire. It was a concentration camp. A lot of people try to correct us and say it was a "relocation camp," not a concentration camp. That sounds a little bit better. But you try stepping out like my brother did, and what happens? In Manzanar people got shot in the back. If they had known my brother had jumped the fence, the watchtower guards would have shot him.

Those boys waited until the searchlight was in the back and it was dark. Nobody saw them. First they tried to catch the freight train that went by every night, but they missed it. Then they saw a used car lot and tried to sleep in an empty car. It was too cold. They wandered around for a little while and then went into a movie theater. The lady who sold them the tickets called the authorities, and they got picked up and brought back to Santa Anita.

Upstairs in the camp grandstand, there was a jail. They were inside a jail in a jail. My brother threw down a note written on toilet paper. He said he knew they were going to be shipped out, but he didn't know where. Within a few days, they quietly moved them out.

They shipped the four boys down to Poston, Arizona. Somebody said they were chained. We didn't know where they were. One of my girlfriends from San Pedro was in Poston [camp]. She saw Masa, and he waved at her. Her parents wrote to my father. That's when we knew where he was.

THE MANZANAR RIOT

The Manzanar riot of December 1942 was one of the deadliest eruptions. Throughout the summer and fall at Manzanar, tensions were increasing. Many felt betrayed by the JACL, some of whose important leaders, like Fred Tayama, were in the camp. Before Pearl Harbor, Tayama had helped organize the Anti-Axis Committee in southern California, reporting to the FBI and naval intelligence agencies "potentially dangerous" individuals in the Japanese community. In November, Tayama and another JACL member were temporarily released from camp to attend a JACL conference in Salt Lake City, where the JACL resolved to petition the government to reinstate the draft for Japanese-American men.

At Manzanar, the mess halls were the largest camp employer, with over fifteen hundred workers. Harry Ueno, a junior chef, organized a union of mess hall workers. Harry had also argued against JACL politicking in camp. Perhaps most significant, he had accused the acting camp director, Ned Campbell, and other administrators of stealing sugar and meat from the prisoners.

On the evening of December 5, Fred Tayama was beaten and hospitalized. He accused Ueno and several others of the attack. Harry denied any participation, but was arrested and taken to a prison outside the camp. Protesters believed Harry was arrested by the administration because of his exposé of the food theft. More than a thousand people gathered at the administration headquarters to demand Harry's return to Manzanar. A negotiating committee of five convinced the administration to bring Harry back to Manzanar. Within hours of his return, the riot began.

Harry Ueno, thirty-four and the father of two children, was born in Hawaii and educated in Japan. He was a vegetable market worker in Los Angeles before the war. Harry had never been involved in any political activities before camp. Jim Matsuoka was six, Sohei Hohri sixteen, and Sue Kunitomi eighteen at the time of the Manzanar riot.

Harry Ueno

On December 5, early evening, six people attacked Tayama. About nine o'clock, "Bang!" on my door. I was already in bed and sleeping. I have to get up at five o'clock in the morning [to work in the mess hall]. When I open the door, I see three jeeps full of policemen. They took me to the police station. They didn't tell me why I was there.

At midnight the chief of police put the handcuffs on me. Acting director Campbell brought his car, and the chief and I were in the back seat. They told me I'm guilty. I said, "I don't know where you're going to take me, but please let my family know."

Campbell said, "No. Where you're going, nobody knows. You're never coming back to the camp."

Then I said, "Mr. Campbell, what you did to the 10,000 people in the camp is very bad." I meant the sugar and all the other shortages. "You're gonna be in a much bigger jail than whatever I'm going in." He was hair-raising mad.

I went to Independence jail. The next morning the chief of police takes me back to camp. He says, "The negotiating committee is out there. So I'm taking you back to Manzanar."

In the Manzanar jail, they had about a half a dozen young men. They said, "Last night a lot of people came and they're gonna be back after dinner tonight." It was the first time I learned that people came over to protest.

Sue Kunitomi

Harry was very popular with all the kitchen people, because he had started a petition drive for a mess hall union. The only block that did not sign his petition was the block in which Fred Tayama's brother was a cook.

We heard a group of men walking by our barracks. My mother

told me to get away from the window. I was working then for the *Free Press* [the camp newspaper], which had some JACL people but was not completely controlled by them. She said, "They may be coming after you," and she turned the lights off. The men went past us. They were looking, I was told, to beat up the director of the YWCA, who was JACL. They couldn't find him. Then they started walking down toward the police station. I guess all the different groups were going to meet there and have some kind of rally for Harry.

Harry Ueno

About six o'clock, a lot of people started coming in the open area between the administration building and the jail. There were sand-bags right in front of the jail and all the way to the administration side. They had maybe thirty-six soldiers with guns lining up in there behind the sandbags. One of the sergeants was saying, "Remember Pearl Harbor! Hold your line!" I could see them out the window. Some young MPs were kind of shaking because so many people were there. The captain was excited. He was walking all over yelling, "Remember Pearl Harbor! Remember Pearl Harbor!"

From jail I can hear and see the crowd. A lot of people come over and shake hands through the window. Some people said, "Come on, get out."

I said, "Where am I going to run to? I have no place to run away." I just shake hands with the people I know.

Sue Kunitomi

There are different stories. From some accounts somebody let go a truck without a driver and aimed it toward one of the stone houses where the MPs were. Others say nothing like that happened. People were chanting and singing in Japanese. Some say a rock was thrown at the MPs, who then threw tear gas into the crowd. On one side, people got pushed back by the gas. On the other side, the crowd was pushed forward.

Harry Ueno

The crowd was building. December 6 was very cold. Around nine o'clock, the MPs went to the other side. I could see through the glass window there. They started putting on masks, so I turned to the front and told the people, "They might throw tear gas. You'd better back out." Some started moving out a little bit. At the same time I noticed the commander of the MPs walking toward the sentry box about 150 or 200 yards away from the jail. Those days the sentry box was four-sided glass, and you could see the light in there. It looked like Ralph Merritt [camp director], the captain, and the police chief. The three men were in conference there. As soon as they come out, the MPs started throwing the tear gas. The crowd was confused and they all were running back to the camp. I could hear the machine gun. I couldn't see it from my position.

By a little after nine, the whole area was covered with smoke. You can't see nothing. I shut the window. By the time the tear gas was clear, I could see one man, not more than ten or fifteen feet away, on the ground face down. Three men tried to take him into the police station. But when a man is dead, he's pretty hard to carry. I open the window and I jump out and helped them carry the body into the jailhouse and put it on top of the table. He was bleeding. He must have been hit from behind at close range. Shot running away. There were eleven of them shot.

According to the Manzanar hospital records, one man was killed instantly, one died within days. Nine had serious gun injuries, with the majority in critical condition.

I knew the one we brought in. James Ito. He's eighteen years old. One man, very strong JACL, was sitting in the back of the table. He saw that dead man, and he pounded the table and he said, "I made a mistake! I couldn't believe the United States could do this!" He was not talking to me or anybody else. He was yelling to himself.

Kitchen bells started ringing as soon as the people started running away from the tear gas. They rang them to alert the people that something's happening. Then the army took us to the Bishop jail, about twenty miles north of Manzanar.

Sue Kunitomi

At around nine o'clock a Caucasian teacher was walking a dog. The teachers lived where the administrators lived, outside the barbed wire. He said he walked right by the riot area when it happened. He heard no orders to shoot, but the soldiers began shooting anyway.

One boy who was killed was eighteen or nineteen. He had a brother in the service.

We didn't hear the shots, but my brother came running. He said, "They're shooting up there!"

My mother said, "Shooting who?"

"The soldiers are shooting the crowd."

She said, "Now they're going to come after all of us. They're going to shoot all of us." My younger sister's boyfriend came running up. "They shot some people up there by the police station, and everybody is running around like crazy!" He was shaking.

Right after that, the kitchen mess hall bells began to ring. They rang and rang throughout the camp. And they rang all night. The jeeps started driving up and down, patrolling. My mother said, "I know they're going to shoot all of us. We're all goners."

I have a report of the ambulance driver about that night. He said both of the young men had already died by the time the ambulance got there. They were shot at close range in the back. The teacher who was walking the dog told me more would have been killed if the machine gun hadn't jammed. I said, "What did you say?" I couldn't believe they had a machine gun.

He repeated, "The machine gun jammed." The soldier couldn't shoot it anymore, and that's why they didn't have as many casualties.

Jim Matsuoka

They rang this bell and everybody stopped whatever they were doing and stood. One of my relatives had a bloody shirt, so I knew something had happened. Years later I talked to a lady who was the sister of one of the younger men that got killed. She claimed he had been shot in the back as he fled. He wasn't charging or attacking. He was running when they shot him. She said they had his bloody T-shirt with a bullet hole in the back. They kept it for years. Finally they buried the thing.

Sohei Hohri

We used to get the Los Angeles papers. There were articles about the camp, which I didn't pay much attention to. Then there was the riot. The papers had a report that the rioters were trying to enter into the bedrooms of the white teachers. They had cartoons: "I predge arregiance to the frag . . ." with the fingers crossed behind the back.

> *After the shootings, Harry Ueno was taken out of Bishop jail and transported to the isolation camps, first in Moab, Utah, and then Leupp, Arizona. He spent a year in different prisons until he was sent to the segregation camp at Tule Lake, where he was finally reunited with his family.*

★ ★ ★

In one of the more remarkable stories of the internment, Ralph Lazo, a Caucasian teenager from Los Angeles, chose to join his Japanese-American high school friends at Manzanar. He was sixteen years old at the time.

Ralph lived with his father and sister—his mother had died when he was five years old. Ralph's neighborhood was racially and ethnically mixed, and he was friendly with kids from diverse backgrounds. Since his father worked long hours, Ralph spent a great deal of time with his friends and their families. When the evacuation orders were posted, Ralph helped his Japanese-American friends as they struggled to sell their belongings. Some twenty-five years after the war, he told a newspaper reporter, "I couldn't figure out why my friends had to go. These people did nothing wrong. I know because I did the same things as they did, except attend Japanese language school, and I wasn't being asked to evacuate."

There are at least two different stories about how Ralph went to Manzanar. There is probably truth in both. According to an article in the *San Francisco Sunday Examiner & Chronicle,* some of Ralph's Japanese-American friends from high school asked him, "What are you going to do when we're gone? Why don't you come along?" Ralph had a paper route of three hundred customers. He made his last deliveries, left his father and sister a note, and then boarded a train for Manzanar.

Ralph died in 1992. In an "In Memoriam" article in the Fiftieth Manzanar High School Reunion materials, William Hohri relates another story:

> Ralph Lazo asked his father if he could go to camp with his friends. His father said, in effect, "Camp? Why not? Sure. And have a good time." When Ralph went through the registration line for camp, he was not challenged for not being Japanese. Days later, the *Los Angeles Daily News* had a headline that read something like, "MEXICAN-AMERICAN PASSES FOR JAPANESE," and Ralph's family realized just what this camp was.

Sohei Hohri knew Ralph in camp:

> It would be no exaggeration to say he was one of the most popular kids at Manzanar. He was certainly one of the most remarkable names of the Manzanar story. He went down to the authorities and said, "You know, you're taking my friends out there. I'm going to go with them." He was from Los Angeles, and he wasn't an orphan. I liked the guy, and he got along terrifically with everybody. He lived in the bachelors' barrack.

Ralph Lazo was drafted into the army from camp, served in the South Pacific, and was awarded a Bronze Star for heroism in combat. Sue Kunitomi Embrey wrote an "In Memoriam" piece about Ralph on the fiftieth anniversary, in February 1992, of the signing of Executive Order 9066:

Ralph was a gentle and kind man, who gained fame after he went along with his Nisei friends to spend the World War II years in the Manzanar concentration camp. While his original intent was to go along with his friends from Central Junior High School, he was outraged at what was happening to his friends and their families.

Over the years, after I met him in Manzanar, Ralph and I used to run into each other. He lived in Mexico for a while and got married there. He was finished with college and soon he was calling me from Los Angeles Valley College where he was a counselor. He would mention a book which had just come off the press about the Peruvian Japanese. Had I seen it? Or he would call and ask me to join him in a panel discussion at some community college, or high school. "I can't do it without you," he would say. And so we went, over the years, doing presentations and workshops, swapping information about books and people.

William Hohri concluded his "In Memoriam" article with this thought:

When 140 million Americans turned their backs on us and excluded us into remote, desolate prison camps, the separation was absolute—almost. Ralph Lazo's presence among us said, No, not everyone. As a nation, as Japanese-Americans, and as his classmates, we need to remember Ralph for his gift of courage and humankindness and embrace him in our hearts with love and gratitude.

Following page: *Children's Village, Manzanar.*

5

THE LITTLEST "ENEMIES":
HOMELESS CHILDREN

The United States military had decreed that anyone with one-eighth Japanese blood was subject to evacuation and relocation. They had exempted people committed to institutions, including orphanages. The Japanese Americans who worked in these agencies, however, were not exempt, and without staff to run the children's homes, the agencies were forced to close.

Before the war, there were three institutions in California for homeless Japanese-American children: the Shonien (the Japanese Children's Home of Los Angeles), the Maryknoll Home for Japanese Children, also in Los Angeles, and the Salvation Army Japanese Children's Home in San Francisco. Some children in these institutions were orphans, with one or both parents dead. Others came from families where one parent had been ill for a long time. Still others were from broken homes, or homes where parents were temporarily unable to care for them. A number of children were born of unwed parents and placed in the institutions for adoption.

The stated purpose of the Shonien was to "provide care for children of Japanese parents, to prevent them from becoming a charge upon the community, and to teach them to become American citizens." As an early lesson in citizenship, the children in California's three Japanese orphanages were swept up in the evacuation that cleared the West Coast of a Japanese presence.

The children were taken from the orphanages and brought by military convoy to the prison camp at Manzanar, about 235 miles northeast of Los Angeles. Children in foster homes were also forcibly removed from their homes and evacuated even when their foster parents were Caucasian. If the foster parents were Japanese Americans, the child was separated from the family and evacuated separately.

Dollie Nagai remembers an orphan girl at the Fresno Assembly Center. "There was one girl who I'd heard had grown up in a Caucasian foster home. She was taken out of that home and brought to camp. I remember her because she had a turban on her head. I think she lost all her hair. I don't know what happened to her."

The orphanage children left Los Angeles in late June 1942. At

Manzanar they were housed in a special area with a decidedly cheerful name for a prison camp, "Children's Village." Unlike the barracks for the ten thousand other evacuees in Manzanar, the three Children's Village barracks had their own running water, toilets, and bath facilities. Children's Village also had its own kitchen and dining room.

During the three and a half years of its existence, Children's Village had a total of 101 different children. Ninety percent of the children were from California. The rest were from Oregon, Washington, and Alaska. Most were Nisei, a smaller number were Sansei, and nearly one in five were children of mixed racial backgrounds. The average age was eight.

Life in Children's Village was similar in many respects to the routine of the prewar Shonien. The directors were the same, and many of the earlier Shonien staff came with the children to Manzanar. Discipline in Children's Village was firm, and the regimen fairly controlled. Chapel service before breakfast was optional, and after breakfast the children went to school. During the first year at Manzanar, very young children stayed at Children's Village. In later years, they attended nursery school and kindergarten with other children in the camp. The older children went to the regular Manzanar school.

Children's Village had its own garden and playground. The Shonien had indeed lived up to its purpose of the Americanization of its charges. As one writer noted,★

> . . .even there [at Manzanar] little boys played the same war
> games as other boys throughout the nation. "Kill the Japs" was
> yelled enthusiastically among the trees of that Oriental garden
> as many a "Jap" was slaughtered by brave Americans with
> Japanese faces.

Manzanar was "American" by other standards as well. By the fall of 1942, the camp had over a hundred softball teams that competed in

---

★Whitney, see Bibliography.

the Manzanar athletic league. There were sixteen teams for boys and nineteen for girls. Children's Village had its own team.

Children's Village functioned as an institution within an institution for thirty-nine months. While in camp, the Village administrators worked to relocate the children to homes outside the restricted military areas, sometimes with adult siblings, sometimes with a parent newly able to care for the child. Young people old enough to work could be released to families who would offer room and board and a small wage. Not all placements were happy. Two teenage sisters sent to New Hampshire to live with a minister and his family were forbidden to speak Japanese. One of the sisters said, "We had no choice but to stay with them, working as a domestic—babysitting, cooking, cleaning. . . . They didn't even attend our graduation. We were better off in the Children's Village."

Others had happier experiences. One eight-year-old Nisei boy in Children's Village was very much wanted by his non-Japanese foster family with whom he had lived before the evacuation. Forced to give him up, the foster parents spent many months trying to get him back. Not until late 1944 did they succeed.

In 1992 Children's Village "alumni" held a reunion in Los Angeles. Few had ever talked to anyone about their "orphan" days. There is still a deep reticence to speak about those long-ago but for many still painful times.

★   ★   ★   ★   ★

Mary Matsuno

Mary had eight brothers and sisters. Her mother had been hospitalized the summer before Pearl Harbor. When the war began, her father, a Terminal Island fisherman, was picked up by the FBI and sent to a Department of Justice camp in Montana. Mary and her siblings were put in the Los Angeles Japanese Children's Home.

From the Shonien, we went to Children's Village at Manzanar. My older sister arranged with the Shonien that she and my brother would come into the Shonien, and as soon as they got to Manzanar, they would be let out. My oldest brother was already at Manzanar. He arrived March 15 because he had volunteered to work on the camp. I read they did that to get the "young studs" off the streets so they wouldn't raise hell.

When you turned eighteen, you had to leave the Children's Village. That was it. You're on your own. I was only there briefly, even though I was fourteen, because I begged my older sister and brothers to take me with them. The four of us got a room in Block 25. Five of my sisters and brothers were left in Children's Village. My little sister was the youngest one in there. She was six or seven months old.

Children's Village had three barracks. The first was the mess hall, rec hall, sewing room, and quarters for the administrative people. The kids slept in the others. I was surprised that two or three of the kids in Children's Village were from Alaska. Alaska, mind you!

At Children's Village, the grownups were very strict with us. They did it for our good, even though we might still feel that it was too much. They didn't like the ones that were mixed blood. They got rid of those kids faster than they did the Japanese. They were put up for adoption as quickly as possible.

It's hard to say why people are so discriminative. You learn about it early when you get discriminated against by your own people, by other children. My mother was sick, and they used to tell us, "Oh, your mother's crazy." It brought us closer together. When you grow up, it takes a while to forgive them. I know my sister doesn't forgive them to this day.

We went to school in camp. It was called Manzanar Secondary High School. I went from the ninth to the twelfth grade. My older sister and I were on the baseball team, the Fighting Nine.

My father came in January 1944. One New Year's, that's all he spent with us. He was sent to camps in Montana, North Dakota, and Crystal City, Texas. He ended up in Santa Fe, New Mexico. This was under the Justice Department. Why does the government do anything, what are the answers? I don't know.

Sohei Hohri

Sohei spent part of his childhood, from ages five to nine, in the Shonien in prewar Los Angeles when both his parents became ill. He was reunited with his family before the war and evacuated to Manzanar as a teenager. His experience as a prewar Shonien child was critical to his understanding of and empathy with the camp children.

After Children's Village was set up, I used to visit there because of the association from my orphanage days. Then, after I graduated from the camp high school, there was a job opening. Since I had been kind of an orphan kid, I had no problem being hired. The pay scale was $12, $16, and $19. I was $16.

There were all kinds of special considerations for the children. The Children's Village building itself was more substantial, and the windows were fitted. They had a hot water heater right in the building. In wintertime, we used to go in that room and sit because it was the warmest place. They had a nice garden, and they probably got better food than the mess halls, but I don't think there was any feeling of complaint. These were orphanage kids. Let them have it.

I had a bed in the boys' ward. I had to be sure that lights were turned off at the right time and everyone got up on time, things like that. I made sure everyone washed, dressed, and went to breakfast. Then they went to school.

There was no radio or television at Children's Village. Every night I used to tell the boys stories. They had a very poor library in Manzanar. I would go through my entire repertoire, including westerns and thrillers. I told them Homer's *Iliad* and *Odyssey,* and the story of Victor Hugo's Jean Valjean. That used to be my favorite book [*Les Misérables*]. I read it about seven times when I was growing up.

Some of the orphanage children are my closest friends. I kept up with them, and I talk to them on the phone every couple of months. Only one family has been very free about talking about their past, and that's a family whose father beat the children up and was finally deported to Japan. Years after the war, all the children went back to

Japan and found the father's grave. They touched the grave and said, "Pop, we forgive you."

There are others I know well, and yet I don't know a thing about their background. In a number of cases, the mother had a "nervous breakdown," and the fathers, for whatever reasons, couldn't take care of the kids.

Several years ago there was a Children's Village reunion. When I went, here were kids I hadn't seen in fifty years. One of them was only six years old when I last saw him. He turned to his wife and said, "Here's the man who told me about Jean Valjean." Another kid told me he remembered the story of Odysseus having to go through the clashing rocks, and how he sent a bird through first. All the other stories, the westerns and thrillers, passed out of their minds. The images from the great writers stayed. One of the boys named his first daughter Cosette. She's the girl in *Les Misérables* that Jean Valjean saves. I didn't realize the impact of these stories on little kids.

At the reunion, Sohei spoke of the ties of loyalty and friendship among those who lived in Children's Village.

In all of America's shameful, illegal internment of Japanese and Japanese Americans, the most shameful episode remains the internment of the orphanage children. Taken not only from orphanages but even from foster homes. What cannot destroy us can only make us stronger. . . . We have been shaken by sudden sorrow. We have been sustained by caring, loyalty, and affection. Three years ago [a friend] . . . said it best with these words: "You are my brothers." The passing years have proven it, and our hearts say it is so: "Sisters and brothers."

Sue Kunitomi

Sue wrote about Children's Village for, The Free Press.

We knew Children's Village was there, but I never played with them because they were younger than I was. I heard from others that they were told not to play with those kids because they were orphans. I said, "Why's that?" They said it's an Asian custom. You do not adopt orphans unless they're related to you, and these are strangers. You don't bring a stranger into your house.

Manzanar was closed in November 1945. It was terrible stuff that went on. The government sent the young people [from Children's Village] all over the country. They had to work in homes where people did not treat them as foster children. Basically, they were like indentured servants. They even separated children [siblings] instead of putting them in one home. One woman I know from Children's Village was sent out to New York and her sister was sent to Connecticut. She said, "We were there in the dead of winter with no decent clothes to wear. We had no money to buy any. These people didn't pay us to take care of their house. The government just abandoned us." For three years, they were in an all-Japanese place. Then all of a sudden they're taken out and sent somewhere where there's nobody they know. Not a friend.

In 1992 there was a reunion, and fifty or more showed up. One person said, "It's a terrible thing, but these kids all felt the shame of being an orphan. That's why they haven't talked all these years."

We said, "You can't let this story go by. It wasn't your fault that your parents died or abandoned you."

They were happy to see each other, but they were remembering all the things that happened to them. They were laughing and they were crying. It was on Memorial Day weekend.

Following page: *Shibayama family in Peru shortly before forced transport to United States.*

6

THE FORGOTTEN PEOPLE:
JAPANESE PERUVIANS IN
U.S. PRISON CAMPS

Several months before the bombing of Pearl Harbor, the U.S. government pressured Latin and Central American nations to arrest those persons considered potential security risks because of their ancestry. Although this included a small number of Germans and Italians deemed "dangerous," virtually all prominent Japanese were to be taken, with no effort made to identify possibly "dangerous" ones.

In a response typical of the nations involved, in late October 1941, over a month *before* the attack on Pearl Harbor, the U.S. Ambassador to Panama notified the State Department:

> The attitude of the Panamanian Government is thoroughly cooperative. . . . Immediately following action by the United States to intern Japanese in the United States, Panama would arrest Japanese on Panamanian territory and intern them on Taboga Island. . . . All expenses and costs of internment and guarding to be paid by the United States.

Similar arrangements were made with other Latin countries. Again, the United States would assume all costs of imprisonment and transfer of the prisoners to the United States.

The issue was not, however, primarily one of security. The United States wanted a pool of hostages that could be traded for Americans trapped in Axis countries. Within months of America's entry into the war, it was clear there was no serious threat of sabotage by Japanese living in this hemisphere. Yet the removal and transport to United States prison camps continued. From 1942 through 1944, over two thousand people of Japanese ancestry were rounded up from their homes in twelve different Latin American countries and imprisoned in United States internment camps. About 80 percent of those arrested were Japanese Peruvians. This chapter tells their story.

*　　*　　*

The first Japanese came to Peru in 1899 to work as contract laborers on the sugar plantations and in the sugar refineries. By 1941, there were more than 25,000 Japanese Peruvians—merchants, educators, doctors, and lawyers, as well as farmworkers. For the most part, the Japanese lived peacefully with other Peruvians. In the larger cities, however, there was increasing hostility to the Japanese community. In May 1940, there was a large-scale anti-Japanese riot in Lima that spread to the city of Callao. Peruvian police stood by while more than six hundred Japanese homes and businesses were vandalized.

After the bombing of Pearl Harbor, Peruvian police began to arrest leaders of the Japanese community, first in the big cities and then throughout the country. School principals, editors, and religious leaders were the first to be taken, and then the prominent business and civic leaders. Many went into hiding in an attempt to avoid arrest, but few succeeded in permanently eluding the authorities. When caught, they lost not only their liberty but their businesses as well, for under Peruvian law, the government could confiscate property owned by an "enemy alien."

The Peruvian police were notorious for their acceptance of bribes. In full awareness of this, a United States State Department internal memorandum stated, "All [Peruvian] police charged with supervision of Japanese should be well paid." The memo went on to suggest that this should be accomplished "even if this necessitates a loan from this government." Libia Maoki tells of one case in which bribery appears to have worked:

> There was a young Japanese Peruvian who worked for a Japan-
> ese baker. He was only fifteen, but he had to quit school to
> help support his family. One evening when the baker's family
> was having dinner, the police came. The baker bribed the
> police. He offered money and this young man that was work-
> ing for him. The young man was not rich enough to give any
> bribe, so he had to go.

From Peru, the prisoners were transported to internment camps in Panama, and finally shipped to prisoner of war camps in the United States.

In July 1942, the U.S. Ambassador to Peru reported to the State

Department on his communications with Peru's President Manuel
Prado:

> In any arrangement that might be made for internment of
> Japanese in the States, Peru would like to be sure that these
> Japanese would not be returned to Peru later on. The [Peru-
> vian] President's goal apparently is the substantial elimination of
> the Japanese colony in Peru.

Unlike most Japanese Americans, the Japanese Peruvians were
interned in camps supervised by the Department of Justice rather than
the War Relocation Authority. Most of the Peruvians were imprisoned in the camp at Crystal City, Texas, along with a much smaller
group of prisoners of German and Italian ancestry. A small number
of Japanese Americans were also in the Crystal City camp.

As Elsa Higashide said of the Japanese Peruvians imprisoned in the
United States, "We are really the forgotten people."

★   ★   ★   ★   ★

Fusa Shibayama

My father was only fifteen years old when he went to Peru to help his
uncle buying and selling coal for stoves. He gradually went on his
own and started a little coffee shop for workers. Then he sold
imported men's dress shirts.

At the time of Pearl Harbor, there were six children in the family,
three boys and three girls. I was about ten, the second from the oldest.
At home we spoke mostly Spanish. Both my parents spoke Spanish.

My grandparents were sent to the United States first. My mother
cried and cried because they were taking them. Then they were sent
to Japan in an exchange of prisoners. They couldn't write to each
other. You're afraid if you write, it's going to make trouble.

Every time my father heard about a ship coming to pick up Japanese people, he would disappear. Where we lived, all the houses on a
block have one roof. I would see him climb up on the roof and disappear. Before the war, he always used to dress in suits and hats—a

businessman. When he went into hiding, he wore a T-shirt, because if he were dressed up like a businessman, they're gonna catch him. They were looking for him, but to this day I don't know where he was hiding. He never told us.

In March 1944, when Fusa was twelve years old, the Peruvian government arrested her mother in order to lure her father from hiding.

They put my mother in jail when my father wouldn't come out. Somebody suggested I go to jail with her, because I'm the oldest girl. The rest of the kids were at home. We had a Japanese housekeeper.

It was a women's jail. They gave us one room with a single bed. They locked the room with a bar and turned the light off. The other women were in a big hall-like room, sleeping on the floor. I didn't know what was going on. I was scared. I cried all the time. I didn't eat anything. My mother is pretty strong. She didn't cry.

We were in jail one night and two days. My godparents, who were Peruvian, got hold of my father and told him what happened to us. If he could bring his family with him to the States, he said he'd come out from hiding. The government said O.K.

Chieko Kato

My father, at the age of nineteen, having studied pharmacy in Japan, went to Peru to open up a drugstore. Thirteen years later, he returned to Japan to marry my mother. Since his drugstore was doing such good business, he was able to open up a department store and a bike shop. He was a member of the Chamber of Commerce.

When the war started, I was about eight years old. There were seven children in the family, myself being the third child. My mom was worried because there were rumors that all the businessmen had to hide because the government was coming to arrest them. I noticed that my father wasn't home most of the time. He used to come home for lunch, or come to see us, but we knew that he wasn't sleeping at home. We children didn't know what it was all about since we were too young to understand. Later on we found out that he had been hiding in the home of one of his employees in the suburbs.

Some men came to our house. They were very friendly and spoke in Spanish. "*¿Como está?*" The maids and the cook were told not to say anything. The men said, "Where's your father?" We said, "We don't know," and they left. Later we found out one was from the United States FBI.

My dad was worried about the business, so one day he went to the store. That's when he got caught. They took him with just the clothes he was wearing. We didn't even know he was caught. Within a week, my mom was notified that she had to pack him a suitcase.

As soon as they took my dad, someone from the Peruvian government took over our business. They stood behind the cash register and took all the earnings. This was the opportunity for Peruvians to take over businesses. They thought the Japanese were doing so well, and they wanted to prosper themselves.

Libia Maoki

I was born in 1935 in northern Peru in a village outside of the small city Chiclayo. Right outside the city was the sugar cane plantation, and my father had a store there. My family was very comfortable. My father also had a pretty good-size bakery in Chiclayo, and he developed other businesses. My mother worked at the store. We had a cook in the household and a chauffeur.

I grew up with Peruvian natives in the village. I didn't go to school until after Pearl Harbor. Then I went to the village school. It was all Spanish. At home we spoke mainly Spanish. The maids were all Spanish. My parents talked to us in Japanese, but we talked back to them in Spanish.

In 1942 my parents had heard that some of the key people, like the newspaper editors, were taken. The government did not want these people to continue to influence the minds of the Japanese Peruvians, I guess. The principal of our school was taken in early 1942.

We were about 300 miles away from the big Japanese population, which was mainly in Lima and Callao. My father continued his business. On January 6, 1943, at night, a detective came to my parents in the village and said to my father, "Sorry, Señor Maoki, but I have to take you."

That next afternoon they got all of the men together in Chiclayo, and we were allowed to see them before they put them into a truck. In the morning the ladies decided to make food for the men's lunch. They were rushing around cooking. Everybody gathered together, and we were giving them packages of foods.

The men were put into a canvas-covered truck. Before they left, they did their *banzai* [hurrahs] and started singing songs that were meant to give courage. They did not want us to cry. I didn't know where my father was going, so I was sad. The mothers were sniffling and singing. I didn't know whether to cry or to sing. I remember looking at everybody and being completely mixed up. The women had tears in their eyes, but the men—they just sang heartily as the truck went away. Singing and waving.

I asked my mother, "Where are they going?"

She said, "We don't know yet, but don't worry." My father was a businessman, and he was always going on business trips to Lima and Callao. But this time, it was so different.

They were taken to Panama in ships all manned by the U.S. military. We got a letter from my father a month later. It was a very brief letter, mostly to wish my sister a happy birthday. My father was in an internment camp in Panama for nearly three months. Then they were taken to Kenedy, Texas [Department of Justice internment camp].

In the spring of 1943, they found out they were going to be shipped to Japan as prisoner exchange. A group of the Kenedy men petitioned and said, "We will not go to Japan. We will not be separated from our families. This is all against the Geneva Convention."*

---

*Rules, adopted by many countries, governing the rights of prisoners of war.

The Peruvian government didn't want an international incident. They sent orders for the families to be taken.

We were excited. We were going to join our dad. We hadn't seen him for about six months. Those were days of preparation. They were happy times. We didn't have to go to school. We played. My sister might have felt it a little bit more, but my brother and I were very protected.

Elsa Higashide

Elsa was born in Ica, Peru, about 230 miles south of Lima. The oldest child in the family, she was five years old at the time of Pearl Harbor. In early 1944, two years after the arrests began, Elsa's father was picked up.

We were too little to know much. We knew that something happened in the world, but we didn't know where the United States was. Japan we knew was across the ocean. It was like a fairy tale place.

My dad was blacklisted as soon as the war started. He was a young man of about thirty-three, and a rather successful one for someone his age. Because he was blacklisted, he was hounded by the police. He had to escape several times. He did not go into the jungle like some of the other fathers and older brothers had done.

He dug a hole under my parents' bed, and that was his hiding place. When you opened the cover, you could smell the earth. It was big enough for him to sleep in. He had a light, some books, and some provisions. Whenever anything suspicious happened, he would hide under the bed in the hole.

After a year of relative calm, one day he said, "As a family, we haven't done anything for a long time, so let's go for a picnic." When we came home, we had dinner. We had just sat down, when there was a knock on the door. The Japanese Peruvians had a code. Each family had a different knock, so you'd know who it was. But the police had somehow caught on. I guess they were watching and they knew the signal. A young boy who was employed by my dad was with us. He was about sixteen years old. Without much thought, he went to the door and opened it. There were four or five policemen with their guns drawn. They apologized, saying, "I'm sorry we have to do this, but it's under the order of the United States."

In the meantime they told my father they were going to take him to Lima in a paddy wagon. He said, "I don't want to travel like a criminal because I'm not a criminal. I haven't broken any laws, I haven't done anything against anybody or the country." He said, "We'll hire a taxi. I will pay." So from Ica, he and a detective went by taxi to Lima.

As they were traveling, he said he thought this may be the last chance. I may not be alive tomorrow. He told the detective, "I know this photographer on the way to Lima. Let's stop for a few minutes so I can take a last picture to send to my family."

It arrived in the mail. It's just a portrait, but no matter from what angle you look at it, it looks like he's looking at you. He really put his whole self into it. No other photo ever looked like that to me. To this day, that's my favorite picture of my dad.

Later, when we found out he was in Lima in prison, my mother took the two oldest, me and my brother, and we went to bring him some fresh clothes. When we came back again, he was gone, and we didn't know where. It was four or six months before my mother knew he was alive. Finally, there was a short letter from him. Letters were being censored, so he wrote it in a kind of short-story form—"The monkey's up a tree"—so my mother knew he was in the jungle someplace. He was in Panama.

At the time he was taken, he had told my mother to keep everything the way it is. He had been wise enough to transfer the businesses to her name because she was a Peruvian citizen [Nisei]. He was in dry goods, import and export, cosmetics, silks, lingerie. In the second letter, he completely changed. He said, "There's a ship leaving the port in Lima. Get on it if you would like all of us to live as a family or die as a family." My mother was very confused, because at first he had said whatever happened, she should keep the business going in order to feed us. Finally, she did as the letter told her. She had to sell everything. But when people know you have to sell, you don't get anything. Here she was a young woman in her twenties, pregnant with her fifth child, and she disposed of two businesses.

Some months after the arrest of their fathers, the children and their mothers boarded ships for transport to the United States.

Libia Maoki

We left Callao in early July 1943 and arrived in New Orleans the 27th of July. I had never been on a ship before. Once we passed Panama, we hit a storm. An older lady, my mother, and I were the only ones in the mess hall. Everybody else was sick.

We didn't think we were going to come back to Peru. My mother had heard that the men insisted on having the family together because we were all going to be sent to Japan as a prisoner exchange. The government was also afraid the Japanese might commit sabotage in the Latin American countries. But by 1943, there were no incidents, and they found out there was nothing to worry about. The Peruvian government knew that, but they still kept on taking more people.

Because we thought we were going to be sent to Japan, we took as many things as possible. We were not restricted. Our ship was one of the lighter ones. We had only a little over 110 people, mostly Japanese Peruvians, and a few Germans and Italians. I took my favorite doll with me, a doll my dad had given me.

We were taken to New Orleans, where we disembarked. They put us on a train to San Antonio, Texas, and then by truck to Crystal City. About a month later, my father joined us.

Art Shibayama

Art, Fusa's older brother, was thirteen when he left Peru.

At home we spoke Spanish and some Japanese. No English. They spoke English on the boat, and we didn't know what they were saying. We were down in the hole, sleeping on cots. No mattresses, just canvas. You barely had enough room to get in there. We were only able to go up on deck once or twice a day for five or ten minutes. People who smoked used to smoke two or three at one time to try and get it in. I think that's the reason I never smoked.

From Callao [Peru], we went through the Panama Canal and on to New Orleans. We were guarded by a convoy of destroyers and submarines all around us. We were hugging the coast. We couldn't go on deck the days we stopped in ports. I heard the women and children in the cabins couldn't open the portholes. I got seasick a couple of days. Some people were sick quite a long time. Out of twenty-one days on the ship, my dad may have been O.K. maybe half a dozen days.

We got off the ship in New Orleans, and they put us in a gym. We had to undress and get in line naked. Then they sprayed us with disinfectant. I was pretty tall for my age, so I was with the men. I know two fellows the same age who were smaller, and they were with the women. These are fourteen-year-old boys. After showers, they put us on a train to Texas.

Chieko Kato

We found out my dad was in Panama. They were digging ditches. Hard labor for the United States government. They took my father in December 1942. In July 1944, my mom heard on the news that the last ship was going to the United States. We thought we had to get on that ship to join my dad. I myself thought we were coming back. We left all our toys, and of course we couldn't pack our dolls. Our maid and cook said, "We'll see you again."

On the ship, we were all sick. All we had to eat was hot dogs and beans every day. We had never eaten that. My brother, who was fifteen, was working. They took him to do KP on the boat, peeling potatoes. He said there were men guarding them with guns and threatening them. Every once in a while he would bring canned fruits to us. Oh, we really loved that!

We were on the boat about three weeks before we landed in New

Orleans. It was very tight. There were seven kids and my mother. We could hear the baby crying in the next room. My mom felt so sorry for the mother with a little baby. She was a lot younger than my mom.

We were happy we were going to see my father, but at the same time we were afraid to go to this new place.

Elsa Higashide

I was seven. The ship took several weeks from Lima to New Orleans. My mother wasn't able to nurse the baby, so we brought cans of milk on the ship. They must have thought we had something terrible in the cans, but it was just milk. American, in fact. Carnation. They threw it overboard. So she had to nurse, and I saw blood. She was under such stress. My mother thought the little baby might die. She was born underweight, and three months later we were shipped out.

On the ship, the hot, steamy pipes ran through our berth. You had to keep the room dark at night for security reasons, and most often the door had to be closed. There was very little air. We were all packed in—five kids, my mother, and I think my auntie and grandma were there too.

On reaching New Orleans, we were processed. All the women and some of the younger boy children were in this huge warehouse-like place with open showers. We all had to be naked. Then they sprayed us with disinfectant from top to bottom. DDT. Maybe because we were from South America, they were afraid of lice and stuff. Then we took a shower, and that was heavenly because on the ship you take saltwater showers. Looking back, though, I'm glad I wasn't a teenager then, because when I was a teenager, I wanted to hide everything.

Fusa Shibayama

They only gave us a few days to get ready, because the ship was leaving. Nobody came around, because they were afraid they would be sent over here too. When we went to Callao, just one family came to say goodbye—a good friend of my mother with her daughter. She was waving as we were leaving.

They had soldiers with guns and rifles watching us on the ship. We had to line up, and they searched us. We brought some food, candies, and fruits, but they threw everything in the ocean as soon as we got on.

My father and my brother were down below. My mother had the two younger boys and the three girls. There was another family of five in the same room—eleven of us—with only four bunks. The small kids were able to sleep three on one bunk. We slept on the floor. No mattress, nothing.

Every time we stopped in some port like Cuba or Panama, all the marines got their rifles and were watching us. We had to go inside the rooms. I guess they were afraid we were going to run away. We had to close the windows, but it was so hot, we opened them up again. There was one sergeant who was so mean. He had a whip. He snapped the whip and closed the windows.

The trip took twenty-three days, I think. A long time. We ate standing up, cafeteria-style. It wasn't good food. We all lost weight.

After we landed in New Orleans, they put us on a train. It was a nice train, a Pullman. After feeding us sauerkraut and wieners every day, all of a sudden they give us Pullman service with a porter coming and fixing the bed, and good food. I was thinking, this must be our last meal, a good meal, and then they're gonna shoot us.

From New Orleans, the families were transported to the camp in Crystal City, Texas, run by the Department of Justice.

Elsa Higashide

When we arrived at Crystal City, my mother wept at the sight of my father's changed physical appearance. Especially his hands. They were all sunburned and calloused and misshapen because of the forced physical labor in Panama.

It is a desert in Texas, and it was very hot. We were deathly afraid of the black widow spiders, because they could bite you and you could die. We were also afraid of what we called the *shi shi* bug. It's a child's word for urine. If the bug landed on you, the whole thing would blow up like a burn. And there were scorpions all over the place. We didn't have that in our home in Peru. Maybe in the jungle, but not in our home.

I remember also how beautiful the sky looked at night. I've never seen another sky like it. We were in the middle of desert and there was nothing else. The stars were incredible. People planted gardens in the middle of the desert, and my dad said, "How can Japan have gone to war with such a rich country? The soil is even rich. You don't have to do anything, and stuff grows practically in front of your eyes." He was from Hokkaido, in Japan, where the soil was very poor and they struggled for subsistence.

In camp there was barbed wire and a trench. When it rained a lot, it would overflow. We were told not to go too near the trench because the guard could shoot us. They think you're escaping. I think they shot somebody in Crystal City, a person who went berserk. He ran towards the fence and got shot.

Our camp was really unique. Unlike the Japanese Americans, they treated us like prisoners of war. We had Germans and Italians, also from South America, and the South American Japanese. The Peruvians had the biggest contingent. Even then we thought there was discrimination, because the Germans and Italians had the better homes. Isn't it interesting, even in camp. They left camp first. Then we were able to move into their homes, and they were much better, like a real house with a shower and toilet.

Before we moved into the German house, our barrack was like an open room that we had to share with everybody in the family. There were five kids, two parents, an auntie, and my grandma and grandpa. We lived in one barrack that was very thinly made, and so you couldn't have any privacy.

Texas heat is intense. The bed was so hot, even at night you couldn't touch the metal part. You'd burn yourself. They had to mop the floors and sometimes spray water just to keep you cool. A friend told me they went underneath their barrack, which was on stilts, to get some sleep.

In the ten prison camps for Japanese Americans, the government tried to curb the use of the Japanese language. In Crystal City it was encouraged, because the government planned to ship the prisoners of war back to Japan.

When I came to Crystal City, I spoke Spanish and some Japanese. In my house it was mostly Spanish, because my mother is a native Nisei from Peru. Her first language is Spanish.

In camp we'd get up in the morning and go to school, which was almost all day, until four in the afternoon. In the beginning, we went to a Japanese school. They wanted to ship us all back to Japan, and so they allowed us a lot of leeway, whereas the other [WRA] camps did not. But as soon as the war ended, my dad told us we'd better study English, so then we went to English school. These were [Caucasian] teachers from outside who came in. Before that, it was people from the camp.

I was a tomboy. In Crystal City when we moved to the German house, there was a big tree, and I remember playing Tarzan in it. I loved running. I was in a school race and I was either first or second. Marbles was the thing to do. We must have bought the marbles in the commissary. They gave us tokens made of something like cardboard. They were different colors for different values.

There was a library, and I remember reading *Cinderella* in Japanese. I always thought it was a Japanese story. I read the *Arabian Nights* in Japanese, but that I knew wasn't a Japanese story because there were pictures. I read about Greek astronomy—the Big Dipper and so forth—all in Japanese.

We had some fun in the camp because we were children. And our parents were so terrific. They didn't show their worries, and they had them. We credit them a lot. We never felt bitterness, and that's also to their credit. I'm sure they felt it at the time, but they were very philosophical too. That's why they hate wars so much. They said war creates these kinds of things.

Fusa Shibayama

After Crystal City was established as a camp, those already there had a welcoming committee for the new arrivals.

Young students dressed like Girl Scouts and Boy Scouts played this Japanese song we knew from Peru. My tears came out. It was a relief. The feeling comes back now.

Every day I went to do the grocery shopping, and then I'd go to Japanese school. We weren't allowed to go to English school. After school I'd meet my girlfriend and we'd go for a walk around camp. Then I'd go home and help my mother do the laundry, or whatever.

In Peru my mother very seldom cooked. The housekeeper made Spanish and Japanese food. In Crystal City, my mother did the cooking. They had cooking demonstrations where the women got together and taught you how to bake and cook different dishes. They gave us rations to buy groceries. My mother used to make sushi and nori. She learned a lot in camp. Of course there's nothing else to do, so you go and learn.

They had to treat us pretty well, because they were claiming they were using us for exchange of prisoners. We had a swimming pool that was used by everybody, Germans and Japanese. I saved my sister and her friend from drowning. The kids were playing, and one let go of the rope. Everybody got scared. They usually had a lifeguard, but they were all watching a baseball game. I could see backs floating on the surface. I didn't know which one was my sister, I just grabbed whoever I got to first. It happened to be my sister. She was half dead. Her friend was already out, and they were getting the water out of her. I went in and got another girl. When I went again, I couldn't see any more. Two girls drowned that day.

Libia Maoki

I was a very carefree child. I wasn't one of these children that worried. As long as I was with my parents, I was happy. The officials in camp said we were very enterprising because we made the most of the situation. We would have variety shows. We also had a Girl Scout troop. The men organized sports events—baseball, basketball, and football. The mothers got into sewing and crocheting groups.

But it was very hard for our parents. I think all of our fathers were very enterprising businessmen. In camp they couldn't do anything. My father worked in the laundry room. Some of the men worked in hospitals as orderlies and some worked in markets. Their pay was hardly anything. They didn't let us know that it was hard for them. Many times they'd be talking at night, but so softly I couldn't hear what they were saying. I was very sheltered from their feelings, but you could sense a worry.

We had to go to Japanese school. Most of us that went to Japanese school were from Peru. We all spoke Spanish. We were all in the same situation. Later we met some of the Japanese Americans. At first we didn't talk to them because of the language barrier, but then they started coming to Japanese school and Girl Scouts, and we did a lot of activities together.

They were preparing us to be sent to Japan. We had to learn the etiquette, language, mannerisms. Every morning at school we lined up in the courtyard in front of our classroom door and had a pledge to Japan. I didn't go to Japanese school in Peru, so the first time I did this was in camp. We had the Japanese national anthem and bowing to the east to the emperor. The Japanese community in camp felt they had to teach us to be part of Japan when we got there. Not to be complete strangers. We had to think Japanese. We had to think we were Japanese.

Kay Uno was a Japanese American whose family was first incarcerated in the WRA camp in Amache, Colorado, and then transferred to Crystal City. She knew many people who were sent from Crystal City to Japan.

The biggest difference from Amache was the "Boy Scouts" and "Girl Scouts." I put that in quotes because they were very militaristic. The Germans also had their scouts, their youth groups. It was all militaristic because the leaders made it so. They were training us to go back to Japan. We had to make uniforms, and we had to do everything in Japanese. I'm tall for a Japanese. They shoved me out in front and made me a leader. We're marching, and I'm supposed to be giving the orders: Left! Right! Only I couldn't remember the Japanese words.

They were sending a lot of people back to Japan. We had quite a few friends from Crystal City that went back in a hostage trade. The leader of the Japanese Girl Scouts and Boy Scouts was real militaristic, with shaved hair and rigid, upright body. He wore a uniform all the time. He was from somewhere in Hawaii. He talked all these people into going to Japan, saying how good it was to be a Japanese and go to Japan. We should go help the Japanese win the war. The irony of it was he never went to Japan himself. He went back to Hawaii.

★　　★　　★

By the end of the war in 1945, nearly half the Peruvian Japanese had been deported to Japan. Those remaining in the camps were considered illegal aliens by the United States government and told to return to Peru or Japan. At first, the Peruvian government refused to allow any of the Japanese to reenter the country. Later, Peruvian-born citizens were permitted to return. That was not, however, a realistic solution, since it would have forced Nisei children to be separated from their Issei parents.

Between November 1945 and June 1946, with no other place to go, over 900 more were "voluntarily" deported to Japan. Many of those felt they had nowhere else to go. Others believed the only way to rejoin relatives still in Latin America would be for everyone to go to Japan. A small number, refusing to believe that Japan had been defeated in the war, thought they were returning to a victorious nation.

Several hundred Japanese Peruvians fought any attempts to repatriate them to Japan. A group of them hired attorney Wayne Collins to fight their deportation orders. While they waited for the court's ruling on their legal case, they were permitted to leave camp—to be "paroled"—if they had a guarantor, a person or company that promised them work or financial support. At that time, Seabrook Farms, in New Jersey, needed laborers for their processing plants. Many of those still in Crystal City traveled east to work for Seabrook. Since life at Seabrook closely resembled camp life, that experience is related here.

Elsa Higashide

There was news the war had ended, and all the adults were excited. Pretty soon they were told to sign these papers for deportation, and that's when my dad and some three hundred other people said, "We don't want to sign this. We don't want to go to Japan. We know if we go, we're going to die, because there's no food or anything." There was pressure, but a few hundred refused to sign, and that's how we stayed in camp until 1946.

One friend had his auntie living in Denver, who sponsored his family. We didn't know anybody, as we're behind barbed wire. How do you get to know an American? Seabrook Farms said, "We'll give you jobs because we need workers." That's how we were finally released from camp a year after the war ended.

We went straight to New Jersey by train. The first ride from New Orleans to Crystal City was a beautiful Pullman train, but from Texas to Seabrook, it was really a junk train. My mother had this white linen suit, and it got all sooty.

Seabrook was like another camp, with barracks but without the barbed-wire fence. We were so disappointed. We thought we were going to live in a house. The Seabrook years were very hard for everybody. My father was working in the plant. My mother cleaned the latrines in the men's dormitories. She'd come home when it was time to feed the baby and then run back. She had never done any job like this. In Peru middle-class families had maids. Some of the Peruvians were a little bit mean to her, saying, "You're degrading all of us by becoming a latrine cleaner." But my dad told her, "Never mind. No matter what it is, if it's an honest job, you do the best you can and you never have to be ashamed." That was a lesson I learned when I was ten.

Later my mother started working at the plant, because they opened up a nursery school and we could take the younger ones. The plant paid better than her first job. My parents would take turns working night shift. Then someone would always be home.

My parents didn't have enough money to buy new clothing, so my mother undid the clothes we had and redid them. Good thing she was clever also with food. We ate a lot of cabbage and hot dogs, but she'd make it interesting with soy sauce. Cabbage is wonderful. You can make all kinds of things, like rolled cabbage, with the cheapest kind of meat.

There wasn't enough money for boots. I was twelve by the time my mother worked nights. My feet were growing, and I was as tall as she was. I'd wear her boots to go to school. We'd share clothing. We never felt poor. But looking back, we realize how poor we were.

They had Seabrook Elementary and Bridgeton High School. We had a Peruvian school in the beginning. Most of us were placed in the Peruvian school, and then a few went to Seabrook school with all the rest of the American people. When you're put into an all-American school, it's harder in the beginning, but you learn faster. It was tough, but we were advanced in math because of my father teaching us at home. In the schools, the Peruvian children left a very good record.

Art and Fusa Shibayama

ART

We got to Crystal City in March 1944, and we were there until September 1946. We thought maybe we could go back home to Peru. We didn't figure we were going to stay here, especially since we didn't know the language. If we went back home, my dad could start all over again. But Peru didn't want us. The only ones they took back were Nisei Peruvians. I could have gone back [without his parents], but what was I going to do? I was fifteen.

My dad didn't want to go to Japan at all. I had friends at Crystal City that went back to Japan. It was sad, and my dad tried to convince a lot of friends, especially the Peruvians, not to go back, but they went. When they got there, they didn't have enough food.

FUSA

We went on a train from camp to Seabrook. There were quite a few people that went at the same time. At Seabrook, the Japanese people from America weren't too nice to the Peruvians. We couldn't speak English—maybe that's why.

ART

At Seabrook, my mother was pregnant, and my dad, working by himself, couldn't feed the family. I had to get special permission so I could work because I was under age. We were packing frozen foods. We had two work shifts, twelve hours a day, and we rotated every two weeks from day to night.

Seabrook Farm had a softball team. Only the workers on the day shift were able to go, because the games were around six or seven o'clock at night. Our team in camp was the Blue Socks. I wore my Blue Socks shirt when we were playing in the Seabrook Farm league, and people started calling me "Blue Socks."

FUSA

At Seabrook we had to start everything from scratch. It was hard for my parents. My mother worked where they make frozen food, sorting spinach, corn, beans. The vegetables came in on belts and they sorted them. My father worked at the platform warehouse where they packed and loaded the trucks. My mother and father alternated day shift and night shift, so there was somebody home for the kids. Before I started working, I used to buy the groceries, do the cooking and laundry, and watch my little brother. I'd have to take my baby brother outside the house because either my mother or my father was sleeping.

After a while I got a job in the Seabrook flower garden. In each season there's different flowers—tulips, daffodils, gladiolas. The menfolks used to cut the flowers and bring them in the barn. We would pack them by the dozen and ship them by the box all over the country.

We were at Seabrook about two and a half years.

*   *   *

By January 1947, several hundred Peruvian Japanese remained in the United States. Not until June 1952 did they become eligible for permanent residency and then citizenship.

Sumi Seo, Jerome

Tetsuko Morita (seated, third from left),
Tule Lake

Joe Norikane, Amache

Betty Morita

Yosh Kuromiya, Heart Mountain

Clifford Uyeda

Elsa Higashide (top left) with brothers and sisters, Seabrook Farms

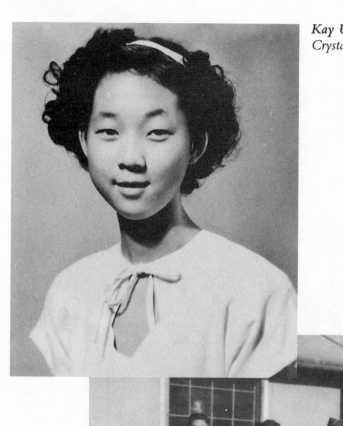

Kay Uno,
Crystal City

*Uno family: **Ernest** (far right) on furlough,*
***Edison** (second from right),*
***Kay** (third from right), Amache*

Lillian Sugita (left),
Hawaii

Mac Sumimoto (top row, third from right),
Crystal City

Don Seki (right)

Dollie Nagai

Harry Ueno (bottom right),
Leupp Prison Camp

Mits Koshiyama (standing center)

"The Crusaders," Jerome

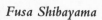
Fusa Shibayama

Art Shibayama

Bert Nakano
(second from right),
Tule Lake

*Libia Maoki (far right) and Chieko Kato
(third from right), Crystal City*

Sue Kunitomi,
Manzanar

Sue Kunitomi Embrey and *Ralph Lazo,*
1991 (courtesy Rosie Kakuuchi)

Following page: *Japanese parents, still*
incarcerated, are handed military medal
posthumously awarded to their son;

Wounded Nisei soldiers.

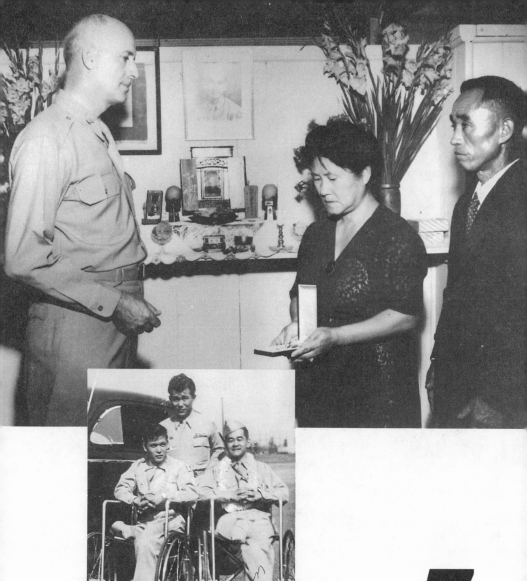

7

NISEI SOLDIERS AND
THE FIGHT FOR
DEMOCRACY OVERSEAS

While their families and friends were locked behind barbed-wire fences and guarded by American soldiers with loaded weapons, by the end of the war some 26,000 Japanese Americans had served in the United States military overseas. The segregated, all-Nisei 442nd Regimental Combat Team (RCT) was, for its size and length of service, the most highly decorated unit in the American military service.

Before the bombing of Pearl Harbor, the United States military had classified Nisei young men as 1-A, eligible for immediate induction. In fact, in the months before the Japanese attack, thousands of Japanese Americans had been inducted into the army and had completed basic training. By early December 1941, some 5,000 were in the military.

Pearl Harbor changed all that. Induction of Nisei was ended. From 1-A, they were first reclassified as 4-F, "ineligible for induction," and then as 4-C, "enemy alien." Many in the service were discharged and sent to the internment camps. Those remaining were assigned permanently to KP (kitchen police) or other generally menial tasks at camps away from the West Coast. In a further demonstration of the suspicion with which they were viewed, they had their weapons taken away.

There were two exceptions to this change of military status for Japanese Americans: the Military Intelligence Service (MIS) Language School and the 100th Infantry Battalion.

★   ★   ★   ★   ★

THE MILITARY INTELLIGENCE SERVICE (MIS)

In anticipation of war with Japan, in November 1941, *before* Pearl Harbor, the army established a language school in San Francisco to train soldiers in the Japanese language for intelligence work. Young Japanese-American men were the logical ones to be trained. After the Pearl Harbor attack, pressure on the Coast forced the MIS to move the school to Camp Savage and then Fort Snelling, both in Minnesota. While the army was recruiting Nisei and Kibei for Japanese-language training, the California State Supervisors Association was advocating barring forever the teaching of Japanese in the United States.

Nonetheless, the MIS school continued its training, and by the time it closed, at the end of the war, it had trained some 6,000 Nisei for military service. MIS-trained Nisei served primarily in the Pacific war zone. They worked on the front lines as well as in field offices, translating captured Japanese battle orders, maps, diaries, and other documents. They also served as interpreters for Japanese prisoners of war.

The work of the Nisei MIS was classified, and little was known of their contribution to the war effort. At the end of the war, however, General Charles Willoughby, Chief of Staff for Intelligence to General Douglas MacArthur, said these young men had shortened the war in the Pacific by at least two years, preventing hundreds of thousands of American casualties.

THE 100TH INFANTRY BATTALION

The formation of the 100th Battalion was the other exception to the ban on Nisei in military service. Originally part of the Hawaiian National Guard, the 100th was formed as an all-Nisei battalion and sent to the mainland for training. In June 1942, more than 1,400 Hawaiian Nisei were shipped first to Wisconsin and then to Camp Shelby in Mississippi.

By September 1943, the 100th Battalion was in Italy, engaged in some of the fiercest battles of the war. In little more than eight months of combat, this unit earned 900 Purple Hearts and was nicknamed the "Purple Heart Battalion." Their exploits were legendary. General Mark Clark, Commander of the Fifth Army, said of the 100th Battalion, "You have written a brilliant chapter in the history of the fighting men in America."

By the time the 100th Battalion was in combat, the government was no longer classifying Nisei as "enemy aliens." Some of the impetus for the change came from the JACL. In November 1942, two delegates from each of the ten relocation camps were given temporary passes to attend a JACL conference in Salt Lake City. The conference members, led by Mike Masaoka, endorsed a resolution urging the government to reinstate military service for all eligible Nisei. Two months later, a delegation of three JACL members made a special trip to Washington to present their case to Secretary of War Henry Stimson. Although some other JACL members disagreed, the three representatives argued for a segregated military unit. If Japanese Americans were mixed with others throughout the armed forces, they insisted, the significance of their military service would be diluted.

At the end of January 1943, Secretary Stimson proposed the formation of an all-Nisei military outfit. President Roosevelt approved the plan on February 1, writing to Secretary Stimson:

> No loyal citizen of the United States should be denied the democratic right to exercise the responsibilities of his citizenship, regardless of his ancestry. The principle on which this country was founded and by which it has always been governed is that Americanism is a matter of the mind and heart; Americanism is not, and never was, a matter of race or ancestry.

This was written by the president less than a year after he signed Executive Order 9066, authorizing the evacuation of American citizens solely because of their race and ancestry.

Not everyone in the military agreed with the new policy of inducting Japanese Americans. On the same day in April 1943 that 2,686 newly enlisted Japanese Americans arrived at Camp Shelby for basic training, General DeWitt, commander of the Western Defense Command, testified before a government subcommittee hearing in San Francisco:

> A Jap's a Jap. They are a dangerous element, whether loyal or not. There is no way to determine their loyalty. . . . It makes no difference whether he is an American. Theoretically he is still a Japanese, and you can't change him.

While the men of the 100th were in combat, the 442nd was in training in Mississippi. By June 1944, the 442nd was fighting in Italy. The 100th Battalion then officially became part of the 442nd RCT. In a critical engagement in the fall of 1944, units of the 442nd freed an American army division. The division of some three hundred Texans was trapped in the forests of the Vosges Mountains in France. Surrounded by German forces, they were in danger of being wiped out. For weeks Allied forces had attempted to free the Texans, known as the "Lost Battalion." Brought in as the situation became more desperate, the 442nd, in a fierce and bloody battle, liberated the Texans, suffering 60 percent casualties, many times the number of Texans they rescued.

The motto of the 442nd was "Go for broke." In their seven major campaigns, the 442nd suffered almost 9,500 casualties. They earned seven Presidential Distinguished Unit Citations; 18,143 individual decorations, including the Congressional Medal of Honor; forty-seven distinguished service crosses; 350 silver stars; 810 bronze stars; and more than 3,600 Purple Hearts. The Congressional Medal of Honor given to Sadao Munemori was one of only twenty-nine awarded during World War II.

General Joseph Stilwell, who commanded Nisei troops in the Pacific, said of these Japanese veterans:

They bought an awful hunk of America with their blood. . . . You're damn right those Nisei boys have a place in the American heart, now and forever. We cannot allow a single injustice to be done to the Nisei without defeating the purposes for which we fought.

The question, of course, remains: should it have to take blood to prove what was always true—that Japanese Americans were as loyal as any other Americans? As William Hohri, imprisoned at Manzanar during the war, has written*:

———

*Hohri, *see* Bibliography.

I do not in any way denigrate the exploits of the Hawaiian 100th or the 442nd Regimental Combat Team. They had a point to prove and they did it bravely and with honor. But frankly, it is not appropriate to make continued references to their bravery as though it were necessary for our being accepted as full citizens. We are all citizens by reason of birth and by law, not by the blood sacrificed by our brothers on the battlefield.

In early 1943, when the government instituted a voluntary military enlistment program for Japanese Americans, camp administrators distributed a loyalty questionnaire to everyone age seventeen and older. Two key and controversial questions (discussed in detail in Chapter 8) asked if the respondents would serve in the armed forces, and if they would forswear allegiance to the emperor of Japan. With a "Yes" response to both, a young Nisei male was eligible for military service.

The army had hoped for approximately 1,500 volunteers from Hawaii and 3,500 from the camps. In Hawaii, where only some 1,100 people out of a Japanese population of 150,000 had been interned, nearly 10,000 young men volunteered. Some 1,200 volunteered from the camps, 800 of whom were accepted. In early 1944, a year after calling for volunteers, the government reinstituted the draft for Japanese Americans. Those who passed the physical were transferred from prison camps to boot camps.

Angie Nakashima

My brother Albert volunteered for the army. These kids were very loyal, which white people can't understand. They think because you don't look like whites, no way can you be that loyal. The majority of the kids we knew who volunteered were plain old gung ho. They wanted to fight for the country.

Sue Kunitomi

Although I finally decided not to, I considered going into the WACS when the recruiting women were in camp. My mother was very worried. I was very patriotic. I really was disillusioned about what had happened, but I wanted to help with the war effort. And I wanted to do something rather than just sit there in camp. "It's still my country," I told her.

Dollie Nagai

In camp at Jerome, Arkansas, Dollie was in a group for teenage girls called The Crusaders, organized by Mary Nakahara, a young woman in her early twenties, who had also been evacuated from California.

The Crusaders was a Sunday school class to start with, but Mary taught real living. She gave us the feeling that camp life was not a waste of time, that our life could have a purpose and a meaning. She got a group of girls together and she started us doing pen pal work with the GIs, the 442nd boys. We were too young to go to the dances, but we were old enough to like correspondence. We'd write group letters. I remember getting letters from the GIs, and I also remember getting letters that came back saying "Deceased," killed in action.

Mary would make up songs about the 442nd infantry. We would feel so good singing. This is my country and they locked us up, but I didn't think of it in those terms.

Mary helped us to feel patriotic. That's why I never felt bitter towards the government. I came from a family of girls and we had no one to serve. It was a feeling of doing for those far away from home, of being grateful for what they were doing. Even though we were in camp, we knew that they were fighting for us, fighting to pave the way so we could go home someday. That's what it was. To be able to go home and live a normal life again.

Ernest Uno

Ernie enlisted from camp in Amache, Colorado.

I was in Amache from November '42 until the following August, when I went into the army. My two brothers went in first. The army was looking for military intelligence experts, so they asked for volunteers, and two of my brothers volunteered. This is before the draft.

Before the war, my brother Stanley was almost three years in the Orient. Stanley was angry with the Japanese. When he came back, he told me of the atrocities he had witnessed. How Japanese soldiers with a rifle butt would beat Chinese civilians. He wanted to get back to the United States. He had no use for the Japanese at all. When he got back, he immediately enlisted in the California National Guard, but when the war broke out, they mustered him out. He was considered an enemy.

In camp, Stanley and Howard said they were going to volunteer because they felt they could qualify for the language school. It was one way of getting the heck out of camp. Stanley's motivation was really that it might get relief for my dad [in a Department of Justice camp]. That didn't happen.

Howard had a wife and a kid who was born in camp. He figured that if he was out of camp and in the army, he could get his family out. They could live on the post or someplace.

When they enlisted, there was still this ban on recruiting or even allowing Japanese Americans in the army. We were still all classified 4-C, enemy aliens. I think Stanley and Howard's classification was changed when they went to Camp Savage.

When I became eighteen, I registered, and I immediately had a 4-C designation. Then, a month later [February 1943], the army came out with this thing: they wanted to recruit Nisei. So I went to enlist. It was a chance to do something. It was a heck of a lot better than sitting and doing nothing, being accused of being an enemy, and being treated as other than a citizen. My mother was very unhappy about it. She felt it was enough that Howard and Stanley enlisted. I should stay and finish school. Finally, she relented. So I went down to enlist, and they turned me down. The doctor said, "Young man, you're not physically fit. You've got this double hernia that would be a liability." When I said I want to get rid of the hernia, he said, "It's a simple operation." So I went back to camp and went to see the doctor.

It took me time to recuperate. Two six-inch scars right in my groin. I was suffering from adhesions. When I went for my induction, the army doctor said, "Who was the butcher that went after you?" But they took me, and I joined the 442nd.

After seeing combat overseas, Ernie returned to the States in September 1945, at the end of the war.

I was living with my sister Amy in Chicago. I told her I wanted to go down and visit Mom and Dad. They were in Crystal City, Texas, in a camp. I had to write to get permission. I got clearance. It took me a couple of days to get down there.

In Crystal City, there was this real dinky hotel, but the people were very cordial. I called out to the camp, and they said I could visit the next day. I'm in full uniform. I caught a cab, and the cabdriver says, "I can't understand. You're in the army and you've got people out there in the camp."

I said, "Yeah, my folks are there." He just shook his head.

My parents were standing at the fence. I got out of the cab and rushed over. The guard immediately said, "Go away. You can't meet here. We have a visitors' cottage." I went in and had one hour to visit. I had had hopes the night I got there about being able to have dinner with my family, sitting at the same table, and Mom fixing something. That all went down the drain. All I could do was visit for an hour in the visitors' cottage. The guard was there for the whole time.

Mom said, "I knew you'd be back. I prayed. You came back, Howard came back, Stanley's coming back. You made it through the war." I broke down. I was terribly disappointed in not being able to really visit with my family. After having risked my life, put my life on the line, it seemed terribly unfair.

I went right back to Chicago. On the bus to San Antonio, I got a seat. At one of the stops, a little old lady was getting off. She put her hand on my arm and said, "Thank you, sonny, thank you," and walked off. Just like that. That touched me. She didn't know me from Adam. She saw me in my uniform.

Ben Tagami

Ben went into the army from camp in Jerome, Arkansas.

I volunteered. I wanted my mother to be able to get out of camp. That was my only reason. This was January of '44, and I was just eighteen.

On the questionnaire, I said I would fight. Allegiance to the emperor? That was ridiculous. I didn't know the emperor or what Japanese people were like in Japan. I remember my mother saying, "Whatever you do, Ben, don't bring shame for your brothers and sister."

There were guys calling me *bakatare*, stupid. I heard a lot of that. I said, "I believe what I'm doing is right. I don't have any allegiance with Japan. I don't know what Japan is like. The only reason I'm in here is because I look like a Japanese, but I don't think like one and I don't act like one."

Although Ben didn't personally encounter racial discrimination during basic training, he knew of others' experiences.

This Japanese American was stationed in Camp Robinson, Arkansas. He went into a drugstore to buy a box of chocolates for his sister, and a guy came out with a shotgun and was shooting at him. Years later I'm in Hawaii and I'm talking to a guy [also a veteran] about strange things that happened. I tell this story, and he looked at me and said, "I'm the guy."

Ben was a soldier in the 100th Battalion. He served with Sadao Munemori and gave a speech at Munemori's memorial.

We were in Italy in '45. It was a mountain where the 100th was the lead battalion to push off. We were the attacking company. The night before Munemori died, we were up in the hills together, reminiscing about what we did as kids and talking about when we lived in California.

He says, "Ben, we're going to go back to Glendale. And whatever you do, remember one thing, don't shame your family, don't bring shame to your country, and don't bring shame to your fellow men. Everything will wash out."

The next day Munemori got through wiping out a machine gun, and a grenade came over and hit him in the helmet. It started to roll by the other guys there. Munemori dove right on the grenade. When they rolled him over, there was nothing they could do for him. Munemori died that morning.

One of the guys he saved was from Hawaii. From 1945 to sometime in the fifties, that guy never had a night's sleep. Then he met Munemori's older sister. He told her how bad he felt, and she said, "I know that if the same thing happened, you would have done the same thing." He broke down. When he went home, it was the first time he slept through the night.

Munemori got the Congressional Medal of Honor for his deeds. He was a private first class. He was from Manzanar, and he was always helping the younger kids like a protective guardian. When he spoke, I listened.

Don Seki

Don grew up in Honolulu and volunteered for the 442nd.

I left the island in March '43. I was twenty that December. They asked for volunteers. It was announced in all the newspapers. Ten thousand volunteered. All my friends went.

We were shipped from Honolulu to Camp Shelby, Mississippi. Mississippi—it's hot, then it's cold in the winter. It's humid and damp. Bugs, chiggers, wood ticks, poison ivy, and poison oak. Disgusting. We wanted to go overseas right away.

Downtown the black people were segregated. Ach, we were sick.

We don't have segregation in Hawaii, so we felt real bad, you know. White water fountain, black water fountain, upstairs for the blacks in the theater, back of the bus.

We had an orientation. Our colonel says, "This is Mississippi. The South. For the whites. Not for the blacks. But you, you're right in the middle. You could go anywhere you prefer." But on the bus they told us not to go in the black section. To spite them, we used to ride in the back. The busman stops and he says, "Get up front." We just stayed. We said, "Damn it, we're going to stay." The blacks don't say anything.

We made a lot of trouble. They'd never seen us kind of guys before. We were strange people. We were there one year. We were sure glad to get out of that place, Mississippi.

Newport News, Virginia, was our port of embarkation. There were a lot of troops, white, black, us. We were fighting with the white guys, and the blacks came to help us. The whites were fighting us because they think we're dirt, you know.

We were there for a couple of weeks, and then on a boat to Italy. I was in the first 442nd group that went over. We had what they called a combat team. We had our own engineers, own artillery. We were about 6,000 guys.

I didn't know I was going into a segregated unit. I thought I was going into the regular army. But I'm glad we weren't with the whites, because we saved each others' life with togetherness. I don't think the white guys would have saved us.

We landed in Naples. Our first campaign was just beyond Rome. This was my first time in combat. Sure, it was scary, especially night-time. I never saw anyone get killed because we were spread out. Some buddies died. In combat it's one of those things. Get killed, wounded. You don't think about it too much.

The 442nd and the 100th Battalion engaged in some of the war's bloodiest battles in Europe, fostering some speculation they were used as "cannon fodder." Don Seki didn't think so.

The way I thought, we're wanted. The heavy fighters. When they couldn't move, stalemate, they use us. Like the Lost Battalion. They got surrounded in France by the Germans. Nobody could get them out. They asked our regiment to get them out, and we did. Our side had heavy losses. We lost more guys than were in the Lost Battalion.

I was in combat nine months. I got hit in France, November 4, 1944, machine gun at night. It's amazing the bullet went the way it did. Just a little different, and I'm dead. It blew off my arm. At first it didn't hurt. When I looked, I saw hardly anything, just the skin dangling. I was in shock. They give you morphine shots. Then after the morphine wears off, you feel it. They took me on a jeep to the field hospital. On the third day the colonel came and offered me a Purple Heart. I said, "Damn it, I don't want it." I was in pain. You don't want anything.

They treated us real nice at the hospitals. The nurses and doctors knew our records, what we'd been through. I was there for about three weeks. I got transferred from France back to Newport News, Virginia. I stayed in a hospital there for two weeks. Then they sent us to Brigham City, Utah. I needed nineteen months of treatment, operations, and physical therapy. We had to learn how to eat with the new artificial limb. Classes in driving, swimming. I wore it for a couple of years. I don't wear it anymore. It's heavy. It's hot.

Even though Don was a soldier and had lost his arm in combat, he was not allowed to return to his home in Hawaii because he would have had to travel through California.

I wanted to go home to Hawaii to recuperate. My brothers were there. But the government wouldn't let me. The war wasn't over, and the Western Division was closed to Japanese. It wasn't really right.

★　　★　　★

In 1992 in Los Angeles and San Francisco, survivors of the Nazi concentration camp at Dachau, Germany, were reunited with some of their liberators, Nisei soldiers of the 522nd Field Artillery Battalion (FAB), part of the 442nd RCT.

Near the end of the war, the 522nd came upon the Dachau camp and found many prisoners dead or dying. Those who could walk had been taken on a forced march to a lake sixty miles away. When the soldiers tracked them down, the German guards fled. Interviewed in 1992 for the Japanese-American newspaper, *Rafu Shimpo,* Clarence Matsumura said:

> Those prisoners were really a sight in their striped uniforms. They were just skin and bones, and they looked so cold. Here I was kneeling down. In my arms sat an inmate of Dachau, and all I could do was hold him as he said, "Please help me." As his body went limp, all I could do was cry. I had to think, What the heck am I doing here? My family was still behind barbed wire in Wyoming . . . here I was in Germany liberating people from camps.

One of the Dachau inmates liberated by the 522nd was Yanina Cywinska, a Polish Catholic, who at age ten was imprisoned with her family because her father was helping Jews escape the Nazis. She was blindfolded by the Germans and expected to be shot. She recalled:

> Next thing I knew, a little Japanese man pulled off my blind-fold. I said, "Go ahead and shoot, get it over with."
> But he said to me, "You are free. We are Americans." I started to touch him, cry and hug. To this day, if anyone says the word "Jap," I become a vicious woman. I adore Japanese people for giving me the chance to live.

The 522nd FAB has never received proper recognition for the liberation of Dachau inmates because their participation was kept secret by the American government. It took more than forty-five years after the war ended for the Nisei participation in the Dachau liberation to become publicly known.

George Oiye and Sus Ito were veterans of the 522nd who organized a photographic exhibit of the liberation. In an interview in a
1992 newsletter of the MIS Club of Southern California, Oiye said
they mounted the exhibit so that their children and their grandchil-
dren "should have an accurate record of what we did."

Betty Morita knew a soldier in the 522nd:

> The brother-in-law of a close friend of mine was with the bat-
> talion that liberated Dachau. They weren't supposed to have
> cameras, but he did, and he took pictures. They were told not
> to talk about it. The government didn't want them to talk
> about it, I guess, because it's so ironic.

Unlike the kidnapping and imprisonment of Peruvian Japanese, the
valor of the Japanese-American soldiers was one story many Americans knew. For those who wanted proof of loyalty, the blood the
Nisei soldiers spilled for America was measure enough.

For others, however, nothing seemed to make a dent in their
racism. A well-known story of postwar discrimination against a Nisei
veteran was the treatment of United States Senator, then Captain,
Daniel Inouye. Captain Inouye, like Don Seki, had lost his arm in
combat. In San Francisco, on his way to Hawaii, Inouye went to a
barbershop. He was in uniform, medals and empty sleeve pinned to
his chest. The barber refused to cut his hair. "We don't serve Japs
here," he said.

Captain Inouye's experience was only one of many instances of
continuing bigotry. In Hood River, Oregon, the American Legion
removed the names of Nisei veterans from the honor roll listing. Betty
Morita's family was affected. "Our second cousin was one of them.
Frank Hachiya. He died in the Philippines. He was one of the interpreters. He was right on the front line and was killed. His name was
on there, and it was erased."

Others appreciated the military service of the Japanese Americans.
Six years after the liberation of the Lost Battalion, the state of Texas

made all men of the 442nd Regimental Combat Team "honorary citizens" of the state.

On July 15, 1946, in a review of the troops, President Harry S.
Truman said to the soldiers of the 442nd RCT, "You fought not only
the enemy, but prejudice—and you won."

Following page: *Mass trial of sixty-three
Heart Mountain resisters;*

Renunciants at Tule Lake Camp.

8

RESISTERS, NO-NOS,
AND RENUNCIANTS

Much has been written to suggest that Japanese Americans walked quietly, some have even implied cheerfully, into the prison camps. It is true there was little organized or violent resistance. But this fact has been transformed into an overbroad generalization about the "true nature" of Japanese Americans. A passive people, according to the stereotype, they understood that military security required their evacuation. In fact the walk to the camps was not so quiet and certainly not cheerful.

A great deal also has been written about the courageous military exploits of the all-Nisei military units that fought Nazism and fascism in Europe and imperialism in Asia. Little, however, has been written about the equally courageous young Japanese-American men who resisted being drafted from the camps so long as their constitutional rights were being denied. Less dramatic, perhaps, than a military charge up a mountain, their battle was for the long haul—nothing less than forcing a reluctant American democracy to live up to its promise of equality for all.

This chapter is about those young idealists. It is also about others who were embittered, angry, or frightened and chose to defy the government in different ways.

Resistance took a variety of forms. There were strikes and riots in the assembly centers and camps, as noted in Chapter 4. Some Nisei renounced their American citizenship and sought *ex*patriation to Japan. Some Issei, denied citizenship in America, requested *re*patriation to Japan.

By far the most explosive issue in the camps was the so-called registration/loyalty questionnaire, distributed in early 1943 to everyone in the camps over the age of seventeen—Issei and Nisei, male and female. The questionnaire had two purposes. The War Department, in a change of policy, was allowing Nisei to volunteer for military service. The department wanted to identify those males who would be eligible to serve. The WRA, a civilian agency, used the questionnaire to identify those who were "loyal" enough to be allowed to leave the camps and settle in the interior states or on the East Coast.

The controversy erupted over two questions, numbers 27 and 28:

Question 27: Are you willing to serve in the armed forces of the United States on combat duty, wherever ordered?

Question 28: Will you swear unqualified allegiance to the United States of America and faithfully defend the United States from any or all attack by foreign or domestic forces, and forswear any form of allegiance or obedience to the Japanese emperor, or any other foreign government, power or organization?

Although the questions were clearly related to military service, they were asked of everyone. The two questions provoked intense discussions, fierce disagreements, occasional family quarrels, and in some camps, bitter fights between different factions.

Angry about the evacuation and disillusioned about American democracy, some answered "No-No" to the two questions. For many of the "No-No boys," as they came to be called, the questionnaire was another outrage in a government pattern of oppression. Others, afraid that a "Yes" answer to Question 27 meant they were volunteering for the army, qualified their answer, or refused to respond at all.

Answering Question 28, about forswearing allegiance to the Japanese emperor, was a wrenching experience for many that literally tore some camp communities apart. Issei were unable by law to become American citizens. They were, therefore, still citizens of Japan, no matter that all had been in the United States for at least eighteen years, most longer. To "forswear" their Japanese citizenship would leave them stateless. The question was eventually rewritten for the Issei, but the damage had been done. Fear and distrust prevailed.

Question 28 posed a different problem for the Nisei, who were American citizens. To be asked to sign a statement to "forswear any form of allegiance to the Japanese emperor" implied they had an allegiance to the emperor. The idea was insulting to many. They were Americans who never had any allegiance to Japan. Some feared it was a trick.

For those not eligible for military service (all Issei and Nisei women), the questionnaire was entitled *"Application* for Leave Clearance" (italics added). Did this mean they would be forced to leave camp? Without homes, jobs, or possessions, forbidden to return to the Coast, many, particularly the older Issei, weren't ready to be thrust out into a hostile world.

In all, nearly 78,000 people in the camps were over age seventeen and eligible to register. After visits by military personnel and pressure from the WRA administration and their JACL supporters, the vast majority answered Yes-Yes to Questions 27 and 28. But it is significant that of the 21,000 Nisei males eligible for military service, some 22 percent answered "No," qualified their responses, or gave no answers at all to the loyalty questions.

General DeWitt, commander of the Western Defense Command, and his associates had argued for the total exclusion of Japanese from the Coast. They believed it was impossible to distinguish loyal Japanese Americans from those disloyal to America. The very idea of a loyalty review, therefore, undermined the general's rationale for the evacuation. He fought against the questionnaire, and went so far as to argue that certain constitutional protections have to be suspended during wartime. He said there should be public education programs to teach people to accept the suspension of civil rights during any future wars.

Although DeWitt failed to convince his superiors, some politicians and government officials continued to fan the flames of anti-Japanese hysteria he helped ignite. Pressure built to segregate those internees deemed "disloyal" from the rest of the camp inmates. In mid-July 1943, the WRA announced a segregation plan. The government chose Tule Lake, one of the larger camps, for the segregants. More than 6,500 people were transferred out of Tule Lake to other camps, and some 12,000 were transferred in. Among the so-called "disloyal," were:

- those who had answered "No," or refused to answer Question 28;
- those who had applied for expatriation or repatriation to Japan;
- those who had some unexplained evidence of "disloyalty" in their files.

★   ★   ★   ★   ★

RESISTANCE TO THE DRAFT

In early 1944, when the draft was reinstituted for the imprisoned Nisei, tensions in the camps escalated. Willingness to serve in the military was no longer a theoretical question. Young Japanese Americans were now being drafted from behind barbed wire to fight for democracy overseas while their families were to remain locked up in America's prison camps.

Of all the forms of camp protest, one is particularly remarkable for its idealism. A combination of political innocence and intellectual sophistication motivated some three hundred young men to resist the draft. Unlike the No-No boys, the resisters said "Yes," they would serve in the army, but only when their constitutional rights had been restored and their families were free to leave the prison camps. When called for their pre-induction physical examination, they refused to appear. They were vilified by those in the camps who supported the JACL. As Mits Koshiyama, a young resister, says,

> We were very naive. We felt the JACL people might know more about the situation than we did. But I never thought they'd sell out our constitutional rights. Wartime JACL thinking was that public image was far more important than fighting for constitutional rights. They felt that if you kowtow and compromise your constitutional rights, or even give them away, finally white America would accept you.
>
> Those of us who thought different were characterized as malcontents, troublemakers. Even to this day they always talk about the 442nd military unit, but when you really study it, what are they trying to say? That the government has a right to

put you in a camp, take away all your constitutional rights, and
then force you into a segregated army to fight for the very
principles that are denied you? I said no, that's wrong. You
can't draft me to fight for something that you're taking away
from me.

The resisters were arrested, prosecuted in court, and pilloried by the
outside press. In some camps, they were attacked viciously by the
camp newspapers controlled by the JACL, which accused them of
everything from naiveté to treason. In fact, they demonstrated a sin-
gular courage and dedication to principle. Most histories have ignored
the resistance movement, or questioned the loyalty of the men
involved. Their story deserves a full airing, and begins this chapter.

Noboru Taguma

*Noboru Taguma's family had farmed in California. He had graduated
from high school the year the war started. Before camp, Noboru had not
been involved in any political activities.*

We got the questionnaire in Amache [camp in Granada, Colorado]. I
said I'm not going in [the army], so I didn't pay any attention. I put
"Yes" to 27 and 28, but I didn't think they were going to draft us
when we were in the camp. I thought it was wrong they put us in the
camps. We learned about the Constitution in high school. This was
violating it. If you're just out of high school, that memory is still
there.

I went to three meetings. There were a lot of objectors. Over half
said they weren't going to go in the army. Then they had a Caucasian
officer come from outside. Every other sentence he said, "Twenty
years in prison or $10,000 fine if you don't go!" When you're eigh-
teen or twenty, you believed it. That changed two of my best friends.
They weren't going to go before they heard him.

But I didn't change. I told my folks I'm not going. I feel sorry for
my parents. They worked so hard on the farm and then they put them
in a relocation center. That's the reason I told the government I

wouldn't go. I told them, when my folks is released, then I'll go. I
got a draft notice, but I didn't pay attention. One night, about 8
o'clock and dark, they picked me up.

*Before their trial, some of the resisters were visited in jail by Minoru
Yasui and Joe Grant Masaoka, both JACL lawyers, who tried to convince them to go into the army. Many were stunned to hear Min Yasui
take this position, for he had earlier violated General DeWitt's West
Coast curfew. When Yasui challenged the curfew, he had asked the
JACL for support. JACL, however, was opposed to test cases, arguing
that total compliance with the evacuation program was necessary to
demonstrate loyalty. Yasui lost his case before the Supreme Court. In a
political twist, he became a spokesperson for the JACL and supported
the policy to draft Nisei from the camps. Noboru Taguma was one of
the resisters whose position Yasui sought to change.*

I went to the youth correctional institution in Colorado first, and
from there to Denver. There were fifteen of us. The guard said, "You
people are lucky. There's two lawyers come to help you." It was Min
Yasui and Joe Grant Masaoka. The guys went to talk to them one at
a time. When they came back, I said, "What happened?" They said,
"You'll find out if you go."

When I got in there, they said, "How do you do, Mr. Taguma.
The first thing I want you to do is go into the army." Min Yasui had
completely turned around and changed.

I got real mad. I told them, "If I was going to go to the army physical, I wouldn't be here in the first place." I was speaking Japanese
because there was a guard listening. I said, "The hell with the JACL!
I have no more business with you guys." I said, "Guard, I want to go
back in." When the interviewing was over, nobody had changed their
mind. That night they put three of us in small solitary confinement
cells.

*Over 300 young men from the camps were brought to trial on charges of
draft resistance. The trials took place during the highly charged atmos-*

phere of the war years. The results varied from courtroom to courtroom. The case against resisters from Tule Lake, for example, was dismissed by Judge Louis Goodman, who said, "It is shocking to the conscience that an American citizen be confined on the ground of disloyalty, and then, while so under duress and restraint, be compelled to serve in the armed forces, or be prosecuted for not yielding to such compulsion."

Noboru appeared before a judge who came to the opposite conclusion.

We pleaded "Not Guilty." We had individual trials, and we were called individually for sentencing. The judge said, "I'm a Republican. I sympathize with you fellas, but most of the people from Amache went into the army. About nine hundred went for the physical and just thirty-five didn't. I have to give you a sentence because you disobeyed the selective service rule."

Everybody got different sentences. I don't know why. My father's friend was a lawyer. He said, "When you go up to the judge, say 'Your Honor.' Don't say anything bad." I was so nervous the only thing I said was "Yes, your Honor." One guy talked back to the judge. He got three years.

When it was my turn, the judge said, "Mr. Taguma, how old are you?"

"Your Honor, what date is today?"

"Today is April third."

"My God, your Honor, this is my birthday. Today is my birthday!"

He said, "One year and a day."

Joe Norikane

Joe was from the Sacramento area and a recent high school graduate at the time of his incarceration.

I liked civics in school. Life, liberty, and the pursuit of happiness, inalienable rights. The teacher said the most important thing is the first ten amendments to the Constitution, the Bill of Rights. Due process, that's one of the main things. You have a right to trial, and you're innocent until you're proven guilty. That stuck with me all the time. You're born with that right, but they didn't give it to me.

They sent us from home to Merced [Assembly Center]. From Merced, they took me to Amache. And in Amache they started saying I have to go into the army. I said, "Hey, that's enough. I'm not going to go. Why should I go? I don't want to defend the concentration camps."

The police chief picked me up, and they questioned me at the camp police headquarters. He said, "I heard you're not going to the draft."

"I'm going to go anytime my rights are restored."

"I didn't ask you that. Are you going to go or not?"

"Yes. I'm going to go anytime my rights are restored."

Four of us didn't go. They didn't do anything then, and I went back to my barracks. There were a lot of No-Nos in our group. The camp director got mad and said, "I'm going to give you one more chance, and I don't want to see so many No-Nos. Change it!" Guys went back and changed it. A lot changed to "No-Yes," or "Yes if drafted" and "Yes."

I didn't want to say "No-No" because I'm true to the United States. It's the only country I know. I never pledged allegiance to another country. I thought about putting "No-Yes," but then I decided I'd better not. I'd probably be separated from my family. So I wrote "Yes, if drafted."

After I got the notice for the physical and didn't go, they picked me up and questioned me. They waited three days, and then the marshal came and handcuffed four of us. My sister was in the camp with her husband. He and I got handcuffed together.

They took us to the U.S. Marshal's office in Pueblo. They asked, "How do you plead?"

We said, "Not guilty." They took us to Denver. We were so innocent, we didn't know anything about law. At least I didn't.

There was a guy from our camp who went into the army. He wrote back to a friend in the Denver County jail who was there for something else, not draft resistance. He said in the letter, "We're try-ing to build up a good reputation, and there's guys tearing it down as fast as we try to build it up." But I knew that the guy writing had volunteered because he got dumped by his girlfriend. He proposed and said, "If you don't marry me, I'm going to volunteer in the army." She said, "Go ahead." And he writes something like that. It makes me mad.

Although they were both from the same camp, Joe didn't know Noboru in Amache. They became friendly in prison in Denver.

In the camp, all our families pooled their money together and got a lawyer. The first five or six guys had individual trials. Then the lawyer said it's not going to work. "Let's plead *nolo contendere.*" That meant we leave it up to the mercy of the court. It's a plea bargain. All of us went and stood up in front of the court and said, "We plead *nolo contendere.*" The judge gave me nine months.

The ones that had individual trials got a lot heavier sentences than we did. My brother-in-law was one of the first. He went up there and started talking in Japanese because he was a Kibei and educated in Japan. The judge looked at his record and said, "You graduated from high school. Why can't you speak in English?"

"Japanese is my stronger language," he said, "and this is my life and death. I want to speak in the stronger language to defend myself." They had to get an interpreter. He got two and a half years.

My friend who was also a resister stood up and said, "Ladies and gentlemen, if it wasn't for the evacuation, if I was back home, I would have been out there fighting with your brothers and sisters or your husbands. If it weren't for being in this concentration camp, I would be fighting shoulder-to-shoulder with your sons." He was a mouth-piece.

Frank Emi

The government's questionnaire provoked the most organized resistance at the Heart Mountain camp in Wyoming. The Heart Mountain Fair

*Play Committee (FPC) distributed three bulletins challenging the gov-
ernment's policies, beginning with the evacuation, held meetings to dis-
cuss the issues, and sent press releases on the group's activities to the outside news media. In Denver, James Omura, English-language editor of
the* Rocky Shimpo *newspaper, was the only one who printed their stories and supported the FPC in his editorials.*

*Frank Emi was twenty-five years old when the war began. He and
his wife and newborn daughter were evacuated from Los Angeles. Before
camp, Frank had not been involved in politics. In camp, he became one
of the leaders of the Fair Play Committee.*

I thought it was really stupid that they expected anybody to volunteer
from these camps. We were treated like enemy aliens, without any
of our rights recognized. To expect us to fulfill obligations without
the rights of citizenship, I thought was basically unfair.

At a public meeting, either the camp Protestant pastor or the associate editor of the Heart Mountain *Sentinel* [the camp newspaper]
urged people to sign the registration "Yes-Yes" and not cause any
trouble. They were JACL. "We have to show the government we're
loyal," they said.

Then Mr. [Kiyoshi] Okamoto got up and gave us a brief discourse
on the Constitution. He said we were all put in here without any
shred of due process, and the United States Constitution says we
should have a hearing before we're put into a place like this.

The more I looked at it, the more disgusted I got at those two
questions. I answered, "Under the present conditions and circumstances, I am unable to answer this question." I put that on both 27
and 28. My younger brother and I made out copies of these two
answers. I figured many people would be confused on how to answer
it. I wrote, "Suggested answers to Questions 27 and 28," and we
posted that around camp.

I was really angry about this. And of course angry about the whole
thing—losing our business, getting thrown in there without any rights
at all. When Mr. Okamoto got up and spoke, I thought, Here's a fella

that's really expressing our feelings. I don't remember who went with me, but we got together with him. He was a soil test engineer from Hawaii, an older man, a Nisei.

Mr. Okamoto was going around the camp giving speeches, talking whenever he could get enough people to listen. He called himself the Fair Play Committee of One. He was considered somewhat of an agitator by the administration. He didn't hold back on his adjectives. He didn't use too much profanity, but he was tough. After we got together, we formed the Fair Play Committee as an organization in 1943.

We used to meet maybe once a week. We would talk about the best way to fight some of the unfair practices going on in camp. We heard some of the civilian employees were stealing meat that should have gone to the internees. We tried to get the block councilmen to protest that.

We looked at the JACL as more or less the spokesperson for the Japanese-American community. Nothing had really polarized yet. The polarization came after the draft issue in the camps.

Frank had originally responded to both Questions 27 and 28 in the same way, stating that under the circumstances of imprisonment, he was unable to answer. At an administrative hearing after the reinstatement of the draft, he changed one answer.

It was clear that if you didn't answer Question 28 [forswearing loyalty to the Japanese emperor] "Yes," you were going to be sent to Tule Lake. I said, "I've never sworn allegiance to the emperor of Japan. I want you to know that. I will change the answer to 'Yes' because I am a loyal American." I didn't want to go to Tule. I thought it was a camp for disloyals and people who wanted to go back to Japan.

In January of 1944, they had instituted the draft in the camps. The Fair Play Committee was holding public meetings at the mess halls. In the beginning, the administration gave us permits, but when they heard what we were talking about, they refused to give us any more permits. We kept holding meetings anyway. The first few meetings were more or less informational.

We were holding these meetings almost every night in different blocks, and we were getting pretty full houses. It was a matter of extreme interest to most of the young men. There was hardly any opposition to what we were saying. We didn't say you should refuse to go. We said we think this is morally wrong, unjust, and maybe illegal to draft people out of camp.

The steering committee was composed of about seven or eight of us who were most active. We had a membership fee of $2 to cover expenses. Up to now we had been giving out information to people to let them make up their own minds. I said, "I think it's time the Fair Play Committee took a real black-and-white stand on this draft issue." Some were a little lukewarm. In the end, those of us that wanted to take a stronger stand prevailed. We put out three bulletins. In the third, we took a very definite stand—we refused to go until all our constitutional rights were restored to us and we're treated like American citizens.

We presented this resolution to a few hundred people at the mess hall. The response was overwhelming that they go along with the resolution. This put us in direct conflict with JACL. They started attacking us. They had some pretty horrendous editorials in the Heart Mountain *Sentinel* and the *Pacific Citizen,* the JACL outside newspaper. We were called everything under the sun. One guy said we were misleading and misguiding the young men, that we were provocateurs, seditionists, disloyal, a second Pearl Harbor.

At the meetings there was almost unanimous approval of our position, but when the notices started to come for the physicals, the majority didn't resist.

Yosh Kuromiya

Yosh, an art student, was eighteen years old when the war with Japan started. He was in the first group of sixty-three from Heart Mountain to be tried for draft resistance.

There was a lot of discussion about the questionnaire. The Fair Play Committee was drawing to our attention the dilemma the questions created. There was no accurate, simple answer. A "Yes" or a "No" didn't really have any meaning at all.

I had no question about my loyalty, even though I couldn't accept what was happening as being constitutionally right. I thought surely this is going to be challenged. We haven't been tried. We haven't been convicted of anything. I didn't think it was going to lead to conscription, although that's what everybody was claiming. You answer "Yes-Yes," and you're in the army, fella. I still couldn't believe that, so I innocently answered "Yes-Yes."

Once you're drafted, you become a part of the machinery. The draft put it right on the table in front of me. It was my own personal problem from that point on. I realized once I sign in, I'm Uncle Sam's property. He can send me wherever he wants to. And I knew where he's going to send me. It was common knowledge we're going to be in a segregated unit. The JACL openly admitted it was their suggestion that there be a segregated battalion in order to more forcefully prove the loyalty of the Japanese. Our loyalty is questioned, and it's important we clear ourselves. That's what the war was all about as far as they were concerned. They didn't really care about the Jews. They didn't care about the Germans. They were too busy clearing our name.

I had a difficult time visualizing myself standing face to face with the enemy with both our guns aimed at each other and deciding who had a better right to shoot first. I envisioned the other person believing in what he was doing. I would have had to question my motives. I would have been there to prove my loyalty to people who had no business questioning it in the first place.

Had the whole evacuation experience not occurred, I would have had no problem at all. I would have felt very righteous. Here was an evil monster [Hitler], and the person packing the gun is representing him. But what had happened to the Jews in Europe could very well be happening to my family in the camps, while I was out there shooting the Germans. There was talk that we were potential hostages should there be a need for prisoner exchange.

When I got the notice for the physical, I ignored it. But I knew they were coming. They weren't going to forget about it. It was just a matter of time. They drove up right in front of our door in a black sedan limousine. These official-looking men in suits and ties came knocking. All the neighbors were crowding around, peering out the windows. I thought it must be humiliating for my parents. They're the innocent victims.

My brother's wife was very upset when she found out. She had just had her first child. She said if she had realized what my attitude was, what my actions would be, she would never have married my brother. I should be more considerate about the baby. "What's it going to be like for him to have a convict for an uncle?" She worked for the *Sentinel,* the camp newspaper run by the JACL.

The car ride to the jail is a complete blank. There were about eight of us on this load. I didn't know anybody except one person I had met in the camp art students' league. We were taken to jail and fingerprinted.

Then we were taken to another jail in Cheyenne. It was terrible. We never got any sunlight, just what reflected off the neighboring brick wall. Some of the fellas were beginning to lose little gobs of hair. Bad nutrition and lack of sunlight. For breakfast, it was a big pie pan piled up with mush and a whole mountain of sugar on top. This was during the war, under rationing. I always wondered how the prisons were able to get so much sugar. It would have been ironic if they stole it from the camps and gave it to us in prison. Most of the mush was dumped down the toilet because we couldn't eat it.

I celebrated my twenty-first birthday in the Cheyenne County jail. It was kind of lonely because I didn't want to tell anybody. No cake, no candles. It's certainly not a conventional thing, and I wouldn't recommend it for anybody else.

I think I would have done it [resisted the draft] even if there was no

Fair Play Committee. But alone, I would have been buried. The Fair Play Committee at least gave us a voice.

In 1942, Gordon Hirabayashi, a student at the University of Washington in Seattle, challenged the military-imposed curfew and the evacuation. He was tried and convicted. He appealed his case to the Supreme Court, which reviewed it along with the case brought by Minoru Yasui. Although Hirabayashi had been convicted at his trial of both violating the curfew and refusing to register for evacuation, the Supreme Court addressed only the curfew and upheld it as a constitutionally valid exercise of war powers. Its decision in the Hirabayashi *case was then cited by the Court to uphold the conviction of Yasui. Many of the young Nisei draft resisters knew of both cases.*

I was one of those interviewed in Cheyenne by Joe Grant Masaoka and Min Yasui. They tried to talk us out of it. They said they were giving us one last chance to redeem ourselves. Needless to say, they were wasting their time.

Min Yasui was my hero when he challenged the evacuation initially. At that point the JACL tried to discourage him. They wouldn't have anything to do with him. When they realized what a forceful lobbyist he was, and after he lost his case, they embraced him and brought him into their fold. And he did a complete turnaround. After that, boy, forget him. You have to be careful when you pick your heroes.

On the other hand, there's Gordon Hirabayashi, who we were fortunate to meet at McNeil Island [prison where Yosh served his sentence]. He was a conscientious objector, a member of the American Friends Service Committee, the Quakers. I admire Gordon Hirabayashi. He didn't do a turnaround. He stuck to his guns.

Mits Koshiyama

After harassment from other students, Mits quit high school in the months after Pearl Harbor and began farming. He too was one of the Heart Mountain sixty-three tried for draft resistance.

Feelings were very high against the draft. I would say 95 percent of the young people were against the draft. But when it comes to actually fighting the government, people change their minds.

A lot of people who were drafted didn't want to go into the army. I give credit to the people who volunteered. Many draftees tried all kinds of ways to get out of the army. Some drank a lot of *shoyu,* soy sauce. It raised your blood pressure. The army got wise, and the induction center held them over for their physical. People in camp said after the boys came back from the physical, you could tell the ones that didn't pass and the ones that did. The ones that passed were in tears.

My brother signed me up to be a member of the Fair Play Committee and paid my $2 dues. He was very interested in it too. But later on he confided in me that you can't fight this racist government. "They're going to put you in jail, lock you up, and forget about you. I'll take my chances with the army." He was a reluctant draftee.

Many people get confused between Fair Play and No-Nos. We were Yes-Yes. When I got the questionnaire, I was about eighteen. I really didn't know what to put down. For Question 27, I scribbled on the paper, "Yes I will fight for this country only if my constitutional rights are returned to me first." On Question 28, I signed "Yes" too. I was Yes-Yes. I had no sympathy for the emperor of Japan. That was ridiculous. I could not understand why they would put a question like this in. It angers me when people say we might be disloyal and pro-Japan. No way! I haven't heard of one resister that talked bad against the United States.

When I got the draft notice, I didn't show up for the physical. I was supposed to go around 6:00 A.M. At nine or nine-thirty that same morning, a federal marshal came with his car right to my door in the barracks and picked me up. I think there were about fifteen of us. They sent us to the county jail in Powell. We stayed there overnight, and the next day they took us to Casper, which had larger facilities. We stayed there approximately a month, until the trial, and then we went to Cheyenne.

The trial of the Heart Mountain sixty-three lasted about a week. They were convicted and sentenced in June 1944.

The trial was really something. Very racial. It was a judge [not a jury] trial. They made all sixty-three of us march down the street single-file to get to the courthouse. There were marshals on the street. I was feeling pretty bad. Are we citizens or not? What are we doing here? Wyoming, of all places.

The judge was not sympathetic at all. We based our case on our constitutional rights. He wouldn't listen. We didn't have an under-standing judge who would listen to both sides. From the begin-ning, he was against us. Our attorney tried his best to convince them that our civil and constitutional rights were violated, but the court wouldn't hear it.

At one point during the trial, the federal prosecutor was rocking in his chair back and forth and all of a sudden he flipped over back-wards. We laughed because it was so ridiculous. He quickly jumped up on his feet and said, "You people laugh right now, but you won't be laughing when you hear the verdict." He let the cat out of the bag there. We were already guilty.

The Judge found the sixty-three guilty and concluded his opinion on a nonlegal note:

Personally this Court feels that the defendants have made a serious mistake. . . . If they are truly loyal American citizens they should . . . embrace the opportunity to discharge the duties of citizens by offering themselves in the cause of our National defense.

On June 26, we were convicted. The judge read us his reasons. He said since we were classified 1-A by the government, all our rights had been returned to us. We were first-class citizens, and we had no right to refuse to bear arms. I couldn't buy that. He said we broke the law. But he won't accept that the government broke the law, the constitutional law, by denying us our day in court before putting us in concentration camps.

We got the sentence the same day. Three years in federal prison. Half of us went to McNeil Island, near Seattle, and half to Leavenworth. I went to McNeil Island. My brother was drafted from camp. Just before he went overseas, he came to visit me in prison. My only visitor. He was a good brother.

★   ★   ★

The sixty-three appealed their convictions. But before the decision was reached in their case, the Supreme Court ruled on two cases involving the evacuation and internment, on December 18, 1944. Fred T. Korematsu was found guilty of failing to comply with the West Coast exclusion orders by not reporting for evacuation. Mitsuye Endo, a Japanese-American woman living in California whose loyalty was not questioned by the government, claimed that she was unconstitutionally detained in a relocation center. The Supreme Court upheld the evacuation order in the *Korematsu* case, but it ruled in the *Endo* case that the WRA had no authority to detain loyal Americans in relocation centers.

On March 12, 1945, the Court of Appeals in the case of the Heart Mountain sixty-three held that even though loyal citizens could not be detained in camps under the new *Endo* decision, as American citizens the young men still owed a debt of military service to the country. "Two wrongs never make a right," the judge wrote. "Neither the fact that [they were] of Japanese ancestry nor the fact that [their] constitutional rights may have been invaded by sending [them] to a relocation center cancel this debt." Their convictions were upheld.

After the sixty-three from Heart Mountain were tried and convicted of draft resistance, Frank Emi was arrested with six other leaders of the Heart Mountain Fair Play Committee and James Omura, the editor of the *Rocky Shimpo*. The eight were charged with conspiracy to counsel draft resistance. The defendants argued that their actions were protected by the First Amendment rights of freedom of speech, press, and assembly. Omura was acquitted, while the seven FPC leaders were found guilty.

Frank Emi

I was exempt from the draft because at that time they were not calling people with children. Out of the seven of us indicted for conspiracy, only three were really eligible for the draft. The reason those of us who weren't subject to the draft entered this fight was because of the basic unfairness of it.

Some wanted to turn a blind eye to the injustice and take the easiest road—go along with anything the government says. The heck with that, you know. This is right and this is wrong. In the same way, I respect those that *volunteered* from the camps and felt they should be loyal to this country no matter what. They're doing the same thing we're doing, only they're doing it the other way. The guys that didn't want to go, who thought it was wrong for the government to draft them but still went along, for them to come back later and criticize us—they're the worst.

When our turn came for the trial, we thought maybe we could get a better shake [than the sixty-three] with a jury trial, but the result was the same. Our attorney was a real sharp attorney for the ACLU, but the ACLU as an organization would not take our case. We had to hire him as private counsel. The head of the ACLU at that time was Roger Baldwin, a close friend of Roosevelt. It was the ACLU/WRA/JACL—sort of an axis there—that were fighting against us.

Our counsel told us right from the beginning we may have to go to the appellate court to get a just decision. Wartime is going to be hard at the lower courts. As he predicted, we lost our case. We were sentenced to four years in Leavenworth Penitentiary, which was a high-security prison.

The appellate court reversed the convictions of the seven FPC leaders on the technical ground that the lower court judge had not given the jury proper instructions. The decision from the appellate court didn't come down until December 1945, after the war had ended. Although Frank and the other FPC leaders had won their case, they remained in prison until March 1946.

The resisters came from the following camps: Topaz, 9; Poston, 112; Granada (Amache), 35; Heart Mountain, 88; Jerome, 1; Minidoka, 40; Rohwer, 3; Tule Lake, 27. Of the 315 draft resisters, 263 were convicted.

RESISTERS AND THE POSTWAR YEARS

In December 1947, President Harry S. Truman granted a full pardon to the young men convicted of resisting the draft. The names of the 263 convicted men were attached to the presidential proclamation, but the individuals were not directly informed of the pardon by the government. Their names were printed in newspaper reports of the presidential action. Joe Norikane's experience was typical: "Somebody had the paper and said, 'Hey Joe, your name's on there. You got pardoned!' "

For many years the Japanese American Citizens League actively condemned the resisters. Books written by JACL leaders have virtually ignored the resisters, recounting only the heroism of the Nisei military men. These tensions within the Japanese-American community continue today. As Jim Matsuoka, a prisoner himself in the camps, says, "Under that stressful situation, people had to cope with things in their own way. They should not be pitted against each other. But when you get powerless people, you wind up like South Africa. They're killing each other."

Some members of the JACL, including past president Clifford Uyeda, have urged the organization to apologize for its attacks on the resisters and others who disagreed with the JACL policy of accommodation to the government during the war. The National JACL has refused to apologize. The Pacific Southwest District of the JACL, in February 1995, however, passed a resolution stating in part,

PSW-JACL regrets and apologizes for any pain or bitterness caused by its failure to recognize this group of patriotic Americans and that by this recognition the PSW-JACL strives to continue to actively promote and nurture the healing process of an issue that has divided our community.

Mits Koshiyama

I'm very glad I stood up. But it took quite a while to feel good about what I did. When the resisters came out of prison, they still felt the sting. The JACL always harped on us. Memorial Day the JACL people got up and call the resisters "dissidents," "traitors," "cowards," whatever came to their mind to hurt us. But we were never against the veterans. Never. Resisters had brothers and other relatives in the 442nd. My own brother was in the intelligence service. And I had two brothers that went into the army after the camp days. People were giving their lives for this country. Why would we speak ill of them?

The change started for me when President Truman gave us our pardon. I felt, Hey, the president gave us a pardon, the government says they were wrong. I'm going to try and be just an ordinary American citizen, work hard, and believe in my rights.

Then the younger people came of age, the Sansei, and they spoke up against the relocation and the evacuation. That gave me a lot of hope. I could feel that people were getting more sympathetic. I went to church one time and a wounded 442nd vet told me, "People are finally recognizing what you people stood for."

Like many, Angie Nakashima didn't think of resisting at the time. But like some today, she gives the resisters the credit due them for recognizing injustice and protesting:

Those that resisted, they were probably the intellectual group. They really did lots of deep thinking. They were a minority, but they were on the right track of course. They were on the right track.

OTHER FORMS OF PROTEST: THE POLITICS OF NO-NO, RENUNCIATION, AND EXPATRIATION OR REPATRIATION TO JAPAN

There were many different reasons why people answered "No" to the loyalty questions. Whatever their reasons, they were all considered "disloyal" by the government. In the fall of 1943, the WRA began the great move of nearly 20,000 people into and out of the Tule Lake camp, the newly designated segregation center for the "disloyals." No-Nos were sent to Tule, and many believed from there they'd be shipped to Japan.

Outside the camps, some politicians and special interest groups pressed for legislation that would make it easy for Nisei to renounce their American citizenship. In July 1944, President Roosevelt signed into law an act that did just that. Inside the camps, particularly at Tule Lake, a parallel pressure grew to renounce. The attorney general had testified before Congress that there were some 300 to 1,000 people at Tule Lake who had said they wanted to renounce. Many times that number in fact filed to renounce.

For some in the camps, there was a logic in renouncing their citizenship. The country seemed to be saying they were not welcome. The hostility of the non-Japanese community, the abrogation of Japanese Americans' rights, and their confinement in desolate camps— all were reason enough for some to choose to give up their citizenship. The next logical step was to leave the country and go to Japan, a return "home" for Issei and the making of a new home for Nisei. After the passage of the renunciation law, nearly 5,700, more than five times the expected number, filed to renounce. Almost all were from Tule Lake.

Sue Kunitomi

It was a terrible time for everybody. [The questionnaire] split families apart. The government makes procedures, but they never think of the human angle.

It was really the way the question was worded. If they had had any sense at all, they would never have put in a question about allegiance to the emperor. My mother had a tremendous amount of pressure put on her to denounce the United States and go back to Japan. She refused. They said, "What are you? Disloyal Japanese?"

She said, "I've got eight kids in this country, three of them in the service. I can't leave them behind. I can't take these kids to a country they don't know."

The father of a friend of mine insisted on going to Japan. The older son wrote No-No and went with his dad. The mother refused to go. She said, "My kids are all American citizens. I'm going to stay here." The father was in Japan for ten years with the oldest son, and the mother was here with the others.

One of the young men in our block went to Japan with his mother. She was a widow, and he was the only son. He was around eighteen. He was shot by an MP the very first week we were in camp. He went looking for scrap lumber, and a guard claimed he was trying to escape. He said he did not hear the guard say "Stop." The guard shot him in the thigh. He was so mad, he signed No-No on the questionnaire. His mother and sister went with him to Tule Lake and to Japan from there. My brother was overseas in Japan with General MacArthur and found him. He had no food and no money and was almost starving. They helped him out. Eventually he came back. He was a young Nisei. He still has the bullet in his leg. They couldn't take it out.

Sohei Hohri

Twenty-six questions were name and address and what do you eat for breakfast, or whatever. Then came questions 27 and 28, and these were asked in person. We went into a room. These were critical questions. I said "No" to 27 and "No" to 28.

There was an army captain there, and he read my answer. He said, "Do you know what you're doing? You're going to have a black mark on your record for the rest of your life."

I said, "I don't give a good goddam." The fellas I worked with used to swear up a blue streak. I would say "Jiminy cricket" or "Gosh darn." But this day I yelled, "I don't give a good goddam!" I was startled. It just erupted out of me.

So I was a No-No. I was going to be sent to Tule Lake and I guess be deported. They were having a second hearing, and my mother pleaded with me. She said, "Say 'Yes' to everything because the most important thing is your family has to stick together." It was like a pre-exam coaching period. My family would ask me things like "If an American battleship is sunk in the Pacific, does that make you feel happy or sad?"

At the second hearing, they asked me a great number of this sort of question. The whole point was, don't say anything to rile the questioner. My mother pleaded with me to be sure to go along with everything they wanted to hear. So I changed from No-No to Yes-Yes.

Yukio Tatsumi

I was eligible for the draft before the war started. All my friends were taken. I was 1-A too, and I was ready to go because I'm a citizen, right? That's our duty. I waited. Maybe I'm lucky or unlucky, I don't know, but I didn't get my draft call. In the meantime, I was put in camp.

When we went into camp, they changed our classification to 4-C. 4-C is "enemy aliens." Enemy aliens, and I'm a citizen! I was born on Terminal Island. They put citizens in camp, tell us we're enemy aliens, and then they want us to volunteer. You know what my answer was on the questionnaire.

What would you do? The questions asked if I'd go in the army. I said, "No." "Will you be loyal to the United States?" I said, "No." That was the feeling. Anger. JACL put a lot of pressure on the No-Nos. I don't think it was courage to put "No." I couldn't say "Yes." That would be a big lie.

I didn't want to go back to Japan. No. That kind of feeling we didn't have. If I wasn't reclassified, well, you forgive what they did putting you in camp, but you go because you're a citizen. I was really devoted before they did that.

Mac Sumimoto

Mac was born in Hawaii and at age five went to Japan with his family. He returned to America when he was eighteen years old, but his parents remained in Hiroshima, Japan.

Among our friends we said, "Why should we say 'Yes-Yes' and go to war for this country when they don't recognize us as United States citizens?" They asked if I wanted to renounce, and I said, "Yes." I signed a paper.

They sent us to Tule Lake. Since I was the oldest son, I thought maybe I should go back to Japan. My sister came from Iowa to visit me at Tule Lake. She said, "I think you should stay in this country." Japan was already losing, and there was no point in going back. That's when I changed my mind about renouncing. I had a hearing at Tule, and they asked again, "Will you fight against Japan?"

I said, "No, I can't, because my family is in Japan, and besides, you put us, American citizens, in camp. I'm not going to change that answer." I changed the second [pledge loyalty to the United States] to "Yes."

Tule was the last camp they closed, and I was there right to the end. After the war was over, they shipped me to Crystal City. I was there a year and a month and got out in '47.

Noboru Taguma

Released from prison after his conviction for draft resistance, Noboru was arrested again while visiting friends in Denver.

A friend said, "Why don't you renounce your citizenship and get your folks to Tule Lake? Then you'll be together." So I renounced my citizenship. I got my birth certificate and sent it to Washington. I wrote and told them to send me to Tule Lake. I said, "I can't do anything now since I came out of the prison. I want to renounce my citizenship so that my folks and I could be together. I'm the eldest one and I have to take care of them."

I didn't get an answer, and I thought it's going to take time. I went to see some friends in Denver. I was with another resister. When we got to the apartment, one of the guys starts singing in Japanese, "You came home at a bad time! You came home at a bad time!"

I said, "Why are you singing that kind of song?" I looked and there were two FBI men waiting. They came up and said, "Are you Noboru Taguma?"

"Yes."

"You're under arrest."

I don't know why, but what can I do, it's the FBI. They didn't tell me the charges. They sent me to Santa Fe, New Mexico. That was a Department of Justice camp. The marshal taking us there was very kind. I asked him, "How come you're nice to us?"

He said, "Well, I'll tell you. My folks came from Ireland, and when they came, they were treated just as bad as you people are now. So I know how it is." Some people are good.

About a month later, the government started having interviews again. Quite a few people went back to Japan from that place. I didn't want to go. I had never been in Japan. The only reason I renounced was to get my family together. Many of us hired Wayne Collins, the lawyer, to take care of getting the citizenship back.

A lot of people got released from Santa Fe. Only forty-seven people were still held. Including me. Then they sent me to the camp at Crystal City in Texas. I don't know why. That's the government. The only thing I can say is they wanted me to have a good time all over.

Like the resisters, No-Nos were condemned by the JACL. But many resisters were sympathetic and understood that "No" answers were another form of protest.

Frank Emi

I think they had every right to take that position. Maybe they were the first dissenters. They had more guts than the ones that criticize them. I really think so.

We try to educate people on the difference between resisters and the No-No people. We're similar, only they did it sooner and under a little different circumstance. They weren't getting involved with the draft.

Mits Koshiyama

The No-No people who got angry at the government, I can't blame them at all. I have friends that did that. But I never wanted to go back to Japan because that was foreign to me. I never wanted to give up my American citizenship.

I had a No-No friend. We grew up together as kids. He was a No-No because he was angry, and he renounced. He was shipped back to Japan in '44 or '45. He's been in Japan ever since. He came back on a visit, and I saw him. He said he regretted it. He liked America and really had no intention of leaving. The evacuation really ruined his life.

Tetsuko Morita

For some young Nisei, the issue of renunciation provoked the first serious act of rebellion against their parents. When Tetsuko refused to renounce, she was pressured intensely to change her mind.

When they were having the renunciations, I was around fifteen. Everybody was badgering me to renounce. I said, "I'm not going to be like the man without a country. I don't want to live in Japan. I don't know how to speak Japanese. I can never make a living if I grow up there. This is the only place I know."

Every day I got it. My folks, and even my uncle, tried to get me to do it. My folks were from the old country. They were Issei. You see, the parents always want to have the kids together. It was a big dilemma for them.

My mother said, "You're the most stubborn one around. You never listen to me."

I said, "I don't care."

My oldest sister and brother renounced. We left camp in November 1945, but they stayed in until March 1946. Wayne Collins was trying to get back their citizenship.

Dollie Nagai

Dollie was also a teenager when she refused to renounce.

At one point in camp, my mother said something about going back to Japan. I said, "This is my country and I'm staying here. You can go if you want, but I'm not going." That was the first time I ever stood up to her. She gave it up because all the rest of the sisters were here.

She was sad, not angry. She didn't know what was going to happen. She had family in Japan, and I guess she thought life would be better there. My mother wasn't a talker, but she came out with that, so she must have had strong feelings.

I'm sure glad she didn't go. I had a lot of friends who had to go because their parents went and took them. I went to the train to see one classmate off. It was so sad to think about. They took them first to a camp in northern California, Tule Lake. It was very traumatic to say goodbye.

SEGREGATION AT TULE LAKE

A combination of factors at Tule Lake made it the tensest of the camps. A rigid and unsympathetic camp director, overcrowding (18,000 squeezed into a camp designed for 15,000), growing frustration on the part of some angry young men, and a truck accident killing an inmate farmer—all finally exploded into strikes and angry demonstrations. For two months Tule Lake was under martial law. Random and unannounced raids were made in the barracks, and people waiting in bathroom, laundry, and coal lines were teargassed for no apparent reason.

Strong factions within the camp pressed other Nisei to renounce their citizenship and urged everyone to go to Japan.

Bert Nakano

Bert was too young to fill out the questionnaire, but both his father and older brother were No-Nos. The family was sent to Tule Lake.

It wasn't long after we got there, three or four months, they pulled my father again. They grabbed him from camp, and this time they took my older brother too. They put them in Crystal City, Texas. No hearing. My dad was a leader, and they didn't want them in camp. To a certain extent he was pro-Japan. That's his country. He wasn't a fanatic. He was a businessman.

Although the pro-Axis group at Tule were very vocal, a lot of people weren't necessarily pro-Axis. Many just felt they had to do something to make them proud of themselves as Japanese. They were surrounded by barbed wire with military police with guns looking down on you. Searchlights. I don't think anybody felt good about that. Probably some of the older folks were in Tule just to be "anti" whatever was out there. But when the war ended, all the politics was gone. Stopped.

My father, who was in Crystal City, wanted to go back to Japan and take the whole family. My older brother, who was with him, was an angry young man by that time. He said, "The hell with the United States!" But my dad had a lot of property in Hawaii. So my brother said, "Forget going back. Japan lost the war. There's nothing there. You go back to Hawaii. I'll go to Japan." He renounced his citizenship and went back to look after the two sisters, grandfather, grandmother, and two younger brothers who were there.

I don't think he would have renounced if we hadn't had family there. Here's a guy who in high school was a football player. He was taking Latin. Straight A's. Planned to go to medical school. That went down the drain. He became a salesman in Japan. When he got his citizenship back, he became a salesperson for a Miami firm that sold liquor and cigarettes to the military in Japan.

Morgan Yamanaka

Morgan was born in California and at age two was sent to Japan for five years with his older brothers. As a Kibei, he was considered suspect by the United States government because of the five years he had spent in Japan. His parents had registered him at birth with the Japanese consulate, thus giving him dual citizenship. After the bombing of Pearl Harbor, Morgan and his brother Al decided to give up their Japanese citizenship "and just be Americans." They were in camp in Topaz, Utah, when the questionnaire was distributed.

We were caught in a bind, Al and I. Al had volunteered for the military and was rejected. I signed up for selective service, and I'm a 4-C-er. It didn't make sense. I think Al and I were just pissed off. I mean, we were good American citizens and all of this is happening. Now they expect us to sign these two questions?

We both signed "No-No." It was out of this feeling of frustration that the No-No came about. Once you get on that track, certain other things were logical. You're already so discouraged that you go to the next logical step: renounce your American citizenship. I gave up my Japanese dual citizenship; now I've given up my American citizenship.

All No-No's from the nine other camps were sent to Tule Lake. The idea was to segregate the "disloyal" from the "loyal." Now I'm a No-No in a segregation center. I renounced, and I requested expatriation in March 1944. It was a continuation of being pissed off. I don't think there were definite thoughts of leaving the United States or going to Japan, especially in the middle of a war. We didn't think that way. It was just a kind of reaction, a steam valve. If you look at the

110,000 people who were in those camps, what other steam valves were there?

Who were now in Tule? You had the Yes-Yes people who refused to leave, some four thousand of them. They had left their homes, gone to an assembly center, from the assembly center to Tule. Now they were being asked to leave Tule and they said no. Then you had the No-No people at Tule Lake, and there were many gradations of No-No: I'm going to say No-No because I want to be with my parents; I'm going to say No-No because I don't know where to go if I did get leave, and if I go, I won't be able to make a living in a strange place; or, I'm going to say No-No because I'm pissed, like yours truly.

You had groups from very pro-Japan to not so pro, to all the way over on the other side. I was probably right in the middle, but not particularly active in any sense. Renouncing in itself had nothing to do with expatriation. There were no plans to ship you back until you asked for expatriation. I requested expatriation, and my parents requested repatriation to go back to their home. All of the family was united in these acts. I think it was the idea of keeping the family together.

I made the application in 1944. Then, when things started calming down, we withdrew our application. What made me withdraw it? I don't know. The stupidity of the act of renouncing maybe, our awareness of what the hell are we doing. I worked with Wayne Collins and that group. Wayne Collins's position was that minors could not renounce their citizenship. Because I was under twenty-one when I signed my renunciation papers, I was part of that group. My brother Al, who was over twenty-one, went into the military and got his citizenship back around 1950. I remember many friends of ours who left Tule Lake to get on the *Gripsholm* [ship exchanging prisoners with Japan] and go to Japan.

One of the saddest things was saying goodbye to those people. Those who went back were not welcome there. And I'm not going to see them again. Never did see them.

At Tule Lake, a stockade—a prison within a prison—was built, and
some two hundred inmates, including Morgan, were kept there, some for
two months.

The administration tried to identify the various leaders of the political
factions and segregate these leaders. So they came up with the idea of
the stockade for "troublemakers." The white administration came
from one end of the camp and the military came from the other end.
It was a squeeze play, and all of the people had a list of names of
approximately two hundred so-called leaders. Everybody was checked
out, and if they fell into that list, off you went to the stockade. There
was my name and my brother's name! I have no idea why. Absolutely
no idea.

All I was doing was playing the guitar, weight lifting, and being
captain of the fire department. No other activities. And Al the same.
So we went into the stockade for whatever reason. We were there
about a month and a half. Two hundred people.

Did you ever see the movie *Stalag 17?* Same thing happened with
us. The colonel came. He wanted to speak about the fact that the
stockade wasn't clean enough for him. We were standing in the snow,
completely surrounded by soldiers. An army half-track, which is a
truck with tank treads, was backed in, and there was a machine gun
aimed at us. They said, "O.K. Some of you guys want trouble. Who
did this?" Nobody answered. We stood in the snow in bare feet all
afternoon. What the hell are you going to do? Soldiers with guns, and
a machine gun aimed at you. We went on a hunger strike for a week.
At that point the stockade had about a hundred and fifty people in it.
On the seventh day, we started eating.

I was in camp four years, from age seventeen to twenty. Six months
after war with Japan ended, I was released from Tule Lake. They kept
me until the end of March. They released my parents and kept Al and
me only. No explanation. We were picked up one day, and then one
day they said, "Go." Strange justice. The whole damn thing was
strange.

★   ★   ★

Issei, of course, could not renounce citizenship, since they were prohibited by law from becoming American citizens. They could, however, ask for repatriation to Japan. Nisei could renounce, and nearly
6,000 did, almost all from Tule Lake. At Tule, 70 percent of the Nisei
declared their intent to give up their citizenship. By June 1945, the
anger had subsided, and thousands tried to cancel their renunciations.
Wayne Collins, one of the few attorneys in the country who fought
for the rights of the internees, brought lawsuits to prevent deportation and restore citizenship. He argued that the renunciations were
made under duress, and therefore should be declared null and void.

Although a lower court ruled in 1948 that all the renunciations
were invalid, the appeals court overturned that decision and required
individual hearings in each case. The last of the cases was finally
resolved in 1968.

Even with the lawsuits, nearly 5,000 people from Tule Lake, the
majority American-born, were sent to Japan after the war ended.
From Japan's surrender to mid-1946, a total of 8,000 Issei and Nisei
left for Japan.

The renunciation law had been passed for the purpose of getting
rid of Japanese Americans. After the war was over, the statute was
declared void by a Joint Resolution of Congress on July 25, 1947.

Following page: *Sign on bulletin board at
Manzanar;*

*On leave from camp, prisoners
topping sugar beets near Hunt, Idaho;*

*Dollie Nagai (center) at school in
Washington, D.C.*

Want to
LOOK FOR A JOB?
Short Time Leave
OR
Indefinite Leave
May Be Granted to Permit You to Go
MOST ANYWHERE
in search of employment

9

LIFE OUTSIDE CAMP

Less than a year after the West Coast Japanese community was evacuated, the government decided the cost of camp upkeep was too great. The WRA Leave Clearance program was designed to identify "loyal" Japanese Americans who could leave camp and go into Caucasian communities.

As long as an internee signed a loyalty oath and could show proof of sponsorship, the WRA encouraged people to leave camp and "relocate" in the Midwest or East to schools or jobs. The vast majority of those leaving camp were between the ages of fifteen and thirty-five. As part of the Leave Clearance application, the prisoners were asked if they would stay "away from large groups of Japanese" and "avoid the use of the Japanese language except when necessary." Equally offensive to some was the question "Will you try to develop such American habits which will cause you to be accepted readily into American social groups?"

Notwithstanding the government's intrusiveness, thousands applied to leave camp. Lists of people and organizations willing to hire Japanese Americans were made available in camp. Clarence Pickett, a Quaker, organized the National Japanese American Student Relocation Council. With church groups across the country, the council helped Nisei students continue their education at colleges and universities by providing scholarships, housing, and general help.

By far the vast majority of those leaving camp went to the Midwest, mainly to Chicago. The big city seemed to offer good opportunities for work and housing. Although most encountered some anti-Japanese bias, all expressed relief to be out of camp.

*   *   *   *   *

Sue Kunitomi

Sue was nineteen when she left camp.

I had got a sponsorship from the YWCA in Madison, Wisconsin, in early '43. I told my mother, I'm leaving. She didn't want me to go because my brothers were up for draft status. I said, "I can't stay here.

I just cannot stay." I told her, "You came from a country to another land where you didn't speak the language. You didn't know the people. You didn't even know the husband you were going to marry, and you lived here for forty years. I've lived here all my life. I can speak English. I know I can get by all right."

"They're going to beat you up," she said.

I said, "I don't think so, but I've got to go and see."

I tried to get into the University of Wisconsin. They told me I couldn't be admitted because they were doing army work. But I had already been cleared. I had my FBI fingerprints, picture, ID card, everything. Someone said maybe I could work in a professor's home. I said, "I'm not going to be a domestic. It's one thing I don't want to do."

I put a small ad in a newspaper in Madison and went to work for a mail-order cheese house. I was there about a year. Then I was living in Chicago with my brother and his family. We had a third-floor flat on the near North Side. When they first looked at it, the landlord said, "Aren't you lucky you're Japanese. There's a restrictive covenant against Chinese, but not against Japanese."

Sumi Seo

I graduated from high school in Jerome [Arkansas] in May or June 1943. They were asking young people to get out of camp, and I wanted to go. The girls who lived in the same barracks with us were out already. My girlfriend wrote from Chicago and said there were a lot of jobs and they were having a lot of fun.

The Edgewater Beach hotel in Chicago, one of the biggest hotels there, said they needed "salad girls." I got the permit to go out, but my dad said, "No, you're not going out." I obeyed him and didn't go. I worked in the hospital at Jerome for six months. But good reports were coming back from Chicago. After six months, my father said O.K., and my mother packed my suitcase. I left camp and got an apartment in Chicago with some girlfriends.

One day when we went to do some shopping, a bunch of women

on the sidewalk started yelling. It was like they thought Japan had invaded Chicago, and they were scared and running away from us. It gave us a funny feeling.

Mary Sakaguchi

Mary had completed a year of medical school in California when she was sent to camp at Manzanar.

I was in Manzanar about a year and a half before I left. There were ninety-six medical schools at that time. I couldn't go back to the Coast, so I wrote to about ninety schools to get into the second year. None of them bothered to answer except three or four. They sent me a postcard that said, "We cannot consider your application because we have military installations on this campus." My return address was obviously the camp.

I asked a professor of physics from UCLA to write a letter of recommendation. I got an A in his class, and he remembered me, I think, because I was Oriental and a girl. His name was Hiram Edwards. One day in Manzanar I got a call from the administration building. There was a Dr. Edwards to see me. I couldn't believe it. He told me he had become an administrator and was now director of relations with other schools. He said, "I recommended you very highly. I spoke to the Dean of Women's Medical College [in Philadelphia], and she assures me you will be admitted." He came all the way to tell me that. There were a few decent people.

Before I left camp, my sister went to the University of Utah. She became a "school girl," doing housework and earning $5 or $10 a month. She took a heavy program at the University of Utah. My mother had told all of us when we were growing up, "I don't ever want you to work for a white person as a servant." My mother had a lot of pride. My sister was forced to do this because there was no other way she could go through school. She got straight A's and was premed. But she had a complete nervous breakdown and was in a mental hospital.

Women's Medical College said I lacked three units of Surface Anatomy. My sister called me from Utah and said that she was in a mental hospital. Since I had to take those three units, I applied to the University of Utah and took the course there. I used to visit her every week. They were very cruel, those people at the state hospital. I went to see the head every week. I said, "My sister's not getting better."

He'd say to me, "It's because your sister is not a Utah resident. She's from California, so we can't really treat her."

I said, "She's here because we were forced out of California."

"You will have to pay $100 a month for your sister's care."

I pleaded with this administrator. "Sir, we lost our farm, we lost our business. If we had our farm, we could easily pay $100 a month." I told the whole family situation. "We were doing very well financially. All of us went to medical or dental school, and our parents paid. But now we have no income. My parents are earning $12 a month in camp. There's no way we can come up with $100 a month."

He said, "We can't treat her unless you pay that $100."

At that time the American Friends Service Committee was a liaison group. I went to them and said, "My sister's had this breakdown, and they won't treat her unless we come up with $100 a month." I think they wrote to California. Somehow California arranged to pay that $100 a month, since she really should have been in a California hospital.

As soon as that money came in, they gave my sister insulin shock treatment, and after one treatment suddenly she was herself again. She said, "What am I doing here? These people are crazy!"

Then it was time for me to go to school. My father came to Utah to take my sister back home to Manzanar.

Dollie Nagai

Dollie was a high school student when she left camp.

I was in Jerome from October 1942 to May 1944. My sisters were already out. Two were working in Washington, D.C., and they sent for me. I stayed with a Caucasian couple who had done missionary work in Africa. They had opened their home to rent rooms to Japanese Americans. I would do light housework, and they let me eat with them. There was no separation. It was really wonderful. They took me in as a member of the family.

Early in the morning I'd get on the streetcar and go to see my sisters while they got dressed. I needed family that much. They lived in one room. That's when the lady I was staying with told my sisters, "You better get an apartment and take her."

When I went to school in Washington, D.C., I didn't know anybody. It was the Jewish kids who would come sit down with me. They were the ones that remembered my birthday. They were the ones that opened their arms and their hearts and made me feel good.

In school there was an "I am an American Day" assembly. This one Jewish girl and I got up and told our stories. She had come from Europe. Sylvia Cohen. She said she saw her parents and all her relatives shot. I don't know how she escaped, but she got here.

Nami Nakashima Diaz

Nami was one of the rare few allowed to return to the Coast, where FBI agents checked on her whereabouts every month.

I stayed in camp five and a half months. Then I got notice they were going to free my older sister and me. We were both married to Caucasians. Within a week we could leave. Avey [Nami's husband] came and got us and brought us home. The rest of the family was still in camp. Shortly after, they were all put on a train and sent out to Jerome, Arkansas.

I had never worked before and I had to find a job. I could live in the Western Defense Command, but I had to have a pass and carry it with me all the time. I went to Los Angeles and got a job in a stationery company. About a month later, Avey went into the navy for two years. First he was based in San Diego. We lived there for three months. He went from there to San Francisco, and then they shipped them out.

I came back to Long Beach, and I was pregnant. The baby was born in 1943. The government kept close tabs. Every month the FBI came to check on me. And two months after my baby was born, I got a pass for him to live in this Western Defense zone. A newborn baby! That's how ridiculous the government became. That left a very bitter feeling.

Joe Norikane

Joe went from camp to prison as a draft resister. He was released on probation and looked for work.

I got out of prison May 28, 1945. The war wasn't over yet. I went to Denver and was a busboy in an American restaurant. My family was still in Amache [camp in Colorado]. I was in Denver six or seven months, and then I went [with friends] to Wyoming. We found a job in Laramie doing construction work at the University of Wyoming. I heard about prejudice against Japanese, but I stayed at the workplace. My other friends went out and heard this old man telling his grandson, "See those two Japs walking over there. The one with the lapel, he's a veteran. He's a good Jap. The other one's a bad Jap."

Clifford Uyeda

Clifford was entering medical school at the time of the evacuation. His biggest problem was raising money for tuition and expenses.

I had no money because all my parents' bank accounts were frozen. Money was a real concern because if I couldn't pay my tuition, I couldn't continue. My mother, my dad, and my sister said they'd look for a job at the camp. They had this very low wage scale. I think they were each getting $16 a month. There were three working, and they'd send me $48 every month.

Then the government announced the navy and army had a specialized training program for all med students enrolled in a Class A medical school. My dean at medical school said I was completely qualified. The only requirements were that you be an American citizen and that you're in good health. They'd pay your tuition and for all the equipment, like a microscope, books, and a living allowance. I applied. The navy said they're not going to train anybody of Japanese ancestry at government expense.

Then my dean said the army should be O.K., because there were about 5,000 Japanese Americans already in the army when the war started. I applied and got another letter saying exactly what the navy had said.

I got a job first at the cafeteria and then later at a hospital doing orderly work, sterilizing things, on call for the nurses, or for patients to be helped, or floors to be mopped—that sort of thing. One time I was working on the cafeteria line, and this man came over and said, "We don't want any Japs around here." This ensign I knew came over and told that guy, "He's an American just like you." I remember him saying that.

I learned that in New Orleans at private hospitals, they were paying $35 for a pint of blood. I figured if I get some iron pills, it will cost me about $3. So I'm making more than $30 each time. I gave one pint every month for nine months. I was becoming anemic. You get very tired and lightheaded. When you wake up in the morning, sometimes you don't know where you are. I had to quit. After a couple of months, I was O.K. I came back to normal.

I was the only Japanese American in my class. My graduation day from medical school was in August 1945, one day before Japan announced their surrender.

Sohei Hohri

I had graduated from Manzanar High School, and I left camp about March of '44 and went to Milwaukee. Those were the hardest working days of my life. I worked in a cold storage plant. Meat would come up from Chicago and it would have to be quick-frozen. I used to work at 30 degrees below zero. Half-sections of steer would come on hooks. Normally, you would have two men working, but there was a labor shortage during the war. The boxcars would come up, and you'd throw these slabs of meat onto hand trucks. Then you'd push them into the cold freezer. You'd work in there twenty minutes with your special gloves on. Then you'd come out and sit by the steam heat to warm up. You'd get drowsy because of the change in the body temperature. Then they'd ring a loud bell, and you'd go back in again.

I'd probably be working there to this day except a friend of my oldest brother started going to the University of Chicago. He came one day and saw me work and said, "You can't do this for the rest of your life." He told me to try for the entrance exam at the university.

I went there on a Saturday. It was an all-day exam. One of the papers we had to read was by Einstein. I think it was an advantage that I almost didn't know who Einstein was. The whole thing was to scare you a little bit. But the questions were straightforward ones that required reasoning. You didn't have to know anything about physics, and you didn't have to know anything about Einstein.

There was a proctor who asked me questions about what I thought the postwar Pacific picture would look like and what my feelings were on modern drama. I was a dead blank. When I finished, she said, "Don't feel bad about rejection. You don't have to go to a big college like the University of Chicago. There are a lot of good colleges all throughout the country."

I was really surprised when I passed. Once I passed, I had to raise money. I took a night job pouring lead. It was terribly hot. It was a striking contrast working in the cold storage all day long and then this heat at night. I was doing two jobs, and I was very tired. But you know at that age, you're indestructible.

Noboru Taguma

Noboru was released from prison and returned to Granada to be near his family, which was still interned at the Amache camp.

I came out of prison November or December of 1944. I went to Granada and got a job in farming for a couple of weeks. I tried to go into the camp, but they wouldn't give me a pass. So I used to sneak in. The guard towers were at the corners, and there was a sewage treatment plant. I went through a gully outside the sewage plant where rain water ran in. The searchlights swept around, and when they passed, I ran halfway. Then when the lights swept back and past, whoosh, I went under the barbed wire.

I ran to my family barrack. My mother cooked and gave me food to take out. I'd rented a place in Granada where we had to cook our own meals, so this was good. I went practically every night. I did this for about one month. Then a friend inside said there's a lot of policemen out at night, so I stopped. When I think about it now, I wonder how in the hell did I do that?

Amy Hiratzka

After Pearl Harbor, Amy's father was arrested by the FBI and sent to the Department of Justice camp in Missoula, Montana. With reference letters from an Episcopal bishop, he was released and allowed to go to Utah, where Amy's brother was living.

In May of '43 we left camp. Eleven months, and we were gone. In order for my father to take us out, he had to vouch for us financially. He worked as a houseboy for an Italian countess in Utah. He worked as a gardener. He worked as a bricklayer. He worked as a railroad worker. Whatever he could do, that's what he did. He was 187 pounds when he went into camp, and he wore a size 42 suit. When he came to get us, he was 137 pounds, and still wore his size 42 suit. We laughed about that.

My parents rented a three-story building and started a place for single men. A lot of them came out from camp. My mother cooked the meals and my father kept up the place.

When we got to Utah, I wanted to finish school. So I went to "school-girl" in this couple's house. You go into a home and you do chores for them in return for your room and board. Then I went to the University of Utah.

I finished in elementary education. The problem arose when it was time for me to teach. I finished in '45, and the war was still going on. The Board of Education said, "We'll have to vote on whether she can teach or not." I knew the dean of girls at one of the high schools. She knew board members, and she talked to them about me. I barely passed, a plurality. I went back there some years later, and one of the board members said, "Wasn't that terrible what we did to you?" I said, "That's what you call war hysteria."

CAMP CLOSINGS

At the end of the war, there were still thousands of people in the camps. The WRA announced the camps would all be closed by January 1946. Tule Lake was the exception. It remained open until late March 1946.

For many still in the camps, the Issei in particular, leaving camp was a frightening prospect. Without homes, jobs, or income, imprisoned for nearly four years, many felt that life behind barbed wire, hard as it was, was safer than venturing out into a hostile white world. When they finally left camp, some followed family and friends to the Midwest, while others returned to their homes on the Coast.

Although there were exceptions, most people who had stored furniture and other goods found their possessions were either stolen or sold. Many had put their goods in churches, assuming at least there they'd be safe. And most had the same experience as Clifford Uyeda. "Our things were in a church, and the church was ransacked. There was nothing left."

For all, it was a time of uncertainty.

Lillian Sugita

My father, me, and my brother left camp and took the bus from Heart Mountain to Montana. We were on our way to Minnesota. My father's friend had settled there and said the people in Minnesota were very nice. My father wanted us to find a place, and then he'd have my mother and the three girls come out.

On the bus we learned it was VJ day. What bad luck that we were traveling that week! It was bedlam. People were all looking at us, and we thought they were going to kill us. Some of them got hysterical. I was never so scared. My brother said, "Don't say anything. Just look down." We were afraid they may say, "What are you looking at?" and the next thing you know, *smack!*

We knew a Japanese man who had a restaurant and hotel in Montana. He served all white people. My father went up to the bus driver and told him we had a friend in Montana. "I think you better let us off because these people are crazy. We don't know what's going to happen." The bus driver said it was a good idea. It was a small town, and he said, "Yeah, I know that place. Let me go down first and get the guy."

People were screaming and looking at us and yelling, "Jap! Jap!" I was petrified. Later on, my brother said his friend in Chicago wrote and said they all locked themselves in because people got guns.

My father's friend came to the bus door. He said, "I don't want people to see you. They're hysterical. No telling what they're going to do." He covered us up with a coat over our heads. We were whisked through the bar into the back. The man said, "You'd better stay here for two or three days. I'll arrange everything." We didn't sleep a wink. We kept thinking, there's all this madness going on out there, and somebody is going to crash the door in and kill us.

We stayed there a couple of nights and then we took the train to Minneapolis. People there were Scandinavian mainly, and they were a lot nicer than others. At the Red Cross they told us it'll take maybe a year before they could send us back to Hawaii. My father decided he wanted to run a small Japanese family restaurant, because Japanese-American GIs were stationed nearby at Fort Snelling.

We all helped in the restaurant. We enjoyed it because we were too traumatized to go outside to work. I felt I couldn't face all that hostility. We probably should have, because you have to face it, but we all opted to stay home.

We stayed in Minneapolis for a year, and then we went back to Hawaii. Unfortunately for my father and many others, they were in camp during their peak. Somehow they never made it back. The government put my father's business on auction rather than return it. They had to pay something like $80,000 to buy it back. Yeah, they had to buy their own business back! It just killed them. They ran it for a few years, but somehow he had lost touch. He had ulcers and sort of gave up. They sold it. My parents were broken, I think. That was the first time I really felt my dad had given up. He had been such a fighter.

Sumi Seo

I was in Chicago in August 1945, when the war ended. I lost my job, and so did my roommate. They were just beginning to open up the West Coast again. We said let's go back home. We went to WRA, and they gave us $25 and a train ticket to Los Angeles.

I didn't really know where to go. The only thing I could think of was the YWCA. Then a housing project in Long Beach opened, and I got an apartment. I wrote to my parents and told them I had a place to stay, so they could come out of camp. My mother and sister came out. My father stayed until the last day. He figured, "What's the use of me coming out? I can't work, I'm too old. I might as well stay and let them feed me until I'm ready to come out."

Jobs were hard to get. Us young kids went to sewing factories. When the Terminal Island cannery opened, a lot of people were saved. My mother finally got a job, and my father worked there. It wasn't hard only for my parents. Look at the people who had had businesses in Los Angeles. Now they were working at the fish cannery. There was no other employment. Some uppity-ups had to do menial jobs to make a living.

For twenty-five years my father had farmed in San Pedro. Now we were in a housing project, but still, you want to live in a home. So I went to the landlord who owned all the land where we had lived. I said, "Do you have any rentals? My dad rented from you and your dad for many, many years, and now we don't have a place."

He said, "No, we don't have no home. Get out, get out!" and he shoved me out of his office.

I went to Mrs. Bennett [the former family friend who had stored things for Sumi's family] and asked her for my furniture. She looked this way and that way to make sure nobody was seeing I'm on her porch. Then she said, "I don't have your furniture. It was stolen. Get off my porch. Go away!"

I said, "O.K., Mrs. Bennett. You don't have it, you don't have it." I didn't fight her because we were taught not to fight back. The word *gaman* means endure, forget about it. That's Japanese culture. During the war, you were not supposed to have any contact with Japanese. End of the war, it's still the same. She didn't want anything to do with any of us "Japs."

But all those years she must have had guilt inside of her. When she died, she willed me her house. And she gave money to my brother.

Jim Matsuoka

Jim was ten years old when he left Manzanar. His family returned to California.

I got out in 1945 when the camp closed. As bad as that was, the world got even harder. We were dumped out with no means of survival except $25 and a bus ticket.

We wound up living in a trailer area. I don't want to say trailer court, because that makes it sound better. If you think of recreational vehicles, wrong, wrong, wrong. I don't know where they got these things, but they were little, old, beaten-up trailers. There were hundreds of them because housing was short, and they had trailer housing areas all over southern California. We lived in the one in Long Beach.

We were all crowded into the trailer. You have four years of camp and two or three years of this. My father never had employment after that. It was only because my two older sisters went to work as nurses' aides that we were living at all.

Amy Akiyama

Amy was eight when she was evacuated. Her family returned to California after camp.

I was put back half a year in school, and that just demoralized me. I thought I was stupid, so I had to take that class over. My father found a job in Oakland as a caretaker of the grounds for the superintendent of the Oakland schools. My mother was very concerned about my sister and me starting school. The superintendent told her, "Don't worry. I've sent a note to the principal explaining that there are two little Japanese girls coming to school and I want everyone to welcome them."

It was an upper-middle-class, very white school. We got on the school bus, and everyone was very patronizing, like, "You can sit in this seat." I just felt it was fake. We were singled out, and I felt very uncomfortable. Then there was a special assembly for us. I thought, I want to fall through the cracks.

At recess time, I never played with anyone. No one ever played with me. The teachers were very nice. There was really no anti-Japanese thing. Just that we were the only Japanese in the school. There was one black boy who was very nice. The kids tried to be nice, except they didn't play with me. Maybe it was me, because I was so super-shy I was unapproachable. That could have been it too. But I couldn't wait to move on.

Years later, I found out my mother wrote to a good friend of hers who was still in the camp, telling her how sad and sorry she felt for Mitsu and me being scrutinized by the rest of the classmates. She was trying to prepare this woman for coming out.

*   *   *

After their release, for many, particularly those who were teenagers in camp, there was a lingering sense of displacement, and a conscious search through the early years of adulthood for some sense of understanding of the world and of themselves.

Ernest Uno

Ernie had, he says, "a good time" as a teenager in camp. But he rushed to enlist in the army as soon as military service opened up.

When I was overseas in France, I saw a dear friend killed. I sought counsel with the chaplain because I couldn't understand the unfairness of life. What kind of God is it that lets an up-and-coming young man with all the promise in the world get killed, and a bum like me, a school dropout, lets me live? Why?

He said, "You never know. God works in many strange and mysterious ways, but you've got to find your mission in life." So in college I was a sociology major. I thought I had to do something in life that was worthwhile for somebody. I guess that's what drove me to go into YMCA work.

Bert Nakano

After the war, I got into a lot of fights. The first day I was back in Hawaii, I wanted to be part of a group. I didn't want to be left out. I went drinking with a bunch of guys, but I was still an outsider. I saw a guy that I had a fight with before I left Hawaii [for camp]. I said, "Hey, you remember me?" He says, "Yeah." Pow! Why would I do a thing like that? I gambled. I had complete disregard for anything. I did what I wanted to do and the hell with the world.

I look in a mirror and I look Japanese. I don't feel good about myself. I don't want to be a Japanese. Maybe I should change my name. You may not be thinking that exactly, but you're not feeling good about yourself. I wasn't angry at the government. Everything is turned inward.

When my mother died [after the war], I joined the army. I was sent to Japan because I had language proficiency. Once I got out of the army, I got married and started working. I said to myself, "Do you want to be a carpenter for the rest of your life?" I started thinking, Why am I this way? Why can't I be like kids who strive for something? I went to Chicago to take up TV repair work. They had a famous school where they train you. I quit that. I figured I'd try college. I took math and English and then the GED exam and got my high school diploma. But I still didn't know what I wanted. First I went into engineering. That didn't go with me. I switched to history. I took a course in Far Eastern studies, Southeast Asia, China, and Japan. I really got into it.

I was going on the GI bill, and I was working at the post office full-time. This black guy who was working with me was going for his master's degree in sociology. He took me down to the South Side, where Malcolm X was speaking, and he says, "Listen to this guy." I saw this interaction between speaker and crowd. I was just fascinated. Then he took me to one of the churches where they were teaching elementary school kids black history and black pride. They were using *Ebony* magazine pictures of famous black people as sort of a textbook. You could see the pride coming out of the kids.

We don't have that in the Japanese-American community. Nothing to bring that type of pride into our community. I said to myself, I got to find out more about myself like these kids are doing. Slowly I got into it.

Roosevelt University was a beehive of activity back then. We didn't have any football games. The kids were all in the lobby arguing about politics, arguing about Mao Tse-tung, arguing about Lenin, arguing about Marx. With a couple of other Japanese Americans who were veterans also, we kind of listened in. I used to insert now and then, "Well, what about the Japanese Americans who were thrown in the concentration camps?"

They'd say, "You are being narrow in your thinking. All men are workers. It has nothing to do with nationality." That didn't sit right to me. I felt there's more injustice than just worker oppression. I felt, We went through this and you guys didn't, so how can you tell me it's the same thing? It's not the same thing.

Without the camp experience, I wouldn't be searching. I felt bad about myself, and that's the reason you start to look. I was all screwed up in my thinking. It was the sixties. The hippies. I got into religion. Buddhism. There was the Zen movement. I went into it more because it was Asian.

At the same time, I'm learning about the Far East. Here was the history of China, which goes back 7,000 years, a great civilization. You're talking about a written history all the way back, the invention of gunpowder, the harness, all these things that were a thousand years ahead of the West. Why should I be ashamed that I'm an Asian? I should be proud I'm an Asian. I started to feel right about myself, to feel good about myself.

Lillian Sugita

Lillian met Bert Nakano in camp, and later they were married. She struggled in her way to find a sense of peace.

In Chicago we couldn't find an apartment. They'd slam the door on you, or they'd tell you right off the bat they didn't want you. Sometimes they'd say, "It's already rented," but then you'd still see the "For Rent" sign. It took many years for all that discrimination to pass.

I was still trying to escape. It took me a long time in Chicago to face up. I think Bert handled it better, mainly I think because he's male. He started dealing with it. He was an angry, frustrated man for many years, but at least he found a way to channel it. For me, I just kept running.

I was running from feeling very insecure, afraid of hostility and not having any confidence in yourself to be able to stand up to it. You get so angry and proud. You keep looking for areas where you're not going to be confronted.

I didn't start playing music again until about 1957. And then I started feeling better about myself. I went to art school and took *shamisen* again. Bert was taking history courses. I was working part-time and teaching music.

We never talked about the camp years, but Bert was beginning to become more political. I was apolitical still. I was going into existentialism and all that abstract stuff. That's how I dealt with it. We were seeking, trying to find some equilibrium, some peace, something to lessen the trouble. It's funny how we both were looking, but we each went in our own way.

Jim Matsuoka

Jim was six years old when he went into camp. After camp, his family returned to California. He worked after high school and then was drafted in 1958.

When I saw people in the army, I thought, They're in desperate shape. Especially the sergeants. I don't want ever to be like these guys. Let me go out and take education seriously. I got out of the army in '60, and I started to go to school at Cal State, L.A. I got my bachelor's and master's degrees in social science.

Going to school in the sixties, you couldn't help but get involved in certain things. The sixties was one of the most remarkable periods of time. At first, my opinion of the anti-Vietnam thing was that these were a pack of draft dodgers. Why don't you go serve your country like everybody else? I did.

Little by little I began to listen. You couldn't help but be affected when you turn on TV and see the war right in your living room while you're eating. I began to question, What in the world are we doing in Vietnam? In my studies, I began to get a historical perspective. I'm thinking, What are we doing in Asia to begin with? Once the questioning starts, it doesn't end.

Then you say, "Wait a minute now, why are these things called 'relocation camps'?" These aren't "relocation camps." By all description these are what we call concentration camps. The big difference between what we experienced and what happened to the Jews in Germany is those were death camps. They were concentration camps/death camps. Ours never got to that point. Nonetheless, they were a far cry from "relocation" camps.

There was nothing at all in my schoolbooks on the evacuation. It was totally ignored. I got very interested in ethnic studies, and I pushed for the first Asian-American Studies class at Cal State, L.A., which I managed to get through the history department. That was in 1969.

I found an instructor who knew very little. I said, "Don't worry about it. We're going to operate it from a different perspective. We're going to make each student a researcher. They're not going to sit there and say, 'You tell me.' We're going to say, 'You look, then tell us.' " But the instructor needed some textbook material, so for a while I was cranking things out. I was doing it as a graduate student. I found it easier to write something than try to find material.

Without a doubt, the sixties triggered this. With the civil rights movement, Vietnam, here we had Watts in '65, you'd have to be almost brain-dead not to question what was going on.

Following page: *Fred Korematsu, Min Yasui and Gordon Hirabayashi (seated) at press conference at time of their* coram nobis *petitions, 1983.*

10
SETTING THINGS
TO REST

After the war, Japanese Americans began to rebuild their lives. Like their parents on first coming to America, they had to start from scratch, finding homes, finding work, building a future. Many have struggled to forget their wartime experiences. Although they often ask each other when first meeting, "What camp were you in?" a great number have never talked to their children about the camps. The pain, and for some a feeling of humiliation, was too powerful.

But the past rested uneasy. In the years since 1945, there have been a number of movements to rectify the injustices of the war years. Researchers and historians began to examine previously classified or undiscovered government documents. Newfound evidence prompted young Japanese-American lawyers to reopen the court cases that had upheld the legality of the evacuation.

Although school textbooks in the past had little or nothing about the World War II story of Japanese Americans, they too are being corrected. On still another front, some former internees have worked to make Manzanar a national historic site. In addition, government policies changed as Congress altered immigration laws to allow Japanese immigrants to become American citizens. And as the pressures of wartime governance ended, officials backed away from the harsh anti-Japanese rhetoric of the war years. President Truman pardoned the draft resisters; Gerald Ford made the first presidential apology for the government's World War II policies, and restored the American citizenship of "Tokyo Rose"; President Carter appointed a commission to examine the wartime excesses against Japanese Americans; and President Reagan signed into law an act authorizing monetary redress accompanied by a letter of apology to each recipient.

With the acknowledgment from the American government of the "serious injustices," as President Bush wrote, committed against Americans of Japanese ancestry during the war, the community is now turned inward to address its internal divisions. Young Sansei and Yonsei, the third and fourth generations, are beginning to question the role played by the JACL during the war years. They are also learning about resistance in the camps. As Yosh Kuromiya, a Heart Mountain resister, says:

It's not so much the government I still have unresolved feelings about. It's more the so-called leaders of the Japanese-American community, the JACL, their response and their justification of their activities. It was an accommodationist position. Go with it, whatever, wherever ordered, in spite of the Constitution.

The government was supposed to be representing the principles of the Constitution. This country is basically an idea. It's a philosophy embodied in the Constitution, and the people in government are there to make that work.

I suppose they [JACL] sincerely felt there was a handicap in being Japanese. Because of the discrimination they no doubt experienced, they felt there was something wrong with being Japanese. We had to wipe out anything and everything that reminded others of our Japanese nature because it wasn't a trusted race.

. . . They really let us down. They had no business assuming a position of leadership if that's the way they were going to deal with it.

In cities across the country, Japanese-American groups sponsor an annual "Day of Remembrance" in February. The event is a historical reminder of February 19, 1942, when President Roosevelt signed Executive Order 9066, authorizing the evacuation. The "Day of Remembrance" serves not only to honor survivors but also to ensure that the younger generations know the community's history.

This chapter takes a brief look at a variety of ways the residue of the wartime experiences of Japanese Americans is finally being set to rest.

★   ★   ★   ★   ★

IMMIGRATION LAWS

From the passage of the first law regulating immigration, in 1790, until after the Civil War, only a "free white person" was eligible for American citizenship. In 1873, the law was amended to include American blacks and "persons of African nativity or descent." In

1922, the Supreme Court ruled, in the case *Ozawa v. United States,* that a Japanese person was not considered the same as a "free white person."

Although the first Japanese arrived in California in 1869, the bulk of the immigration from Japan began in the 1880s. It ended in 1924, when immigration was cut off by passage of the Japanese Exclusion Act. Thus for their entire history in the United States, Issei immigrants had been forced to remain aliens.

In 1952, Congress passed the Walter-McCarran Immigration and Nationality Act, which eliminated race as a bar to citizenship. The law, however, set restrictive quotas for different nationalities, with a quota bias against Asians. President Truman, critical of the restrictive quotas, vetoed the bill, but Congress overrode the veto, and the bill became law.

Although the Asian immigration quota was indeed very small, Japanese aliens for the first time were allowed to become citizens. With their imprisonment as "enemy aliens" still fresh in their memory, many Issei applied quickly for their naturalization papers.

The new law also affected the Japanese Peruvians still in the country. Before they were brought into the United States, they were forced to surrender any passports or visas they possessed. On their arrival, without any official papers, the U.S. Immigration Service declared them "illegal aliens" and interned them in prisoner-of-war camps.

Since they had entered "illegally," at the end of the war they were still considered illegal aliens. Without legal status in America, they could be deported. The Immigration Service advised them to go to Canada or Mexico and reenter legally. They were then given permanent resident cards dated at the time of this second entry. Those who hired attorney Wayne Collins, however, did not have to leave the country and reenter. Furthermore, they received their residency cards with the date of entry made retroactive to their first arrival in America. This "date of arrival" would become critical in the Peruvians' later application for redress (see pages 205–208).

Chieko Kato

Through the help of attorney Wayne Collins, Chieko's Japanese-Peruvian family was able to become permanent residents and then citizens.

We got deportation orders, and that's when we hired Wayne Collins. My parents didn't want to go to Japan. My father wrote a letter in Spanish to a bishop for help. He said, "All I know is I do not wish to go back to Japan. I believe if we go back to Japan together with these children, it is a sort of crime that I am committing to kill them. Japan at present time is not fit to accept my children who are all foreigners to Japan."

We were one of the last ones to get out of camp. It was July 1947, and we went to Stockton, California. There was a Japanese foreman for a Caucasian farmer who sponsored us. Our house was a little shack. We didn't have a toilet. We had to go to the outhouse. We used to hate going to the bathroom, especially at night. We had to go to school and learn English. That's when it hit me. I felt insecure. I started in the sixth grade. I didn't know the language. I stayed up all night many nights, trying to translate with the dictionary. Most of my friends spoke English. Even the Japanese girls that lived in the neighborhood all spoke English.

We thought, Why do we have to be here? Why couldn't we have gone back to Peru, where we had our home and comfortable living? But my dad said it can't be helped. *Shikataganai, shikataganai,* that's all he kept saying.

Fusa Shibayama

After the war, when she was living in Chicago, Fusa, also from Peru, married Mac Sumimoto. Mac, an American Nisei, had renounced his citizenship as a protest against the evacuation. Fusa's family, following the Immigration Service's instructions, went to Canada and reentered the United States "legally."

I didn't go to Canada from Chicago, but my brother and my sisters did. My whole family got green cards but me. Immigration said I couldn't get my green card. I think it was because Mac wasn't a citizen at that time.

I wanted to become a citizen because I didn't want this to happen again. I went to night school. Mr. Nakano was teaching the Constitution. I used to go once or twice a week, and he gave me a book to study. My son was just born, so somebody had to watch him at home. Mac would study at home from my book. We both went for the test at the same time and got our citizenship. We went out to dinner and celebrated.

MANZANAR AFTER THE WAR

Beginning in the late sixties in southern California, three former camp inmates—Sue Kunitomi (Embrey), Amy Uno Ishi, and Jim Matsuoka—regularly visited schools to speak to students about the evacuation and internment. But as Jim says, "It wasn't as if things were being done on a weekly basis. The whole issue of the camps more or less held the back seat to Vietnam and all the other things that were going on at the time."

Asian-American studies programs, however, had begun to be introduced into college and university curricula in the 1960s. In Los Angeles, Japanese-American students became interested in Manzanar, some two hundred miles northeast of the city. They organized a "pilgrimage" to the site of the former camp. No barracks remained, but the guardhouses at the entrance to the camp still stood. Jim and Sue were part of the first pilgrimage. The Manzanar pilgrimage is now an annual affair.

Jim Matsuoka

The very first one was either in '68 or '69. It was in the dead of winter. We did that to make sure people realized that Manzanar was no picnic. In April, it's a beautiful place, but in December, it's harsh. We held it by the cemetery, where they have a big stone monument. When people ask me how many people are buried there, I say a whole generation is buried. They made prisoners of us and killed off our will to struggle and fight.

Sue Kunitomi (Embrey)

As director of the Manzanar Committee, Sue was instrumental in the fight for landmark status for the camp.

In 1970 or '71 a group of us applied to the state of California to make Manzanar a landmark. It took about a year for them to approve that designation, but they didn't want our wording describing Manzanar for the bronze marker. After about a year, there was a tiny press article that they had rejected our wording. They didn't like the words "racism, economic greed, concentration camps." They argued it was mostly war hysteria. They said it was not California, but the U.S. government that did it. "Don't blame us," they said.

I said, "If it was just hysteria, how come it was only the Japanese and not the Germans and Italians? It was a deliberate attempt on the part of politicians and everyone else to get us out of there. And even the government called them 'concentration camps.' "

Finally, at a meeting in Sacramento, one person argued to the government representative, "You're sitting there saying you're not going to let us describe our own experience. That's what it is, a description from our point of view, not your point of view. We want these words on the plaque. It's the same racism that put us in the camp."

That was in 1973, and we left in the words "racism" and "concentration camps."

The final inscription was approved as follows:

In the early part of World War II, 110,000 persons of Japanese ancestry were interned in relocation centers by Executive Order No. 9066, issued on February 19, 1942. Manzanar, the first of ten such concentration camps, was bounded by barbed

wire and guard towers, confining 10,000 persons, the majority
being American citizens. May the injustices and humiliation
suffered here as a result of hysteria, racism and economic
exploitation never emerge again.

In 1985 the National Park Service designated Manzanar a Historic
Landmark. Then, in 1992, a Manzanar bill passed both houses of
Congress, and the former prison camp was declared a National His-
toric Site. The bill passed on February 19, 1992, the fiftieth anni-
versary of President Roosevelt's signing of Executive Order 9066.
The vote was 400 to 13. President Bush signed the bill into law on
March 3.

"I'm relieved," Sue told a reporter, "that something is going to be
done to protect the site, because so many people are concerned about
making sure that their history is there, that the story is told and the
public knows about it."

TOKYO ROSE

Hollywood World War II movies about American soldiers in the
Pacific all have at least one scene of an attractive woman of Japanese
ancestry speaking English with an American accent on a radio show
beamed from Tokyo to the Allied troops. In insinuating tones, this evil
woman works to undermine army morale. In these movies, her broadcasts are always ridiculed as propaganda, although they are depicted as
sometimes successful on war-weary GIs. She is called "Tokyo Rose."

The real story of "Tokyo Rose" is instructive in how a political
myth can be created and enshrined in the national consciousness. It is
also a story of Japanese Americans working to correct an injustice and
to set the record straight.

During World War II, Radio Tokyo had a propaganda program
known as *Zero Hour*. It was broadcast specifically for Allied soldiers
in the Pacific. The program was directed by three prisoners of war, an
Australian major, an American captain, and a Filipino lieutenant.

The *Zero Hour* broadcast Western music, news, and propaganda reports. Although eighteen English-speaking women announcers read scripts written for them, the belief grew that one woman alone, dubbed "Tokyo Rose" by soldier-listeners, was Radio Tokyo's voice of propaganda. Iva Toguri, a Japanese American stranded in Japan during the war, was accused of being that one voice.

Toguri was born in Los Angeles in 1916. She graduated from UCLA in 1941 with a B.A. in zoology. When her mother's sister who lived in Japan became very ill in the summer of 1941, Iva went to Japan to help care for her. Trapped there after the war began, she was pressured relentlessly by the Japanese police and government officials to renounce her American citizenship. She consistently refused.

In America, Toguri's parents were considered "enemy aliens" and were removed from their home on the Coast and imprisoned in the camp at Gila River, Arizona. In Japan, Iva was the "enemy alien." Hounded by the Japanese police and under pressure from her relatives to move out of their home, she began to scrounge for work. Finally, she found a part-time job as a typist for Radio Tokyo. Later she became one of the female voices on the *Zero Hour,* functioning essentially as a disc jockey.

When Japan surrendered to the Allies, in August 1945, reporters flocked to Japan and began to search for "Tokyo Rose." Although told by a Radio Tokyo writer that there was no such person, some reporters nevertheless bribed witnesses to identify Iva Toguri as "Tokyo Rose." After a year's imprisonment, she was cleared by the army and the Department of Justice. When the press reported that "Tokyo Rose" planned to return to America, there was a great public outcry by commentators and political groups to keep her out. The protests worked, and she postponed her trip.

With new press demands for information identifying Toguri as "Tokyo Rose," she was arrested again in 1948 and brought to San Francisco for trial on charges of having committed eight acts of treason. The U.S. government recordings of the *Zero Hour* broadcasts that had previously cleared her had been destroyed. And so the evidence at trial consisted only of testimony from supposed witnesses to these acts. These witnesses were later discovered to have lied.

Toguri continued to insist she had only worked as a disc jockey. The fact that she had earlier turned over all her scripts to the authorities certainly supported her belief she had done nothing wrong. Some thirty years later, when interviewed on the CBS show *60 Minutes,* she said "I gave them the information. In fact . . . I turned over my scripts—I mean, whatever!—because what was there to hide?"

After fifty-six days of trial, the jury was deadlocked. Pressured by the judge to come to a decision, the jurors finally acquitted her of seven of the eight counts of treason, convicting her of one. On the *60 Minutes* program, the foreman of the jury said, "There was a great deal of anti-Japanese prejudice existing throughout the country, especially here in California, and that had some effect on the jury. Of that, I am quite certain."

Iva Toguri was sentenced to prison and fined $10,000. She served six and a half years in a federal penitentiary. Convicted of treason, she had her American citizenship taken away.

Beginning in 1954, Toguri supporters have argued that she was framed. They unsuccessfully sought a pardon from Presidents Eisenhower, Johnson, and Nixon. Then, in 1974, the JACL at its national convention passed a resolution stating,

> Iva Toguri was the victim of wartime hysteria and became a scapegoat for her alleged role as "Tokyo Rose." . . . It is now apparent that much of the evidence and the conduct of her trial were highly questionable and prejudicial and that in view of the motivations and climate of public hysteria at the time of the trial the verdict is a blot on the integrity of American jurisprudence.

Clifford Uyeda

Clifford Uyeda was a leader in the JACL national campaign to restore Iva Toguri's American citizenship.

The JACL resolution sounds nice, I thought, so I went to JACL and I said, "What are you doing?" They said, "Nothing." Finally, I got hold of Iva. She said JACL told her they passed this resolution, but that was the last time she heard about it. I thought we should do something. That's when I contacted Wayne Collins Jr., the son. [Wayne Collins Sr. had volunteered to represent Toguri without fee at her trial. He died in 1974.]

All of the Tokyo Rose meetings were held right here [Clifford's house]. I called twelve different people, and about six or eight came. We said, What shall we do to get her citizenship back? We had no idea which way to go.

I went down to the library right here in San Francisco and looked at the microfilm of the trial, which was held here from July 15 to the end of September 1949. I read everything. One of the reporters said the account of the two who testified against Iva is almost word for word the same. They're using the same phrases [he said]; they sound like they were coached together. It was their testimony that put her in prison. You have to have two persons testify to the same act [of treason].

Then, in 1976, suddenly there was a newspaper article in the *Chicago Tribune* from a man who was a Far East correspondent. He interviewed the two people who had testified against Iva. They were both American Nisei in Japan during the war working for Radio Tokyo. They said, "We were coached two hours a day for one month on what to say. We had to cooperate because the government said if we didn't, they'd put us on trial [for treason]." This information did not come out until 1976. In 1977, we finally got the pardon for her, and she got her citizenship back.

With press reports establishing that the testimony against Iva Toguri was perjured, major U.S. newspapers—including the Denver Post, Honolulu Advertiser, Los Angeles Times, San Francisco Chronicle, San Francisco Examiner, Seattle Post Intelligencer, *and* Washington Star—*wrote editorials in 1976 calling for a presidential pardon.*

Governmental officials, civil liberties groups, and even an Oregon post of the Veterans of Foreign Wars called for a pardon. In January 1977, on the last full day of his presidency, Gerald Ford granted Iva Toguri a full pardon. Her American citizenship, which she had at great personal risk refused to renounce when the Japanese demanded it, was at long last restored to her.

THE REDRESS MOVEMENT

When Japanese Americans were driven from their homes and imprisoned, they lost their possessions, their jobs, their freedom. Middle-aged Issei became old before their time. Young Nisei lost a sense of order in their lives. Fifty years after her imprisonment at age eighteen at Manzanar, Sue Kunitomi looked at a mound of broken plates and cups scattered on the weed-covered grounds of the camp and said, "Broken china, broken lives."

Property losses have been estimated at several hundred million dollars. In 1948 Congress passed the Japanese American Evacuation Claims Act to pay some minimal compensation for property losses suffered as a result of the evacuation. Under the strict limitations of the act, only a small fraction of the money lost was ever repaid. Sumi Seo's family filed a claim under the act:

> My sister filled out the papers. She put in the claim for losing
> so much acreage of string beans and tomatoes. I went with my
> dad to the hearing so he could get his money. We had to go
> and testify in some big auditorium in Los Angeles. My father
> got $250 or $300. He was scared to put down what his actual
> loss was.

One can try to estimate property losses in dollars and cents. But how do you assess an injury to liberty and human dignity? How do you pay for lost hope, fractured innocence, betrayal of social trust? Edison Uno, a teenager in the camps, was one of the earliest voices calling for redress for the violations of constitutional rights as well as property losses. In 1947, at age eighteen the youngest president of a JACL chapter, he first raised the idea of redress and reparations. He argued for redress through the years until his death in 1976.

In 1978, JACL, under the leadership of Clifford Uyeda, undertook a national campaign for redress. Shortly before his election as president, Uyeda had chaired a JACL committee that published a pamphlet calling for redress:

> German Jews experienced the horrors of the Nazi death camps. Japanese Americans experienced the agonies of being incarcerated for an indeterminate period. Both were imprisoned in barbed wire compounds with armed guards. Both were prisoners of their own country. Both were there without criminal charges, and were completely innocent of any wrong-doing. Both were there for only one reason—ancestry. German Jews were systematically murdered en masse—that did not happen to Japanese Americans, but the point is that both Germany and the United States persecuted their own citizens based on ancestry.
>
> . . . Redress for the injustices of 1942–1946 is not just an isolated Japanese American issue: it is an issue of concern for all Americans. Restitution does not put a price tag on freedom or justice. The issue is not to recover what cannot be recovered. The issue is to acknowledge the mistake by providing proper redress to victims of injustice, and thereby make such injustices less likely to recur.

The movement for redress grew on several fronts. In 1978 Bert and Lillian Nakano helped form the Los Angeles Community Coalition for Redress. Two years later the group became the National Coalition for Redress and Reparations (NCRR), a key organization in the redress battles through the 1980s.

On still another front, in 1979 the National Council for Japanese American Redress (NCJAR) was founded, with William Hohri as chairperson. The goal of NCJAR was to obtain monetary damages for Japanese-American victims of the government's World War II exclusion and imprisonment policies.

In 1980 Congress passed a bill calling for a commission to study U.S. wartime policies against Japanese Americans. President Jimmy Carter signed the bill into law, establishing the Commission on Wartime Relocation and Internment of Civilians (CWRIC). The stated purpose of the commission was to review the facts and circumstances of the evacuation and incarceration policies and to recommend "appropriate remedies." The commission held hearings in 1981 in six cities around the country, at which hundreds of Japanese Americans testified about their wartime internment experiences. Several government officials responsible for the evacuation and internment also testified. Commission staff reviewed thousands of government documents, some previously classified. The Commission issued its report, *Personal Justice Denied,* in 1982. The report was a powerful indictment of the government's wartime actions. It charged that "racism, war hysteria, and failure of political leadership" were responsible for the "grievous wrong" committed against Japanese Americans. The recommendations to Congress included a one-time $20,000 payment to each survivor.

Five years after the commission issued its report, Congress passed the Civil Rights Act of 1988, which extended an official apology to Japanese Americans for the government's actions and granted the recommended $20,000 in redress. Although President Reagan had opposed redress, when it became clear Congress overwhelmingly supported it, he reluctantly signed the redress bill into law. The first redress payments were made in 1990 by President Bush.

The Japanese-American community had not been united in the struggle for redress. Three organizations—JACL, NCRR, and NCJAR—each approached the issue differently. JACL had urged the creation of the Commission on Wartime Relocation and Internment of Civilians, believing that "fact finding" was necessary to persuade Congress and the public to support monetary compensation. NCJAR believed the commission was a delaying tactic, that the insult and

injury to Japanese Americans needed no further proof, and that a lawsuit demanding payment of damages was the only real way to fully
spell out the grievances of the community. NCRR was most concerned with educating and activating the Japanese-American community to the need for redress. It wanted to break the pained silence of
the victims and engage them in the battle to regain their own dignity.

There were also those in the Japanese community who did not join
the struggle, believing that the government would never acknowledge the wrongs done. Still others feared a stirring up of more anti-
Japanese racism.

The voices in this section express the range of feeling about the
volatile issue of redress.

Clifford Uyeda

To me, Michi Weglyn's book [*Years of Infamy: The Untold Story of
America's Concentration Camps,* published in 1976] is what really gave
the Japanese Americans finally some documented reason for going
after redress. *Personal Justice Denied* [1982] is the report of the commission, but Michi was the first one to really bring all that out. A lot
of academics say Michi doesn't have a degree. So what? The two most
effective researchers in Japanese-American history are two women,
Michi Nishiura Weglyn and Aiko Yoshinaga Herzig, and neither has
a degree.

In 1978 we [JACL] put out a booklet called *Japanese American Incarceration: A Case for Redress.* We sent it to all the media with over
200,000 circulation and most of the major TV and radio stations, so
that people would at least have a background on it.

Bert Nakano

We decided we wanted to get the community involved. Within
JACL, people like Edison Uno were pushing for redress, but nothing
much was happening. Sometime around 1980 we made a call to grassroots organizations all over the United States to come to Los Angeles
for a conference to try to form an organization. Four hundred fifty

people came from around the country. We decided that the name was going to be the National Coalition for Redress and Reparations [NCRR], a coalition for all the survivors. I was elected as the national spokesperson.

By the time we formed the organization, we were splitting apart, because Bill Hohri wanted us to help organize and do fund raising for his class-action suit. NCRR said no. A class-action suit is fine. We don't disagree with that. But our Nisei and Issei are getting older. Any kind of a lawsuit is going to take years and years, and it's very expensive. So we decided we would not discourage NCJAR from doing that, but we felt the fastest route to redress was the legislative route.

I was working for Pan Am at the time. I would get up at four o'clock in the morning and get to work at six. I used to go to meetings and get off at midnight, go to sleep at one o'clock and get up again at four. We thought that this was something we must do. It made me feel real good.

Ben Tagami

I had mixed feelings. If they're going to give it to me, fine. If they don't, fine. It doesn't make no difference. It wasn't that I was against it. I wanted the government to come out and make a statement. When I visited Sparky Matsunaga [Senator from Hawaii] in Washington, he says, "Ben, we can't let people ever forget that this happened." From that moment on, I realized that we gotta fight like hell for the redress. It's not for me. It's for all the others. They suffered just as much as I did. If they want it, fine. If they don't, they can always return the check to the government.

Amy Akiyama

We wanted an apology. I would have been happy with that too. But money attached really perks people up. I just keep thinking, God, I wish my mother and father were here to hear the apology or some kind of acknowledgment that this was indeed very wrong. That's what I regret. That's what makes me most angry when I think about it. All the people that really suffered more so than their children like myself, people that died or were really affected psychologically or physically by just becoming older than their time. I feel very mad and angry for them.

Sumi Seo

In 1975, before the commission hearing, a white couple lived in our apartment building. They heard about the evacuation, and they asked me, "Is it true what happened to you during the war?" I thought, Oh, my God, how am I going to answer? I was in tears. Then I told them, "Yeah, it happened. We had to leave everything and go, like the government told us."

When I worked at Douglas Aircraft, some people made me feel like I was the enemy. One day we were all having lunch together. One woman was talking about how her relative was hurt in the Pacific. They all talked about "those damn Japs." They were saying it on purpose at me.

When the redress movement was beginning in 1979, '80, one of the girls pointed her finger at me and said I was a Jap, and regardless of what kind of Jap, I'm still a Jap. I said, "One of these days you're going to have to pay me for all this rigmarole you're causing me. One of these days the government's going to pay me." I said it out of the clear blue sky. And you know, it came true.

When we marched for redress in front of the federal building, there weren't too many Niseis. It was almost all Sanseis and Yonseis. Everybody said, "You guys are crazy, you'll never get it." I was kind of ashamed at first, but I believed in it so much, I didn't care.

NCRR said we need housewives, not just doctors and lawyers and teachers to testify [before the commission]. I said, I don't know the first thing about testifying. I never spoke in front of an audience. I don't know what to do. So I got my tape recorder and I talked into it. They wrote out exactly what I said. It wasn't any good, but it was all typewritten and ready for me to testify.

Some Nisei are ashamed of what happened to them. But with the redress movement, talking got easier and easier. It got real easy when we went to the commission hearing and let it all out. Everybody was crying. It was a big relief.

At the hearings, this one Caucasian woman talked against redress. In high school in camp, we had graduation annuals. Everybody that took pictures for the annuals is smiling. This woman said, "Heck, those kids never suffered. They're having fun." She talks about the "good times" everybody had. Some white people like that try to deny these things happened. They want to erase it. All the white people have to do is say, "I'm sorry for what happened during the war. It's something terrible that happened."

> To be eligible for redress, a person must be of Japanese ancestry, must have been a U.S. citizen or permanent resident during the period December 1941 to June 1946, and must have been alive on August 10, 1988, when the redress bill was signed into law. The government has estimated that of the 120,000 people interned, only half were still alive in 1988.

Nami Nakashima Diaz

I felt they're never going to give us anything. Absolutely not. Sumi [Seo] was very active for it, and thank God for people like her. She dragged me to meetings. I went to three, four, or five of them. All I could think of was, There sure are a lot of bright young Japanese kids coming up. I filled out my forms, but I never thought it would happen. I never thought the government was going to pay us anything.

Of course they waited until half the people were dead, so they couldn't get it. If the veterans who fought died before the certain cutoff date, their families didn't get the money. They fought! That was the worst.

Amy Hiratzka

When I was interviewed, I said all I want is not any reparations for what happened. I just want to work towards the fact that this doesn't happen to anyone again. I accepted the $20,000 for my daughter. I think of the blacks. I think of the American Indians. Their plight has been just a chronic series of ups and downs and unfair treatment, lack of justice.

Avey Diaz

When they gave this [redress] money to the people, the government sent me a letter saying because I wasn't of Japanese ancestry, they couldn't consider me. I mean, I was in with all of them, and then they send me that.

And my brother-in-law Albert fought so hard in the 442, saw a lot of discrimination, and he passed away before. His children and his wife got nothing. My brother-in-law was one of many who fought and never got anything. I say that's wrong.

Angie Nakashima

On the issue of should they or shouldn't they give us redress and reparation money, I thought if they do that it's going to stir up all this hatred and animosity again. And I don't want to go through all that again. And it did stir up a lot of stuff. There are people that resent it and think you shouldn't have gotten it. They're not going to say that to you in your face, but they're thinking it inside. I know that. Ninety percent of the people are. But if they're going to pay the money out, well, I'm going to take it.

Frank Emi

I supported redress. Oh, yeah. In '83 this guy at Cal State, L.A., asked me to come and speak about our resistance movement [the Heart Mountain Fair Play Committee]. It was the first time I really thought about it. After the program, some students from the school said they were really surprised there was resistance. "We've never heard of any. We thought everyone went quietly like sheep." They said they'd like to hear our story at their NCRR meetings.

Before this, I was not involved. I had read about it in the newspa-

per, but maybe I was cynical. I thought it was just another government commission making a lot of noise. When I went to an NCRR
meeting, I saw how dedicated these Sansei were about getting redress
even though they weren't involved. I thought this is something I
would like to help in. I joined them, and I've been active ever since.

A lot of the veterans are against redress. They're too proud to get
involved. Ninety-nine percent of the people said, "You'll never get
it." I had a big argument with someone at a Day of Remembrance
meeting. He was saying, "You NCRR guys are just spinning your
wheels. The government's not going to pay you a penny, and besides,
you're going at it the wrong way. You've got a bunch of commu-
nists in your group." We got into a hot argument. Later he told my
brother, "I thought Frank was going to haul off and hit me." I told
him, "Look, if you're so damn smart, why don't you come over to
our meeting sometime and show us how to do it?" He didn't take
me up on it.

Kay Uno

I was asked to come to Honolulu when the first checks for the redress
reparations were given out. They had a ceremony at the legislature,
but I couldn't go. It was too powerful. I was angry because Edison
[Kay's brother who died before the passage of the redress law] worked
so hard. He was the first one to say we should have redress and reparations. When he was eighteen, he was president of a JACL chapter in
Los Angeles and he raised that question. They fought him. "Don't
bring that up. We're getting along all right. Don't rock the boat."
Later on, because he kept at it, they finally did it.

Edison told us in the United States a thing doesn't mean anything
to anybody unless they have to pay for it. If you just ask for a letter of
apology, that's all you'll get, and nobody will remember it. You make
it controversial by asking for $20,000. It's not a sense of money wind-
fall. Oh, no. It's a sense of this is how we could get attention for it.
And it did. Get attention, and then you can start educating people.

People don't give Edison the credit that he deserves. He was the kind of person that if you opposed him, he wouldn't let you go. He would ask you out to coffee and talk and talk. Pretty soon you thought it was your idea you were telling him. He had that gift.

I was angry that the redress presentation did not include a clause that gave Edison recognition. When President Reagan signed the bill, you had to be alive to get redress, and Edison was already gone. Hana [Kay's sister], who spent her own money to go to lobby for this, had died. Amy [another sister], who had done all this education of everybody and spent a lot of her own time and money doing this, she was gone. I was angry that there wasn't some way that their families could get the reparations.

Mary Matsuno

Monetary benefit. This is the system that's already established. That was the only way you could go, even though a lot of them didn't want that. Like my brother said, they should have given the money when we needed it. Not now when we don't need it. Not that we're not thankful, but the benefit and the feeling would have been better for our parents than for us.

Mary Sakaguchi

Actually, it never even occurred to me until the idea was raised, that we should be compensated. We as *Japanese* would not have asked for money. That's what [Senator] Hayakawa [who spent the war years in the Midwest, not in a camp] said, but we were *Americans*. We're not Japanese. And that's the American way of handling things. You compensate a person for a wrong committed. So I was for it. It would never have occurred to me to ask for it, but once it started, I thought we were justified in asking.

Morgan Yamanaka

I was pretty much anti-JACL until redress. The redress idea started with the 1970 JACL convention in Salt Lake City, I think, when Edison Uno brought up this issue. I went with the redress idea, not

JACL. I became the area coordinator for northern California for the redress movement. Then I became a regional director for Alameda, Contra Costa, San Mateo, San Francisco, and Marin. So I was very active.

I think the fact that the redress movement came up is good, because people won't forget. They say, "You got your twenty grand." If I was the only one, and my case was going up to the Supreme Court for twenty grand for my four years, no way. I wouldn't accept it. I'd keep the fight open. I know the courts said Vietnam vets that marched in Washington, D.C., were eligible to get $10,000 a day for the days they were arrested without their constitutional rights being protected. Ten thousand dollars a day, and $20,000 for four years? Well. So if I were the sole person getting twenty grand, I would not accept it. But to me the issue is more important.

NCRR came later in the picture. JACL was not really looking favorably at NCRR, and I was the only JACL person who went to NCRR meetings. I said, "Look, I don't give a damn who they are as long as they're going to help this redress movement." At NCRR meetings they said, "You're JACL," and I said, "So what? I don't give a damn who you are. There's an issue here."

California Congressional Representative Norman Mineta, who had been a child in the camps, testified at the commission hearings:

I realize that there are some who say that these payments are inappropriate. Liberty is priceless, they say, and you cannot put a price on freedom. That's an easy statement when you have your freedom. But to say that because constitutional rights are priceless they really have no value at all is to turn the argument on its head. Would I sell my civil and constitutional rights for $20,000? No. But having had those rights ripped away from me, do I think I am entitled to compensation? Absolutely.

*   *   *

When the Peruvian Japanese were brought to the United States and imprisoned, they were considered by the government to be illegal aliens. Unless their immigration status was made legal, they were ineligible for redress.

Libia Maoki

In 1949 when we were in Berkeley, we got a Notice of Deportation from the Immigration Department. My father went to the attorney, Mr. Collins. I heard that Mr. Collins had filed a class-action suit. We filled out the Petition for Suspension of Deportation and we sent it in. I had to do a lot of the writing for my dad. We didn't hear from them for a long time. I was about sixteen when we were called to go to San Francisco to the Immigration Department for a hearing. I remember getting all dressed up. They asked all of us individually as children if we wanted to stay in the United States, or would we want to return to Peru. I said I wanted to stay with my parents. In 1953 we finally got a letter, saying that we have been granted permanent residence retroactive to the date of our arrival. When we received our green card, the date of entry shows 1943. That made us eligible for redress.

Elsa Higashide

When we got on the ship in Lima, we were processed by United States military people. That's why we are hurt, and some of us are angry that they tell us we don't qualify for the redress.

My dad, my husband, and I have worked for Peruvian redress for over ten years. Our Peruvian people are scattered all over and loosely organized. Only a few of us happen to have the documentation. We really are the forgotten people.

At the commission hearings, my father testified in Japanese, and my husband translated. My father first had to go to Panama Canal Zone, where they were made to work as prisoners of war. Right there it was a violation of international law, because he was a civilian. My father had no hearing, nothing, when he had to leave Peru.

Justice Goldberg [one of the commission members] said, "That is really kidnapping." I had never thought of it like that before. He said,

"If you're taken by force without any hearings or any explanation about why you're being taken, that's kidnapping."

We really hadn't thought about all this until just before the hearing. We went to Chicago on the weekend, and we stayed at my brother's place. That's when we started to write, cutting and rewording. We aren't real writers, so we had difficulty. Things were coming back. My tears started to flow, and I couldn't stop it. I thought I would be all right at the hearing, because I already cried so much, but when I began to speak about my mother, I started crying and I couldn't go on. Justice Goldberg said, "Are you all right?" They gave me water, and then I said I'd like to continue.

After, Justice Goldberg came down from the dais. He took that time. He could have just rushed off. I think I'll treasure that always.

Art Shibayama

Art was fourteen years old when he was brought from Peru and interned in the camp at Crystal City, Texas.

In my case, we were trying to get our permanent residence as soon as we went to Chicago after camp and Seabrook [in 1949]. We went back and forth to the immigration office. In the meantime, I got drafted in April 1952. I'm supposed to be an illegal alien, and they drafted me.

One day while I was in the service, my section leader looked at my records and he said, "How come you're not a citizen?" When I told him, he said, "That's ridiculous. I'll get you a green card." My papers went to Washington and came back saying I was an illegal alien.

After I got out of the service, I went to the immigration office, and they told me I had to go to Canada and reenter the states before they can give me my citizenship. That was 1955. I was in the service between 1952 and 1954. I was in Germany and France. Even though I had been in the service, they made me wait five years for my green card.

The Peruvians that Wayne Collins handled qualify because they received their green card retroactive to the day they entered the States. But Immigration didn't do that for us. The date of our green card is the date we received the card when we made a "lawful entry" from Canada. ORA, the Office of Redress Administration, is trying to get INS [Immigration and Naturalization Service] to make everybody retroactive to the day we actually entered. If they won't do that, we have to get new legislation.

★   ★   ★

In March 1983, the National Council for Japanese American Redress [NCJAR] filed a lawsuit against the United States government demanding redress for the mass evacuation and detention of the war years. The lawsuit described economic and psychological losses and extensive deprivations of constitutional rights.

NCJAR asserted that there had been no military necessity for the wartime actions against Japanese Americans. In his decision on the lawsuit, federal Judge Louis Oberdorfer acknowledged the evidence of government misconduct regarding the military necessity argument. Nonetheless, he dismissed the case. Forty years had passed since Japanese Americans had been forced from their West Coast homes. The judge ruled that the lawsuit was barred by the statute of limitations—that is, it was filed too long after the events in question. After several appeals, Judge Oberdorfer's opinion was upheld, and in 1988 the case was dismissed.

Although the lawsuit itself was in the end unsuccessful, some believe the fact of its existence may well have had a significant impact by providing an additional impetus for Congress to pass a redress bill. As Yosh Kuromiya, a Heart Mountain resister, has said:

I supported the redress movement and William Hohri's test case. I was behind the case even more. He was suing the government for the evacuation and the internment, the whole thing. I think his efforts laid the groundwork for the congres-

sional action. If Hohri's test case had ever succeeded and the
government was found guilty, everything would have been out
of control. The amount of redress could be a horrendous thing
in itself. William Hohri's initial amount was over $200,000 for
each evacuee. After seeing that, I think the government realized they'd better do something and unruffle the feathers. Even
though William Hohri doesn't get credit for this, I personally
feel that case made all the difference in the world. Otherwise,
they'd still be jerking us around.

Jim Matsuoka

We deserved our redress. We have a right to redress. It shouldn't be
counterposed to others. Afro-Americans as well as American Indians,
or anyone who has a grievance against the government, should bring
it up, the way I see it.

Redress was almost like a resurrection, people coming back to life.
At that time, in '69, we were certainly a dead bunch. Because of the
anti-Vietnam movement and the fact that I was a social science major
and became heavily involved in the community, when the redress
came, it was like the culmination of so many different things. Now it
was time to call America to account. In the process, it was a healing
thing. This is the only way we're ever going to come out of what we
were in.

You don't stick people in a camp and four years later say, "Well,
that's that. Goodbye. Hope you have a nice life. Have a nice day." It
doesn't work like that.

If they simply gave us the money, it wouldn't have changed anything. We would have spent it and we would have been the same
people—browbeaten, downbeaten, with nothing to say. Prisoners, so
to speak. But if we struggled back and fought this thing and in the
meantime freed ourselves and became whole again, that would be a
magnificent victory.

One person who testified said, "Somebody said, 'Why did it take us
so long to complain about this and ask for redress? Why forty years

later?' " He said, "We're finally getting out of the camps. We are now, just now, getting out of the camps." And many of us are still in there.

THE COURT CASES

At the same time the redress movement was in full swing, Japanese Americans were working on other fronts to correct the injustice of the war years. The United States government had claimed that "military necessity" required the exclusion and imprisonment of the West Coast Japanese-American population. On the basis of this argument, Gordon Hirabayashi, Minoru Yasui, and Fred Korematsu had all been convicted of violating military regulations governing the movement of Japanese Americans on the coast (see Chapter 8).

The argument for military necessity was made in the *Final Recommendation* and *Final Report* of General DeWitt. The first was submitted on February 14, 1942, and the second was dated June 5, 1943. In the reports, DeWitt claimed that Japanese military attacks on the mainland of the United States were "probable." He asserted that the 112,000 Japanese Americans on the coast were all "potential enemies." He said:

> The Japanese race is an enemy race and while many second and third generation Japanese born on United States soil, possessed of United States citizenship, have become "Americanized," the racial strains are undiluted. . . . The very fact that no sabotage has taken place to date is a disturbing and confirming indication that such action will be taken.

In his *Final Report,* DeWitt had cited many instances of radio and light signals from the West Coast to assist Japanese military efforts. But the Federal Communications Commission, which monitored all West Coast transmissions, and the FBI had both investigated the reports of illicit shore-to-ship signaling and reported to DeWitt that there had been no espionage activity by Japanese Americans.

In addition, Lieutenant Commander Kenneth Ringle of the Office of Naval Intelligence, an expert on Japanese intelligence, concluded in his reports that the vast majority of Japanese Americans were loyal to the United States, and that individuals who were possibly dangerous were already in custody. He stated,

> The entire "Japanese Problem" has been magnified out of its true proportion, largely because of the physical characteristics of the people. . . . It is no more serious than the problems of the German, [or] Italian . . . portions of the United States population.

Ringle and the FBI both concluded that total exclusion was unnecessary, and that individual hearings were sufficient. But these facts didn't support DeWitt's claim of danger based on race, and so he ignored them and asserted that "military necessity" required total evacuation.

When Hirabayashi, Yasui, and Korematsu challenged the curfew regulations and the exclusion from the Coast, the Justice Department gathered information to prepare for its argument before the Supreme Court. It reviewed not only DeWitt's *Final Report* but also the information from the FBI, the FCC, and Naval Intelligence, all of which contradicted DeWitt's report. After a discussion within the Justice Department, its lawyers decided not to tell the Supreme Court about the reports that contradicted DeWitt. Thus deprived of crucial information for their consideration, the Court relied heavily on the arguments of "military necessity" and upheld the convictions.

In 1983, forty years after Fred Korematsu's conviction for resisting evacuation to an assembly center, he filed a special petition called *coram nobis* to correct judicial errors that he claimed had resulted in a complete miscarriage of justice. Korematsu argued that his conviction should be set aside, because newly discovered evidence showed officials of the War Department and the Justice Department had altered and suppressed relevant evidence. Within weeks, Hirabayashi and Yasui also filed *coram nobis* petitions.

After a hearing in 1984, federal Judge Marilyn Patel overturned

Korematsu's conviction. She stated that the military necessity argument was based "on unsubstantiated facts, distortions, and representations of at least one military commander, whose views were seriously infected by racism." Judge Patel concluded that,

> the government had deliberately omitted relevant information
> and provided misleading information in papers before the
> court. . . . The judicial process is seriously impaired when the
> government's law enforcement officers violate their ethical
> obligations to the court.

Hirabayashi and Yasui's convictions were later also vacated. Since the *coram nobis* petitions were decided on the basis of errors of *fact*, the Supreme Court rulings of *law* in these cases still remain as law, no matter how limited and discredited.

These wartime court cases are a powerful lesson. Whenever "military necessity" is asserted as the basis for policies that abridge constitutional rights, one must be scrupulously careful to separate fact from prejudice.

EPILOGUE

World War II left a collective scar on the Japanese-American psyche. As Sue Kunitomi says, *"Personal Justice Denied* [CWRIC Report] describes this as the watershed for Japanese-American history. The way we raised our kids, our perception of what the country means to us, all that comes out of this experience in the camps.''

For many there is a denial of any anger or bitterness; for others, those emotions have taken years to surface. For some, the experience has left a residue of mistrust. As one person said, "The real legacy is I am very self-conscious when I'm among Caucasians. I have a hard time getting over anger. About any white. And that's very unfair of me, because we have so many wonderful friends." He added, "People say, 'You've got to learn to forgive and forget.' I can forgive, but I can't forget. The scars are too deep."

Whatever the particular baggage an individual Japanese American carries from the war years, most have successfully rebuilt their lives. But not all have been as successful in dealing with the painful residue of the past. Some tried to ignore it. Others did the opposite and became politically active. They were driven by the belief that only with the vigilance of a socially conscious public can the rights set forth in the Constitution be made secure.

The voices in this chapter reflect a range of thoughts and emotions expressed some fifty years after the evacuation and imprisonment. Yukio Tatsumi sets the context: "I think [Executive Order] 9066 was a mistake. In a way, you couldn't blame President Roosevelt. There was war against Japan. But not against *me*. You see, *that's* the mistake. *That's* the mistake."

★   ★   ★   ★   ★

Jim Matsuoka

The worst thing about the camps was the bit-by-bit crushing of the spirit. There was nothing subtle about the message. What you could do, where you could go, and what they called you wasn't subtle at all. It was out front. The most terrible thing is they begin to break your spirit and make you dislike yourself.

You can't be a prisoner without feeling it. And it affects you the rest of your life. You learn right away that you don't speak out. You keep your mouth shut. The nail that sticks up gets hit in the head. You go along with things because you don't trust anything or anybody. You close into yourself. Nisei love the characterization of themselves as the "quiet Americans," until they realize they're not quiet. They've been incarcerated.

One of my best friends was the past president of the Prisoners of Wars of America. He pointed out the similarities between the former [camp] internees and prisoners of wars. You don't become outspoken, because there's no point to it. All you do is bring problems to yourself. You become more individual—not individually assertive, but individually isolated—because you trust no one.

In many ways I have these scars.

Frank Emi

Frank was a leader of the resistance group, the Fair Play Committee, at Heart Mountain.

I can't understand not telling your kids. It could be that some felt a little ashamed that they didn't resist. Quite often you hear people say, "I didn't feel I could put my head up until this redress thing went through, and I got a load lifted off me." I never felt that way. I never felt I was humiliated, or I was ashamed. I was just angered. I also never thought about it too much afterward, because we won our case. We took on City Hall and we beat them at the appellate level.

When there's a principle involved, you should stand up for it even if you have to pay a price. I have no regrets at all. I'd do it again. I think it's important to let people know that not everybody submitted quietly. There were some that did think there was a principle worth fighting for.

Clifford Uyeda

This type of thing did happen in the United States, and it could happen again. The Constitution is there, but unless you are watching it, the Constitution really is just words. People have to make it work.

I think most people internalized it. You have to make some kind of an excuse for what happened to you. But somehow the excuse is always inner-directed instead of to someone else. If they could say, "It's somebody else [at fault]," I think it's much healthier, but they don't. Another good example would be people who are raped. They take the blame on themselves.

So much of the Japanese community is still insular and turned into itself. If we don't learn from our experience of what happened to us and look at other people and understand what happens to them, then it doesn't mean anything, not even the redress. If you don't understand that other people also suffer, it all meant nothing.

Dollie Nagai

Ever since the camp, I don't like Arkansas, and I didn't like anybody from Arkansas unless they were black, because I knew what they had gone through. I have a good Caucasian friend, and it turns out she's from Arkansas. She laughed and introduced me to her parents and said, "Dollie doesn't like people from Arkansas." We became very close.

In 1972 my family drove across the U.S. We stopped at a truck stop in Arkansas. It was late at night, and we sat down in the back. There were five of us. We waited and waited to be served. People all around us were getting water, menus, and still they didn't serve us. This one black fellow at the counter kept looking at us, and he knew what I was feeling. I told my kids, "I'm going to go up and ask them."

"Don't make a big fuss. Don't start anything," they said.

I said, "I'm just going to ask them. Period." I went up and said, "Are you prejudiced? We've been sitting here for the longest time and you've served everybody around us but us. If you're prejudiced, just say so and we'll walk out." I guess I wasn't as tactful as I thought I was going to be. The guy got all flustered. "Oh, no."

The food was lousy.

I don't know why I was so blunt. But by then I was boiling, and being in Arkansas brought it out. It started something with my kids. In Kentucky this lady was staring at us, and they stared right back at her. "She's staring at us, we can stare at her."

I never turned against the country. This was my country. This was the only place I knew. But I turned against anything Japanese. I gave up my Japanese name. I never gave my children Japanese names. Now they're turning around and giving Japanese names to their children.

When I went to Honolulu, I could not go to see Pearl Harbor. I was so resentful when I saw those Japanese tourists. I hated anybody or any group from Japan. It was a Caucasian friend, a social worker, who said, "You're going. The next trip, I'm taking you. You need to see that place once." And she took me. If it weren't for her, I probably still would not have seen Pearl Harbor, because what they did there is what caused this to happen to us. That was in the 1950s. It took me a long time to get over it. And I still have conflicting feelings.

Sue Kunitomi

My son was in the first grade and made friends with a young kid up the street. One day his mother came over and said her son wanted to start visiting with my son. That happened to be a day when the Santa Ana was really blowing in Los Angeles. It's this very strong, hot wind. As she was leaving, she said to me, "Don't you love this wind? It's so nice."

I said, "No. It reminds me of Manzanar." I had never said anything like that before to anybody.

She looked at me. "Oh, were you in one of those camps?"

I said, "Yeah, I sure was." I didn't know anybody who knew about them.

"You'll have to tell me about it," she said.

During the Vietnam War, I shocked myself. They had the court-martial of these young soldiers for the Mylai massacre. At one point they asked a soldier, "Didn't you realize you were shooting human beings?"

He said, "It was the order. We were told to destroy the village in order to save it."

I blew up. My kids were sitting there looking at me. I said, "God, were we lucky to get out alive from Manzanar." They looked at me like "Boy, she's really gone off her rocker." I shocked myself because I thought, How could such a strong feeling come out so late, almost twenty years later? It was something I needed to settle with myself— my relationship with my country, how I feel about my country.

I was interviewed for an article, and the reporter asked me, What was the result of all this experience? I said, "I've become very anti-war." To me it seems a waste of human resources. During the Vietnam War, when the war had already gone on for ten years, it suddenly occurred to me, If it goes on any longer, both my kids will be going. I thought, My mother sent three sons to war. Why do I have to send two of mine? I just can't do that. So I started marching.

A lot of times people say, "You don't sound very bitter." It has to go beyond bitterness. Bitterness doesn't do you any good. If you can work on something, it's helpful. I think the pilgrimages [to Manzanar] have been healing for me.

There are different ways people have reacted. One fellow I know has been asked to speak several times. He says, "I can't do it. I break down and cry. With all those people looking at me, I'd feel so embarrassed that I'm crying my eyes out, and here I am, an old man." He said, "It's in my head every day, every day."

I said, "You gotta make peace with it." He hasn't talked about it, and now it's coming out. It's taken him all this time.

My mother never talked about it much, until one time she said, "You know they sent us to the desert. Manzanar is a desert. And that's where they sent us." It described it all.

Bert Nakano

It's not in the history books. It's not anywhere. Unless you delved into it, went to the library, and made a special effort to try to learn about it, it's not there. That's the reason why Michi Weglyn's book is so very important. That was the most comprehensive, straightforward book that came out.

It was a revelation for many young people when they first read it, because their dad and grandfather didn't talk about it. These kids said, "It happened to our people. What the hell's going on here? Why aren't we informed about these things?"

We didn't really tell our kids until the redress started. Usually, you try to protect your child from getting too angry, too "anti." You want them to grow up with a sense of confidence in themselves, not to delve into something that is very negative and disagreeable. But eventually I felt that I had to tell them about it and talk about it. We went through the whole civil rights movement back in the '50s and '60s. You start to instill in your child this whole thing about justice, equality.

Avey Diaz

I was a longshoreman. After the war, when I came on the waterfront, I took an all-Japanese work gang on the docks just because there was so much prejudice. The longshoremen, Anglo people that are poor and have only their color, were real mad against it. That's still a problem today. They judge you physically. Well, they couldn't do it to me. We worked with all other nationalities, but we had a gang of all-Japanese. I heard rumbles, but I happened to have a fellow who was a

Japanese with a black belt, and he looked it. When they rumbled, I'd tell 'em, "Go tell *him,* he's right over there. You tell him how you feel." And you know, they really quieted down.

I feel this is a country for all of us. My wife gets after me because sometimes she thinks I'm overaggressive, but I'm not. I see things different, the injustice of it. When my kids grew up, I made sure that nobody would pick on them that way. No Anglo or any other race, and I've done a good job with them. My son, he's a nice guy, and my daughter, she may be overaggressive even to me, but you know, I like her that way. This way in our society they're going to make out. They're polite, but they know where they're at all the time. And they know they got backing in me as to whatever happens.

Nami Nakashima Diaz

It could easily happen again. Oh, I think so. But it's never going to happen to me again. I'll go away. You won't catch me. I'll go to Mexico. In those days, we were so law-abiding. If the law told me to rub my nose in the dirt, I guess I'd do it. My mother was strict with us. The law was the law. You never questioned it. Now, to me? No. Absolutely no.

Like many Japanese Americans who were in the camps, Nami didn't tell her children about her camp experiences for many years.

I never told them. I don't know, it was something that we didn't want to think about. It was like a mad dream, an awful experience. My kids didn't know anything about it until all this started coming out with the redress. Then I felt maybe it's time to start saying things, letting them know how I feel and what happened.

But I've never told them really how angry I do feel. I never told them how I think the United States didn't do the right thing. I don't believe everything the United States prints in the papers for us to read.

People look different, but if they're raised in a country, they can be very loyal to that country. I guess it's always going to be that looks make a great deal of difference. People take you for what you look like, and that isn't always so.

Amy Hiratzka

I wouldn't wish on others what I went through, being interned with no freedom of choice. The worst part of being locked up is that you've experienced freedom once and now you could not be free. Freedom is a very valuable thing. You don't think about it until you're denied it.

People who helped, they took their chances. And very quietly, they did it. It's really what you believe in, isn't it? That's the strong force, the strong element that pervades one's life, rather than the unsureness or anxieties and fear that may take over.

With me, I am very sure of what I believe, and I'm not afraid. I'm not afraid. That's something that I learned. I was nineteen at that time, and this is what I learned: I'm not going to be afraid of standing up. I don't feel anger. More than being angry, what came to me was what my life will be as a result of that. And it wasn't negative. It was a very positive thing. I must not be prejudiced against people because of what they look like. I didn't know this at the time, but I got that more than anything. When I went to New York City, I went to Harlem to teach in a day-care center there. In Hawaii I worked with retarded children and in a penal system with juvenile delinquents for fourteen years. Just two weeks ago and again tomorrow I'm going to testify against raising the bus fare. I always give testimony for the disenfranchised people. This will be my third testimony as a private citizen.

Amy Akiyama

I'm always fearful that something like this might happen again. Not to me maybe, but just in the world. I see the neo-Nazis. That scares me to death. And these ultraconservatives like Rush Limbaugh and people like that. I think they could do something like this again. Not necessarily to me but to whoever will be vulnerable. I think I'm more fearful of racism since that whole experience.

Chieko Kato

Chieko was brought from Peru to prison camp.

To this day I feel I have to struggle with my English. I didn't go to school when I was young enough to learn all the grammar. Maybe if my language was better, I could do different things. I would have been more confident.

Libia Maoki

Libia and her family were also brought from Peru to a prison camp.

I have a small spot of anger because of what happened to my parents. I put myself in their place, and I'm a little bit older than my dad was when he first came to America. To see him work so hard, not knowing the language, not being able to do anything . . . I feel so bad for them. It makes me sad. And I think the anger is justified.

Today Libia lectures on panels and at workshops about the Japanese-Peruvian experience.

I'm a mild one, not a real activist. But I feel our story has to be told, because there's nothing in the history books in the United States. Even for the story of the Japanese-American internment, there's only a small paragraph. It's something U.S. citizens and children should know happened right here in the United States. It could happen again. It almost happened two years ago when the Gulf War started. The FBI started interrogating Arab people. A group of Japanese, I think JACL and NCRR, spoke up against this kind of interrogation of U.S. citizens.

Yosh Kuromiya

One of the negatives of Japanese culture is that it's so group-oriented. Once you're regarded as outside of the fold because you dared to question the policy of the group, you're forever banished. So nobody questions. Resistance was not typically Japanese.

Japanese people themselves, the very people who were interned, are in a deep state of denial. So many can't accept the fact that some of us behaved in ways they didn't think were the Japanese way. We resisted.

It's hard to resist [without political power], but it still doesn't excuse not stating your position, no matter how futile it might be. It may not change a single thing, but it will hopefully start people thinking, and that is important.

Lillian Sugita

Working for the redress was like anger directed in the right place. Finally. The whole movement became a catharsis for everyone. Everyone needed to do that, including those who dragged their feet in the beginning. It's a liberating thing. If only people can realize that it's the process of struggle that frees you.

Sue Kunitomi

Every time my older sister moved, I'd find boxes of Kleenex, paper towels, toilet paper, and canned goods. I'd say, "Where do you think you're going?"

"Oh," she said, "I don't know. I just buy this stuff." Other people have told me similar stories. It's because of the evacuation experience. We have this pack-rat mentality.

I used to do that. Whenever we went anywhere, I'd pack everything in my suitcase. My husband would say to me, "Why are you taking all that stuff? If you run out, we can buy it in a drugstore."

One day when we were packing for a trip, he said, "You know what it is, it's that camp experience of yours." I thought about it and decided he was probably right.

I still cannot eat orange marmalade. I don't care how expensive and nice it is, I cannot eat it. I cannot eat apple butter. That's what they served us. The first time a friend of mine served orange marmalade, her mother burst into tears. The same thing with Fig Newtons. I don't like to eat Fig Newtons, because that's what they gave us. These little things, I guess, hang on.

The biggest problem we have in our country is human relations. When you don't know what makes another person tick, you have all these prejudices. The textbook my son had in the eighth grade was very controversial because it put in things, though not a lot, about Manzanar, the Holocaust, and something on black history. A lot of conservatives in California didn't want any of that. A friend of mine was working with the PTA, trying to get that adopted in her school. She got death threats. These people are crazy. They don't want anybody to have an open mind.

I talk to kids in schools about the constitutional issues, and the fact that we were held for three years without any charges against us, without a hearing of any kind. There was still a Constitution on the books, and the courts were open, but the leadership was not willing to grant us our rights. You've got to protect everybody's rights, not just your own. Otherwise, your rights aren't worth anything.

Angie Nakashima

It could happen again very easily. Very easily. I don't think it's possible to do anything about it, to tell you the truth, because I don't believe in human behavior ever changing. That's in us, bred in our genes. It could be too much immigration of one particular nationality. It could be against anybody, even the Irish or the Scottish people. If there's too much, then there's fear. And with fear there's resentment, and then there's antagonism.

Morgan Yamanaka

Without political power, some small, individual, powerless groups can get into this bind. I think ethnic Japanese would never get into this bind now. We have senators, we have representatives, we have mayors of cities. No way would this happen to ethnic Japanese. But some small group of people with no power, yes. In '42, there was nobody fighting for the rights of the minority, such as the ethnic Japanese. So my idea is keep the issue alive.

Mits Koshiyama

We always bore the scar of being called disloyal. Even today most of us are apprehensive of this trade war with Japan, a fear that someday the same thing that tied us in with Japan is going to hurt us again.

A lot of resisters haven't talked to their children at all. I told my kids about it right away. I never had any shame. My kids believe in America. They haven't experienced the discrimination I have. I don't want them to worry about something that may never happen to them in their lifetime, but I tell them to be wary of it. Don't take your citizenship for granted. You know what happened to the Jewish people in Europe. If you're not guarding against things like that happening, it could happen again.

We all want to be accepted as Americans. For some of us, it's a very hard road. Just because we might look different and we might dress different or talk different and eat different foods, it doesn't make us any different from any other American. Our dreams are all the same.

Mary Sakaguchi

After I had finished my [medical] internship, I went to Japan because my husband had a job. We came back after a year and a half and bought a farm. I'd been a housewife for seven years when I started to work as a general doctor for the state hospital in Pomona. The head of the hospital was a refugee from Germany, and one day he said to me, "You're still angry about what happened to you during the war."

I was shocked. I said, "No I'm not."

"Yes you are," he said. "You're still angry."

Shortly after that I went to an exhibit in the museum in Glendale. That was about fifteen years after camp. They showed photographs of Manzanar, and I couldn't stop crying. I saw all those pictures, and it brought back all those bad memories. That was the first time I shed any tears.

I was asked to testify for the hearings in 1981. Actually, I didn't want to. It's one of those things you don't want to think about or remember. Some of the people in the community said to me, "Look, you're a doctor. You went through it and you should talk about it." So I decided, All right. It took me three nights to write up my testimony. And I cried for three nights. Then I went to the hearings. Originally, I was only going to stay to say my part and leave. Once I started hearing other people's testimony, I couldn't believe what I heard. I sat there and cried for another three days. So I think I got part of it out of my system.

Mary Matsuno

The thing is, it happened. The older ones should have done something, but they weren't geared for it. They were always under the father and mother's protective wings. They weren't mature enough. They didn't know how to react.

The evacuation changed all our lives. I'm not a pessimist. I think things happen for the best. That's the only way you should take it, because otherwise you go in the dumps. Hey, we got to go all the way to the other side of the United States, not just the West Coast. Before the war, there was not even a handful in all the other states. Professionals only practiced within their own race. This way they could expand through hard work. People who were placed out of camp made damn sure to be a good example. They were going out there before all the rest of us. They'd better set a good example, or else we're dead.

Harry Ueno

Young people should know what happened. They think the United States is better than any other country, and the Constitution is so solid. But there's a dark side. People who know what happened during wartime, well, they won't let it happen if they know. If they don't know, it could repeat again.

Elsa Higashide

You know, it's strange. I don't know where I got this, but I always felt I was just a citizen of this earth. If the person was nice, I liked them, period.

Sohei Hohri

I never want to say "ouch." I can take it. I don't want to make any kind of statement that "Yeah, you hurt me." I know who you are. I know what you did, but you didn't hurt me.

In the long haul, I'm still working on what it is that actually took place. Not so much the factual side, which is interesting, but on the emotional side, and on the area of understanding. How to describe it, what words. The terrible things that are done to people and that are being done all over the world today, and were done in the past in our lifetime—how to describe it.

I'm most interested in the people who were involved in setting the whole thing up and how they justified it in their mind. At the time, I didn't have any of the ideas I hold today. For instance, that we were kidnapped. Or that we were mugged, not by rednecks, but by graduates of the Harvard Law School who wrote their theses on constitutional law. These are the guys that did us in.

The most important thing is to try to be clear. To say that Roosevelt is a racist, or any put-down word, doesn't help. I'm trying to understand. We all have to think about things we don't know, like the Harvard-educated people who did it—wanting to do you in and still maintain decorum and a judicious tone. That's the area I'm interested in. I'm trying to understand what's going on.

Art Shibayama

I didn't tell my kids. I don't know, I never got around to it, I guess. I was interviewed in *The Mercury News,* and then Fusa [Art's sister] and

I were interviewed by the paper. After that my daughter started asking about camp.

The newspaper reporter had never asked her dad about his camp life. Her dad died, and now she's doing this for her dad, interviewing people about camp.

We went to the Tule Lake pilgrimage in '79 because my wife was there. They had four busloads from Sacramento, two or three from San Francisco, and one or two from San Jose. Out of all those buses, there were about a dozen Isseis, a handful of Niseis, and all the rest were Sanseis. All the children wanting to know. This friend of mine said, "We're not going to go to a motel. We're going to rough it. Bring your sleeping bags." We slept in the cafeteria on the floor with the kids.

The next morning we got up, washed, and got in the breakfast line. The line was long, about the length of a basketball court. The Sansei looked at us and said, "Hey, you guys don't have to stand in line. Go in the front."

Kay Uno

Everybody always says, "Oh, you're little Kay-chun. Nothing affected you. You were protected." For years and years I had a sound in my head and I didn't know what it was. In the sixties, doctors tested and tested me. I had water shot into my ears and all kinds of other tests. Nothing. One doctor said it was ringing. I said, "I don't think so. It's a sound I can't even describe, but it's there all the time."

In the late seventies or early eighties, I went to Denver for a convention. I had been in camp in Amache, Colorado, and I wanted to rent a car and drive there. One of the women took me.

The barracks were gone, but there were some bricks and barbed wire. I stood on a hill and I could see the way the camp was laid out. I had this vision. It was a picture of a bunch of us playing in the shower room. The mess hall bell rang, and we dashed out. We ran into an older lady and made her drop her soap and towels. I turned around and picked up some stuff and handed it to her. That all flashed before my eyes.

I put the tape recorder on and did a narration. When we got back in the car, I played the tape back, and I screamed, "That's it! That's the noise in my head!" It was the wind through the sagebrush and the grass. The sound matched exactly the noise in my head. When I turned the recorder off, the noise in my head went off, and I've been free. I've never heard it again.

GLOSSARY

BAKATARE: stupid.

BANZAI: a Japanese patriotic shout or cheer of encouragement.

GAMAN: to endure.

INU: literally "dog." During the time of the internment, an "informer," someone who gave information to government or prison camp officials, was called an inu.

ISSEI: first generation. The Issei were born in Japan, and were the first generation to live in America.

KAMIKAZE: literally "divine winds." During World War II, Japanese air force pilots in the kamikaze corps performed suicide missions by crashing their planes into such enemy targets as American ships. Now, generally refers to some form of suicide mission.

KIBEI: a Japanese American (Nisei) born in the United States, who spent at least five years in Japan, usually in school.

NISEI: literally "second generation," but the Nisei are the first generation to be born in the United States. They are the children of the Issei.

NORI: thin sheets of dried sea vegetable that are black or dark purple when dried, and are used in making sushi.

SANSEI: literally "third generation," but the Sansei are the second generation of Japanese Americans to be born in the United States. They are the children of the Nisei.

SHAMISEN: a three-stringed instrument, like a lute.

SHIKATAGANAI: an expression often used by the Issei, it means "it cannot be helped."

SHONIEN: literally "children's garden." Shonien was the name of the Japanese Children's Home of Los Angeles.

SUSHI: a traditional Japanese dish made of rice rolled with vegetables, fish, or pickles, wrapped in nori, and sliced into round pieces.

TOKONOMA: the place in a Japanese home where one displays an art object.

YONSEI: literally "fourth generation," but the Yonsei are the third generation of Japanese Americans to be born in the United States. They are the children of the Sansei.

CHRONOLOGY

This is a selected chronology of the major events referred to in this book.

1941 NOVEMBER 1. A Japanese Language School is established by the army in San Francisco.

NOVEMBER 7. Curtis B. Munson submits his report, "Japanese on the West Coast," to President Roosevelt, stating, "There is no Japanese 'problem' on the coast."

DECEMBER 7. The Japanese navy attacks the U.S. Pacific fleet at Pearl Harbor.

The FBI arrests over 700 Japanese resident aliens considered "dangerous enemy aliens."

The Southern California chapter of the Japanese American Citizens League (JACL) forms the Anti-Axis Committee.

DECEMBER 8. The United States declares war on Japan.

DECEMBER 11. Some 1,370 Japanese are detained by the FBI.

DECEMBER 15. Secretary of the Navy Knox issues a press statement alleging an "effective fifth column" at Pearl Harbor. The statement is false.

1942 JANUARY 5. Japanese-American men are classified 4-C, "enemy aliens," for purposes of military registration. Many Nisei soldiers are discharged or given menial tasks.

JANUARY 29. Attorney General Francis Biddle establishes certain prohibited areas on the West Coast (harbors, airports, power lines) and orders removal of Japanese, German, and Italian "enemy aliens" from such zones.

JANUARY 30. War Department representative Colonel Karl R. Bendetsen tells the West Coast congressional delegation that the military approves of the idea of evacuation.

EARLY FEBRUARY. An 8:00 P.M.-to-6:00 A.M. curfew is imposed for enemy aliens living in "restricted" areas on the West Coast. A five-mile travel ban is also imposed.

FEBRUARY 12. Walter Lippmann's syndicated column entitled "The Fifth Column on the Coast" is published.

FEBRUARY 13. Pressure builds for evacuation of Japanese from the Coast. The West Coast congressional delegation sends President Roosevelt a letter urging evacuation of "all persons of Japanese lineage," citizens as well as aliens.

FEBRUARY 14. Lieut. Gen. John L. DeWitt, commander of the Western Defense Command, recommends evacuation of the Japanese in a memorandum to Secretary of War Henry Stimson.

FEBRUARY 15. The FBI has 2,192 Japanese in custody on the mainland, and 879 in Hawaii.

FEBRUARY 19. President Roosevelt signs Executive Order (EO) 9066 authorizing the Secretary of War to establish military areas from which any persons so designated may be excluded. This order sets the stage for the forced evacuation and imprisonment of nearly 120,000 Japanese Americans.

FEBRUARY 20. Secretary of War Stimson appoints Lieutenant General DeWitt to carry out the evacuation under E.O. 9066.

FEBRUARY 21. Hearings of the House Committee on National Defense Migration (the Tolan Committee) begin on the West Coast and continue until March 12. The purpose is to investigate problems of enemy aliens on the Pacific coast.

FEBRUARY 25. The Navy orders Japanese Americans on Terminal Island in Los Angeles Harbor to leave their homes within forty-eight hours.

MARCH 2. General DeWitt issues a proclamation declaring parts of Washington, Oregon, California, and Arizona as military areas.

EARLY MARCH. Voluntary evacuation begins. Some 8,000 people move eastward. Many go to the eastern part of California and are eventually evacuated when all of California is declared a restricted zone.

MARCH 11. Colonel Karl R. Bendetsen is named director of the Wartime Civil Control Administration to carry out the first stage of the forced evacuation to assembly centers.

MARCH 14. General DeWitt designates Idaho, Montana, Nevada, and Utah as military areas.

MARCH 18. President Roosevelt creates a nonmilitary agency, the War Relocation Authority (WRA), to carry out the relocation of Japanese Americans to permanent prison camps. Milton S. Eisenhower is named director.

MARCH 21. President Roosevelt signs into law an act making it a federal crime to violate a military order issued under the authority of E.O. 9066.

The first group of Japanese Americans moves from Los Angeles to a camp at Manzanar.

MARCH 23. General DeWitt orders the removal in one week of all people of Japanese descent from Bainbridge Island in Puget Sound.

MARCH 24. General DeWitt extends the curfew and travel restrictions to *all* persons of Japanese ancestry, including citizens.

MARCH 27. The voluntary evacutaion ends when General DeWitt issues a "freeze" order, effective March 29, forbidding further voluntary migration of Japanese from the West Coast.

MARCH 28. Minoru Yasui violates the Portland, Oregon, curfew restrictions in order to challenge the constitutionality of the order.

APRIL 7. Governors or their representatives from ten western states (Nevada, Idaho, Oregon, Utah, Montana, Colorado, New Mexico, Wyoming, Washington, and Arizona) meet at Salt Lake City with WRA director Eisenhower. All except Governor Ralph Carr of Colorado protest against resettlement of Japanese Americans in their states.

MAY 7. The National Japanese American Student Relocation Council (a non-government group) is set up through efforts of the American Friends Service Committee to help evacuated students continue their education at colleges outside military areas.

MAY 8. The first group of evacuees arrives at the Poston prison camp in Arizona.

MAY 16. Gordon Hirabayashi violates the Seattle curfew and exclusion restrictions to challenge the constitutionality of the orders.

LATE MAY. The governor of Oregon signs an agreement with the WRA for release of camp inmates to work in sugar-beet fields. The first group of Japanese-American prisoners leave the Portland assembly center to do farm work in eastern Oregon.

MAY 27. The first group of evacuees arrives at the Tule Lake prison camp in northern California.

MAY 30. Fred Korematsu violates the exclusion order and is arrested in San Leandro, California.

JUNE. The Military Intelligence Service Language School opens at Camp Savage, Minnesota.

JUNE 1. Manzanar changes from an assembly center run by the army to a prison camp under the administration of the WRA.

JUNE 5. The Hawaiian Japanese American 100th Infantry Battalion is formed and sent to the mainland for training.

JUNE 17. Dillon S. Myer replaces Milton Eisenhower as director of the WRA.

JULY 13. Mitsye Endo files a court petition asking to be released from prison camp on the grounds that the WRA had no authority to detain a loyal and law-abiding citizen.

JULY 20. The first group of evacuees arrives at the prison camp at Gila River, Arizona.

AUGUST 7. According to General DeWitt, the evacuation of more than 110,000 Japanese Americans from the West Coast is completed.

AUGUST 10. The first group of evacuees arrives at the prison camp in Minidoka, Idaho.

AUGUST 12. The first group of evacuees arrives at Heart Mountain prison camp near Cody, Wyoming.

AUGUST 27. The first group of evacuees arrives at the Granada prison camp (Amache) in Colorado.

SEPTEMBER. The 100th Battalion arrives in North Africa and moves to Italy.

SEPTEMBER 11. The first group of evacuees arrives at the Topaz prison camp near Delta, Utah.

SEPTEMBER 18. The first group of evacuees arrives at the Rohwer prison camp near McGhee, Arkansas.

OCTOBER. More than 8,000 camp prisoners are temporarily released from camps to work on farms to save the beet and potato crops.

OCTOBER 6. The first group of evacuees arrives at the Jerome prison camp near Dermott, Arkansas. Jerome is the last of the ten camps to open.

OCTOBER 12. On Columbus Day, President Roosevelt declares that Italian aliens are no longer considered "enemy aliens."

OCTOBER 30. The last assembly center is closed with the transfer of inmates from the Fresno center to the prison camp at Jerome, Arkansas.

NOVEMBER 14. Prisoners in the Poston camp mount a community-wide strike that takes over a week to settle.

NOVEMBER 17. JACL holds a convention in Salt Lake City, with delegates given temporary passes from the camps. The convention passes a resolution calling for the reinstatement of military service for Japanese Americans.

DECEMBER 5. In Manzanar, Fred Tayama, a JACL official, is attacked. Harry Ueno, organizer of the Kitchen Workers Union at Manzanar, is arrested for the attack.

DECEMBER 6. The arrest of Ueno at Manzanar precipitates a riot. MPs fire into a crowd of prisoners, killing two and wounding at least ten others. Ueno and fifteen others are arrested. Later they are shipped to a WRA isolation center for "troublemakers," first at Moab, Utah, and then Leupp, Arizona.

1943 JANUARY 28. Secretary of War Stimson announces plans for the formation of a segregated combat team of Japanese-American volunteers from Hawaii and the mainland.

FEBRUARY. With the distribution of a loyalty questionnaire, Army enlistment and leave clearance registration begin at most of the prison camps.

Nearly 10,000 Hawaiian Nisei volunteer for military service. Some 1,100 volunteer from the camps on the mainland.

JUNE 21. The Supreme Court upholds the military-imposed curfew in the Hirabayashi and Yasui cases. The Court refuses to address the constitutionality of the exclusion orders raised by Hirabayashi.

JULY 31. The Tule Lake prison camp is designated as the segregation camp for "disloyals."

MID-SEPTEMBER TO MID-OCTOBER. Some 8,500 "disloyals" are transferred from other camps to Tule Lake, and over 6,000 Tuleans are transferred to other camps.

OCTOBER 15. The death of a prisoner in a truck accident leads to a farm strike at the Tule Lake prison camp. Within weeks there are mass demonstrations at the camp.

OCTOBER. The all-Nisei 442nd Regimental Combat Team begins training at Camp Shelby, Mississippi.

NOVEMBER 1. Military rule is established at Tule Lake in the face of mass demonstrations.

1944 JANUARY 14. Military rule ends at Tule Lake.

JANUARY 20. Secretary of War Stimson announces that Japanese Americans once again will be subject to the military draft.

FEBRUARY. Nearly 2,000 more prisoners are brought to the segregation center at Tule Lake.

FEBRUARY. The Fair Play Committee at Heart Mountain prison camp is formed to protest against the denial of constitutional rights to Japanese Americans, to challenge unfair prison camp practices, and ultimately to challenge the government's policy of drafting young Nisei men from the camps while their families remain imprisoned.

MARCH. Some 315 young men from different camps refuse to go to their Army physical examinations. They are arrested and imprisoned until their cases come to trial.

APRIL. Joe Grant Masaoka and Minoru Yasui, JACL representatives, visit some of the draft resisters in various jails, trying to persuade them to drop their resistance.

JUNE. The 442nd Regimental Combat Team lands at Naples, Italy. Mid-June, the 100th Battalion and the 442nd meet up, and the 100th becomes part of the 442nd.

JUNE 12. In the largest mass trial for draft resistance in Wyoming, sixty-three prisoners from Heart Mountain are tried, found guilty, and sentenced two weeks later to three years' imprisonment.

JUNE 30. Jerome prison camp in Arkansas, the last to open, is the first to close. The internees are transferred to other camps.

JULY. Seven leaders of the Heart Mountain Fair Play Committee and newspaper editor James Omura are arrested and charged with conspiracy to promote draft resistance.

JULY 1. President Roosevelt signs into law an act permitting United States citizens to renounce their citizenship in wartime while on American soil. Before the passage of this law, U.S. citizens could not renounce their citizenship unless they were living in a foreign country.

JULY 29. Federal court Judge Louis E. Goodman dismisses the indictment of twenty-six Japanese-American internees from Tule Lake charged with draft resistance. The judge concludes, "It is shocking . . . that an American citizen be confined on the ground of disloyalty, and then . . . be compelled to serve in the armed forces, or be prosecuted for not."

OCTOBER. The 442nd RCT rescues the Lost Battalion, suffering 60 percent casualties.

NOVEMBER. James Omura is acquitted of conspiracy, but the seven Heart Mountain Fair Play Committee leaders are convicted and sentenced to three years' imprisonment.

DECEMBER 17. By public proclamation, the government lifts the West Coast mass-exclusion orders. The proclamation is effective January 2, 1945. Although the mass-exclusion orders are rescinded, individuals may still be excluded from the coast.

DECEMBER 18. In the *Endo* case, the Supreme Court holds that the WRA has no authority to detain loyal citizens. But in the *Korematsu* case, the court upholds the evacuation orders as a valid exercise of military authority. Justices Murphy, Roberts, and Jackson dissent against this "legalization of racism."

The WRA announces that all the prison camps will be closed before the end of 1945 with the exception of Tule Lake, which will remain open until 1946.

1945   JANUARY. The Hood River, Oregon, American Legion removes the names of seventeen Nisei soldiers from the community honor roll.

JANUARY 8. The home of a returning internee in Placer County, California, is firebombed. This is the first of thirty incidents of violence against returning Japanese Americans that took place over a ten-month period.

MARCH 12. The Court of Appeals upholds the convictions of the Heart Mountain draft resisters.

APRIL 12. President Roosevelt dies.

MAY 14. Secretary of the Interior Harold L. Ickes, one of the few government officials to protest against the forced evacuation, publicly denounces the West Coast incidents of violence and terrorism against returning Japanese Americans.

AUGUST 6. The United States drops the first atomic bomb on Hiroshima.

AUGUST 9. The United States drops an atomic bomb on Nagasaki.

AUGUST 14. Japan surrenders to the United States.

AUGUST 15. VJ day (Victory over Japan) is proclaimed.

OCTOBER 15 to NOVEMBER 30. The prison camps at Granada, Minidoka, Topaz, Gila River, Heart Mountain, Manzanar, Poston, and Rohwer close.

DECEMBER. The Court of Appeals reverses the conviction of the Heart Mountain Fair Play Committee leaders on technical grounds. They remain in prison, however, until March 1946.

1946   MARCH 20. Tule Lake, California, the last prison camp, closes.

JUNE 30. The War Relocation Authority program is officially terminated.

1947   JULY 25. The renunciation law, passed in 1944, is voided by a Joint Resolution of Congress.

DECEMBER. President Harry S. Truman grants a full pardon to the draft resisters.

1948   The Japanese American Evacuation Claims Act is passed, offering limited monetary reimbursement for property losses to those forced to evacuate.

1949   OCTOBER 7. After a trial that lasted fifty-six days, Iva Toguri, called "Tokyo Rose," is convicted of treason and sentenced to ten years in federal prison and a $10,000 fine.

1952   Congress passes the Walter-McCarran Immigration and Nationality Act, which establishes restrictive quotas for immigration, and for the first time removes the restrictions that prohibited Asians from becoming citizens.

1969   DECEMBER. The first pilgrimage to Manzanar is organized. It has since become an annual event.

1973   Manzanar becomes a California Historical Landmark.

1976   FEBRUARY 19. On the thirty-fourth anniversary of Executive Order 9066, President Gerald Ford by proclamation officially acknowledges the "national mistakes" of the war, declaring, "February 19 is the anniversary of a sad day in American history. . . . We now know what we should have known then—not only was the evacuation wrong, but Japanese Americans were and are loyal Americans."

Years of Infamy: The Untold Story of America's Concentration Camps by Michi Weglyn is published. The book, written by a Nisei who had been interned in one of the WRA prison camps, is an exposé of U.S. government policy regarding Japanese Americans during World War II, and enables many Nisei to begin to talk about their evacuation and camp experiences.

1977   JANUARY. On his last day in office, President Ford issues a presidential pardon for Iva Toguri.

1978   The Los Angeles Community Coalition for Redress is formed. Two years later the group becomes the National Coalition for Redress and Reparations, a key organization in the redress battles through the 1980s.

1979   MAY. The National Council for Japanese American Redress is formed. NCJAR tries to organize support for a redress bill in Congress.

1980   JULY 31. President Jimmy Carter signs into law an act creating the Commission on Wartime Relocation and Internment of Civilians (CWRIC). The purpose of the commission is to review the facts and circumstances of the evacuation and incarceration and to recommend appropriate remedies.

1981   CWRIC holds hearings in six cities around the country at which hundreds of Japanese Americans testify about their wartime internment experiences.

1983   JANUARY 19. Fred Korematsu files a petition for a writ of error (*coram nobis*) challenging his conviction in 1943 for violating the evacuation orders. Shortly thereafter, Minoru Yasui and Gordon Hirabayashi also file coram nobis petitions.

MARCH 16. The National Council for Japanese American Redress files a class-action suit in federal court for monetary restitution for 120,000 victims of the forced evacuation.

CWRIC issues its report, *Personal Justice Denied*. The report is a powerful indictment of the government's wartime policies.

1984   APRIL 19. Judge Marilyn Hall Patel grants Korematsu's petition and vacates the forty-year-old conviction. Subsequently both Yasui and Hirabayashi's convictions are also vacated.

MAY 17. Judge Oberdorfer dismisses the NCJAR class-action suit for redress. The dismissal is ultimately upheld by the Supreme Court.

1985   The National Park Service designates Manzanar a National Historic Landmark.

1988   AUGUST 10. Five years after CWRIC issued its report, *Personal Justice Denied,* President Reagan signs the Civil Liberties Act of 1988 into law. The act authorizes redress payments for surviving Japanese-American internees.

1990   The first redress payments are made by President George Bush to surviving internees.

1992   FEBRUARY 19. A Manzanar bill passes both houses of Congress, and the former prison camp is declared a National Historic Site.

ACRONYMS

ACLU	American Civil Liberties Union
AFSC	American Friends Service Committee
CWRIC	Commission on Wartime Relocation and Internment of Civilians
FAB	Field Artillery Battalion
JACL	Japanese American Citizens League
FPC	Fair Play Committee
MIS	Military Intelligence Service
NCJAR	National Council for Japanese American Redress
NCRR	National Coalition for Redress and Reparations
ORA	Office of Redress Administration
RCT	Regimental Combat Team
WRA	War Relocation Administration

CAMP SITES

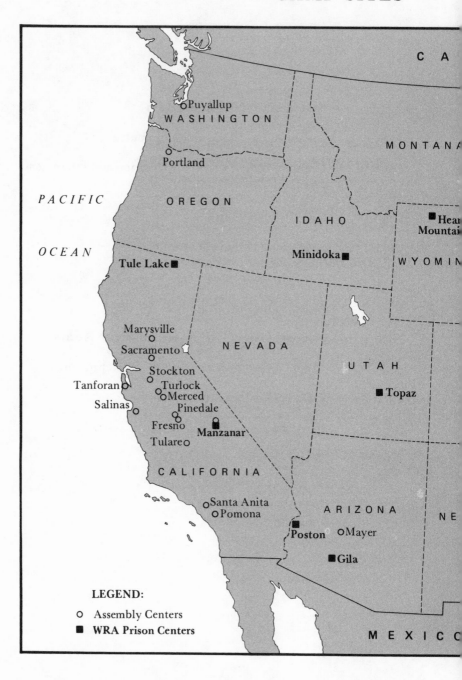

LEGEND:
○ Assembly Centers
■ WRA Prison Centers

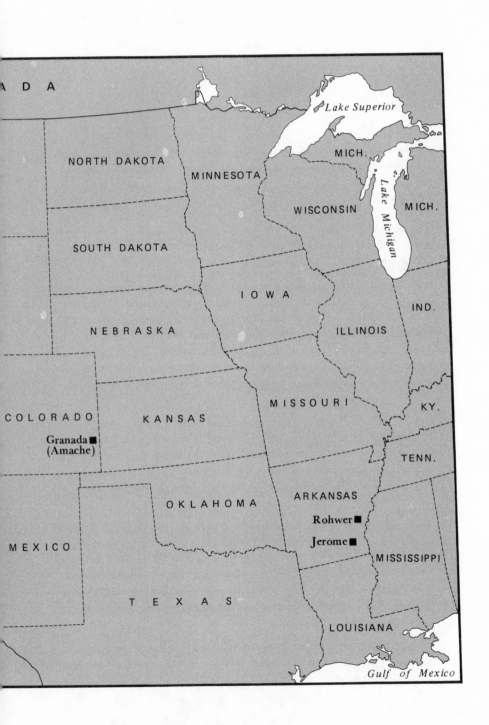

WHO'S WHO

AMY AKIYAMA: Amy entered seventh grade when she returned to northern California with her family at the end of the war. After high school, she went to art school, and then moved to New York. "One time some friends started talking about summer camp, and I said, 'Oh, I was in a camp too. I went away for three years.' Everybody said, 'What camp was that?' And I told them. They were shocked. Most people are not aware of the details." Today Amy Akiyama Berger is the art director of Cuisenaire, a company that produces educational materials for children.

AVEY DIAZ: Avey, a Mexican American, went to the Santa Anita assembly center with his wife. He was drafted into the Navy from camp. After the war, Avey was a longshoreman. He organized an all-Japanese-American work gang. About the anti-Japanese prejudice during the war, Avey says, "Because I was married to a Japanese woman, they tried to put that prejudice on me. Fortunately I come from a father that came from Mexico, from people that fought revolutions. I wouldn't put up with it." Avey Diaz lives in southern California and is now retired.

NAMI NAKASHIMA DIAZ: Nami was released from camp early because her husband was not of Japanese ancestry. She remained in California during the war, working at whatever jobs she could find. She had to carry a special pass with her throughout the war years, and was checked on every month by an FBI agent. Nami Nakashima Diaz lives in southern California with her husband, Avey.

FRANK EMI: After the war, Frank worked at a produce market in Los Angeles and then as a gardener. He passed the civil-service exam and was hired by the United States Post Office. After retiring from the Post Office, he worked for ten years for the California State Unemployment Office. Now fully retired, he does volunteer work teaching judo to children. Frank Emi speaks on panels and at workshops about the Heart Mountain Fair Play Committee, which he helped to organize.

ELSA HIGASHIDE: From prison camp, Elsa and her family moved first to Seabrook Farms and then to Chicago, where she completed her education. After living for several years in Japan, Elsa now lives in Hawaii, and works for a realty company. With her father and her husband, she has worked for more than ten years for redress for Japanese Peruvians. In 1994, Elsa Higashide Kudo and her husband published *Adios to Tears,* her father's autobiography, which includes the story of his kidnapping from Peru and wartime imprisonment in the United States.

AMY HIRATZKA: Amy was in junior college when she was evacuated. Her diploma was mailed to the Gila River prison camp. After camp, she and her family lived in Salt Lake City, where she went to the University of Utah and earned a degree in elementary education. She taught school in Utah and then in New York City. Interviewed once on a television program about the camps, she said, "You see what fear does to people. That's what was rampant. It was kind of a wholesale guilt by race." Amy Hiratzka Mizuno continues to be politically active in her community, working with civil rights and peace groups, among others.

SOHEI HOHRI: After finishing high school at Manzanar, Sohei left camp to work in Milwaukee. He passed the entrance exam for the University of Chicago and went to school there for several years. He left to go into the army in 1946. After a tour of duty in Japan, he returned to the University of Chicago. Sohei was a student of the humanities with a particular interest in art. After graduation, he went to Paris on the G.I. bill to study painting. He returned to America after nearly seven years and worked as the curator at the New York Yacht Club. Upon his retirement, the Yacht Club named the Sohei Hohri Rare Book Room in his honor.

CHIEKO KATO: Chieko was fourteen years old when she and her family left the Crystal City internment camp for Stockton, California, where her parents worked for a Caucasian farmer. She lives in northern California and works as a lead clerk specialist, supervising a group of people in the management information systems division of the county mental health department. Chieko Kato Moriguchi has begun to speak on panels about the wartime experiences of Japanese Peruvians.

MITS KOSHIYAMA: After serving a prison term for draft resistance, Mits returned to California, where his father worked as a gardener and his mother as a housekeeper. Mits worked briefly for a cement mason, but discriminatory union practices limited his advancement. Then he and his brother began a wholesale flower business, growing and shipping chrysanthemums across the country. As his own boss, Mits says, "For the first time in my life I felt free from discrimination. Japanese Americans came back and worked real hard. If we weren't evacuated and incarcerated, we would have benefited from the American dream. Probably twenty years of our life was spent trying to come back to a normal life." Mits Koshiyama is now retired.

SUE KUNITOMI: After the war, Sue returned to California and received a teaching degree at Cal State, Los Angeles, and a master's degree in education from the University of Southern California. She taught elementary school and worked at UCLA in the Asian-American Studies Center in resource and curriculum development. She has taught Asian-American Studies at different colleges, and lectures to students in grades nine to twelve about the evacuation and internment. As director of the Manzanar Committee, Sue Kunitomi Embrey was central to the campaign to have Manzanar designated a National Historic Site.

YOSH KUROMIYA: After serving a prison sentence for draft resistance, Yosh returned to California and tried to earn a living as an artist. "Finally," he says, "like everybody else, I settled for gardening." He also took night classes in horticulture and earned a degree in landscape architecture from Cal Polytech, Los Angeles, combining both his art and gardening interests and skills. Yosh Kuromiya is now retired.

LIBIA MAOKI: Libia's dream was to become a teacher, but after the war, she went to work to help her family. She worked for an insurance company and then for the Japanese consulate. At present she is employed by a charter bus company. Although not a schoolteacher, Libia Maoki Yamamoto in fact has begun teaching: she speaks at workshops and on panels about the story of the Japanese-Peruvian internment in America. "I feel," she says, "our story has to be told, because there's nothing in the history books."

MARY MATSUNO: Mary and her family left camp in October 1945, and went to Long Beach. "We got a trailer for the girls and one for the boys. We cooked in the girls' trailer." She says, "The only jobs that were available to us were within our own race." After she was married, she worked at a number of different places and eventually became an office manager. Mary Matsuno Miya, with her brothers and sisters, helped to organize the Manzanar Children's Village reunion in 1992.

JIM MATSUOKA: Jim was ten when the war ended. After high school, he worked in the aerospace industry, and was drafted in 1958. In 1960, he went back to school and received his bachelor's and master's degrees in social science. He helped start an Asian-American Studies program at Cal State, Los Angeles, and in the 1970s began to lecture in schools about the internment. Jim Matsuoka is presently a counselor and associate director of the educational opportunity program at Cal State University, Long Beach. "It's sort of an outgrowth of the camp experience. Having lived a low-income life, I relate to this program. Many of our students exhibit camplike tendencies. They have walls around, but you can't see them."

BETTY MORITA: After camp, Betty, age twelve, and her family lived for a number of years in Chicago, where she met her husband, Art Shibayama. She worked for an insurance company, and then moved with her family to California in the early 1970s. She and her husband bought a service station, and Betty Morita Shibayama was the bookkeeper until her retirement.

TETSUKO MORITA: After the war, Tetsuko worked as a baker in the schools, and then in a department store. Her husband didn't tell her for almost fifteen years that he had served a prison sentence for resisting the draft during the war. Tetsuko responded, "You guys did the right stuff. I would have done the same thing, too, because it was unconstitutional." Tetsuko Morita Norikane retired in 1991 and lives in northern California.

DOLLIE NAGAI: In 1947, Dollie and her family returned to Fresno, California, where she earned a degree in sociology. After working for a number of years at the Fresno County Welfare Department, she returned to school for a social work degree. She worked as a medical social worker and was then employed by the Los Angeles County Department of Children and Family Services. Dollie Nagai Fukawa is now retired.

BERT NAKANO: A year after the war ended, Bert and his family returned to Hawaii. After serving in the Army, he married and went to Chicago, where he took the GED exam and got his high school diploma. He tried different jobs and then went to college while working full-time at the Post Office. He and his wife, Lillian, moved to California in 1964, where they became involved in grassroots political organizing in Los Angeles' Little Tokyo. As a founder and national spokesperson for the National Coalition for Redress and Reparations, Bert was deeply committed to the redress movement. "Our whole purpose," he says, "was to get the community involved." Bert Nakano worked for Pan American Airlines until his retirement. He and his wife live in Gardena, California, where he continues to be politically involved.

ANGIE NAKASHIMA: After a year in camp, Angie and her sister left camp to find jobs in Chicago. She worked for a brief period as a domestic, and then for the YMCA business offices. She was married in Chicago and returned to California at the end of the war. Angie Nakashima Kato says about the internment experience, "I feel angry for my mother, for what she suffered. And for my dad, too, knowing he lost his business. But not for myself. I know I should, but I don't."

JOE NORIKANE: After serving a prison term for draft resistance, Joe went first to Denver and worked in a restaurant and produce market. With friends, he moved to Wyoming to do construction work at the University of Wyoming in Laramie. In 1946, Joe Norikane returned to California and worked in farming and gardening until his retirement. He and his wife live in northern California.

MARY SAKAGUCHI: Mary left camp to finish her medical school studies in Philadelphia. When she completed her medical internship, she and her husband moved to Japan for a year and a half and then returned to California. After seven years as a housewife, she went to work as a doctor for the state hospital in Pomona. Dr. Mary Sakaguchi Oda is currently in private practice in Northridge, California.

DON SEKI: Don had volunteered for the 442nd Regimental Combat Team, and was wounded during battle. He was discharged from the hospital in 1946 and went to Japan to work at an Air Force base in a civilian position. Don's parents had moved back from Hawaii to Japan shortly before Pearl Harbor. He found them in their old village, and helped to support them. After six months, he returned to Hawaii and then moved to Los Angeles, where he attended business school. Don Seki worked at the Long Beach Naval Shipyard as a payroll comptroller until his retirement.

SUMI SEO: As soon as the West Coast restrictions against Japanese Americans were lifted, Sumi returned to Los Angeles and worked at whatever jobs she could find. She learned the trade of making buttonholes and was paid fifty-five cents an hour. In the early 1950s, she began to work at Douglas Aircraft. She took time off to raise four children, and then returned to work at Douglas until her retirement in 1983. When the redress movement began, Sumi became involved with the National Coalition for Redress and Reparations and testified before the Commission on Wartime Relocation and Internment of Civilians. The redress movement got her started as a community activist and, she says, "I've been shooting my mouth off ever since." Sumi Seo Seki lives in Long Beach, California, with her husband, Don.

ART SHIBAYAMA: Although the government classified Art as an illegal alien, it drafted him into the army in 1952. After his discharge, he lived in Chicago. In the 1970s, he moved with his wife, Betty, to the West Coast, where they owned and operated a service station until retirement. Art Shibayama is active in the fight for redress for Japanese Peruvians.

FUSA SHIBAYAMA: After camp at Crystal City, Texas, Fusa and her family went first to Seabrook Farms in New Jersey and then to Chicago. In Chicago, she met and married Mac Sumimoto, who had also been in the Crystal City camp. In 1966, they moved with their two children to San Jose, California. Fusa Shibayama Sumimoto was working for a clothing store at the time of her death in 1994.

LILLIAN SUGITA: A year after the war ended, Lillian and her family returned to Hawaii, where she married Bert Nakano. She and her husband moved to Chicago, where Lillian went to art school and began to study and play the *shamisen*, an instrument she had played before the war. Lillian worked part-time and taught music. After briefly living in Japan ("Forget that place for women!" she says. "Japan was terrible about chauvinism."), she and her husband moved to California in 1964, where she worked at various secretarial positions. Along with her husband, Bert, Lillian was a founder of the National Coalition for Redress and Reparations. Today Lillian Sugita Nakano plays the *shamisen* in a group with her nephew, a pianist and composer who writes compositions on internment camp themes. Their group has played in America and Europe.

MAC SUMIMOTO: After camp, Mac moved to Iowa, where his sister lived, and then to Chicago. He married Fusa Shibayama in Chicago. Mac had renounced his citizenship in camp, and Fusa was a Japanese Peruvian. They studied together for their citizenship exam, which they both passed. Before his retirement, Mac Sumimoto was the chef in an American steak house restaurant he owned with a friend.

BEN TAGAMI: After serving a tour of duty in the 100th Infantry Battalion, Ben reenlisted in the Army. He was stationed in San Francisco, where he taught cooking and baking at the Army camp before he was sent overseas to Japan. "It was," he says, "a strange feeling. I look at those people. They look like me, but they don't think like me." After about a year and a half, Ben Tagami returned to the United States and worked at a produce market until his retirement.

NOBORU TAGUMA: After serving a prison term for draft resistance, Noboru was sent to the Crystal City camp in Texas and then to Seabrook Farms in New Jersey. He went on a brief trip to New York and then returned to his hometown of Sacramento, California, and worked as a farmer until his retirement. Noboru Taguma's son Kenji has been active in Asian-American studies programs, organizing exhibits about the World War II Japanese-American draft-resistance movement in general, and his father's resistance activities in particular.

YUKIO TATSUMI: Before his forced evacuation from Terminal Island, Yukio had started to work on a fishing boat. After the war, he returned to California and began fishing again. Then Yukio opened an Oriental market in Long Beach, which he owned and operated until he sold it and retired. Yukio Tatsumi is active in Terminal Island reunion activities and is president of the Terminal Island Association.

HARRY UENO: Harry was released from Tule Lake in February 1946. He decided to go into farming. Although he had no farming experience, his wife had grown up on a farm, and they were hired together. "We worked very hard, thirty days out of a month, but we were lucky enough to stay healthy." Harry worked as a sharecropper, and then bought ten acres in Sunnyvale, California, which he farmed until his retirement. In 1986, the story of Harry's internment experiences was published in *Manzanar Martyr: An Interview with Harry Y. Ueno,* by Sue Kunitomi Embrey, Arthur A. Hansen, and Betty Kulberg Mitson.

ERNEST UNO: With the experience of the camps fresh in his mind, and having seen a close friend killed during battle, "I thought," Ernie says, "I had to do something in life that was worthwhile for somebody." After his discharge from the Army, he went to school and received a degree in social work. He worked for the YMCA from 1950 until 1980, when he retired from his position as a branch executive. Ernest Uno has recently been ordained as a deacon in the Episcopal Church. He is the chaplain for a 442nd veterans' club, and does volunteer work at a hospice program.

KAY UNO: After the war, Kay went to the University of California School of Nursing and received her degree in 1955. She married and moved to Hawaii, where she worked as a health counselor in a special high school program for abused children, runaways, those who had attempted suicide, and drug users. Although officially retired, Kay has remained a community activist. She teaches adult literacy classes, and has helped organize "Hawaii: A Part of the American Tapestry," a multicultural program demonstrating the rich diversity of Hawaiian society. At meetings and conferences, Kay Uno Kaneko shows a video slide presentation called "American Concentration Camps: The Japanese-American Experience," which was created by her sister Amy Uno Ishi.

CLIFFORD UYEDA: Clifford graduated from medical school and specialized in pediatrics: "I think it was because the most forward-looking, progressive doctors were in pediatrics. Progressive meaning that you're always looking to do something new, in a different way. They talked more about preventive medicine, not just doing things after somebody is ill." Although he believed the JACL had not effectively represented Japanese Americans during the war, Clifford became involved with the group to work first on an Issei history project and then in the struggle to secure a pardon for Iva Toguri, known as "Tokyo Rose." He was the national chair of the JACL campaign for redress. Dr. Clifford Uyeda is active on behalf of many groups suffering discrimination, not just Japanese Americans. He believes, "If we don't learn from our experience to look at other people and understand what happens to them, then it doesn't mean anything, not even the redress."

MORGAN YAMANAKA: When Morgan left the Tule Lake prison camp in March 1946, he went to Chicago and stayed with a friend who worked in a restaurant. Morgan got a job first as a dishwasher and a short-order cook, and then in a factory making radio cabinets. After a brief trip to New York City and Washington, D.C., he returned to San Francisco and completed his education. He first attended City College and then transferred to the University of California at Berkeley, graduating with a bachelor's degree in sociology. Morgan switched to the school of social welfare, earning a master's degree in social work. After several different jobs, he began to teach at San Francisco State University. Today Morgan Yamanaka is a professor of social work education at San Francisco State University.

SELECTED BIBLIOGRAPHY

Much of the material in this book is taken from interviews I conducted with Japanese Americans who, during World War II, were removed from their homes and imprisoned in the internment camps. To prepare for the interviews, I read extensively about the evacuation and internment. The following is a selected list of these books and other materials:

Armor, John, and Peter Wright. *Manzanar*. Photos by Ansel Adams. New York: Times Books, 1988.

Bosworth, Allan R. *America's Concentration Camps*. New York: W. W. Norton, 1967.

Chuman, Frank F. *The Bamboo People: The Law and Japanese-Americans*. Del Mar, CA: Publisher's Inc., 1976.

Commission on Wartime Relocation and Internment of Civilians. *Personal Justice Denied*. Washington, D.C.: U.S. Government Printing Office, 1982.

Daniels, Roger. *Asian America: Chinese and Japanese in the United States Since 1850*. Seattle: University of Washington Press, 1988.

———. *Concentration Camps, USA: Japanese Americans and World War II*. New York: Holt, Rinehart and Winston, 1971.

———. *Prisoners Without Trial*. New York: Hill and Wang, 1993.

Daniels, Roger, Sandra C. Taylor, and Harry H. L. Kitano. *Japanese Americans: From Relocation to Redress*. Salt Lake City: University of Utah Press, 1986; 2nd ed., Seattle: University of Washington Press, 1991.

Drinnon, Richard. *Keeper of Concentration Camps: Dillon S. Myer and American Racism*. Berkeley: University of California Press, 1987.

Embrey, Sue Kunitomi, ed. *The Lost Years: 1942–46*. Los Angeles: Manzanar Committee, 1972.

Embrey, Sue K., Arthur A. Hansen, and Betty K. Mitson, eds. *Manzanar Martyr: An Interview with Harry Y. Ueno*. Fullerton, CA: California State University Press, 1986.

Gardiner, Harvey C. *The Japanese and Peru, 1873–1973.* Albuquerque: University of New Mexico Press, 1975.

———. *Pawns in a Triangle of Hate: The Peruvian Japanese and the United States.* Seattle: University of Washington Press, 1981.

Gesensway, Deborah, and Mindy Roseman, eds. *Beyond Words: Images from America's Concentration Camps.* Ithaca: Cornell University Press, 1987.

Higashide, Seiichi. *Adios to Tears: The Memoirs of a Japanese-Peruvian Internee in U.S. Concentration Camps.* Honolulu: E & E Kudo, 1993.

Hohri, William Minoru. *Repairing America: An Account of the Movement for Japanese-American Redress.* Pullman, WA: Washington State University Press, 1988.

Hosokawa, Bill. *Nisei: The Quiet Americans.* New York: William Morrow, 1969.

Houston, Jeanne Wakatsuki, and James D. Houston. *Farewell to Manzanar.* Boston: Houghton Mifflin, 1973.

Kogawa, Joy. *Obasan.* Toronto: Penguin, 1981.

Kuramoto, Ford H. *A History of the Shonien, 1914–1972: An Account of a Program of Institutional Care of Japanese Children in Los Angeles.* San Francisco: R and E Research Associates, 1976.

Myer, Dillon S. *Uprooted Americans: The Japanese Americans and the War Relocation Authority During World War II.* Tucson: University of Arizona Press, 1971.

Okubo, Mine. *Citizen 13660.* New York: Columbia University Press, 1946; 2nd ed., New York: Arno Press, 1978; 3rd ed., Seattle: University of Washington Press, 1983.

Rostow, Eugene V. "Our Worst Wartime Mistake." *Harper's* 191 (1945): 193–201.

Uchida, Yoshiko. *The Invisible Thread: A Memoir.* Englewood Cliffs, NJ: J. Messner, 1991.

———. *Picture Bride.*: Northland Press, 1987 Flagstaff, AZ; 2nd ed., New York: Simon & Schuster, 1988.

Uyeda, Clifford, ed. "Nikkei Heritage." San Francisco: National Japanese American Historical Society, published quarterly.

Weglyn, Michi. *Years of Infamy: The Untold Story of America's Concentration Camps.* New York: William Morrow, 1976; 2nd ed., Seattle: University of Washington Press, 1995.

Whitney, Helen Elizabeth. "Care of Homeless Children of Japanese Ancestry During Evacuation and Relocation." Master's thesis, University of California at Berkeley, 1948.

Yamada, Mitsuye. *Camp Notes and Other Poems*. San Lorenzo, CA: Shameless Hussy Press, 1976; 2nd ed., Latham, NY: Kitchen Table: Women of Color Press, 1992.

INDEX